"Can Ana come, too?"

Rico looked into Anamarie's blue eyes. "You bet." He got up, feeling a little unsure of what was ahead of him, but he could do no less.

"That's so nice of you to take him."

Rico placed Dustin on his feet. "Go tell the sheriff thank you for letting you stay with me. Then we'll go."

"'Kay."

Rico needed a minute to talk to Anamarie. She picked up the sippy cup, which hadn't broken or leaked onto the floor. "I might need your help. Are you available?"

She smiled one of her trademark smiles. "You bet."

They walked back to the bakery with Dusty between them. Mickey trailed behind. Rico carried the duffel bag and quilt over his shoulder, and thought this was a slice of heaven being together with Anamarie and Dusty. It was almost like a family. It was almost real. The *almost* kept him from thinking any further. Happily-ever-after wasn't in his future. It never had been.

Dear Reader,

The Texas Rebels series began in Harlequin Western Romance, and I'm so happy to continue the series for Harlequin Heartwarming.

Jericho Johnson's life hasn't been easy, but he's grateful to the Rebel family for giving him a home. Even so, he never feels as if he fits in, and he yearns for a family of his own. But he's a loner by nature and feels that will never happen. Until Anamarie Wiznowski smiles at him. She gives him hope that they could have a future together. These are two people who want the same thing: a home and a family. But the struggle to get them there was a tearjerker. I shed a few tears over their story.

I have to say Jericho is the kindest hero I have ever written. I was so glad to give him his happy ending. It's been a long time since I visited Horseshoe, Texas, and I hope you enjoy the visit and Jericho and Anamarie's journey.

With love and thanks,

Linda

PS: You can email me at Lw1508@aol.com, send me a message on Facebook.com/authorlindawarren, find me on Twitter, @texauthor, write me at PO Box 5182, Bryan, TX 77805 or visit my website at lindawarren.net. Your mail and thoughts are deeply appreciated.

HEARTWARMING

A Child's Gift

———

Linda Warren

⟨H⟩ **HARLEQUIN**® HEARTWARMING™

Recycling programs
for this product may
not exist in your area.

ISBN-13: 978-1-335-51094-5

A Child's Gift

Copyright © 2019 by Linda Warren

Printed in U.S.A.

www.Harlequin.com

Two-time RITA® Award–nominated author **Linda Warren** has written over forty books for Harlequin. A native Texan, she's a member of Romance Writers of America and the RWA West Houston chapter. Drawing upon her years of growing up on a ranch, she writes about some of her favorite things: Western-style romance, cowboys and country life. She married her high school sweetheart and they live on a lake in central Texas. He fishes and she writes. Works perfect.

Books by Linda Warren

Harlequin Western Romance

Texas Rebels

Visit the Author Profile page
at Harlequin.com for more titles.

The heroine in this book is a great cook.
So I dedicate this book to Tammy Medina,
my friend, my right hand, for all the marathon
cooking days in my kitchen.

CHAPTER ONE

JERICHO JOHNSON WASN'T a complicated guy; the simple life suited him just fine.

Like this morning, driving in the early dawn with the morning dew glistening off his windshield, the beam of his headlights piercing the wall of darkness as he drove into Horseshoe, Texas. Simple. Quiet. Perfect.

A two-story limestone courthouse, over a century old, stood as sentinel over the two-thousand-plus citizens. Large gnarled oaks gave it a bygone-days presence. At the top was a Gothic-like clock tower that never had the correct time. Most people in Horseshoe set their watches by it, making them a little off. Time-wise.

At this hour there wasn't much going on in the small town, but the lights were on in the diner and in the bakery. He pulled in at the bakery.

It was Tuesday morning. No fanfare. No balloons. No confetti. Just plain ol' Tuesday—his favorite day of the week. For about two years now he'd been picking up kolaches for the guys at Rebel Ranch every Tuesday morning. That was his excuse to see Anamarie Wiznowski. He liked Anamarie more than he wanted to admit, but nothing could come of their relationship. Her parents, especially her mother, would never allow her to date an ex-con.

When people turned away from him or avoided speaking to him, he felt sure those words were branded on his forehead. He was a loner and he wore a stone-like expression, as some people called it. He tried not to care what people thought of him, but each snub cut a little deeper on the inside. Until he met Anamarie, he'd kept to himself.

He tapped on the glass door and Anamarie hurried from the back. It was mid-May and the tepid south wind nipped at his clothes as the hint of summer whistled through the trees. She opened the door and he lost all train of thought at the smile on her pretty face. A hairnet covered her hair and a big apron adorned the front of her jeans and blouse. She'd never looked lovelier to him. Her blue eyes sparkled as bright as the morning dew. He never grew tired of looking at her.

Unlocking the door, she said, "Good

morning—come on in. Your coffee's ready. I'll be with you in a minute."

Jericho removed his hat and stepped into the bakery with its black-and-white-checkered floor, breathing in the heavenly scent of fresh-baked kolaches. He never tired of that, either. In an hour or so the place would be swarming with eager customers. He glanced toward the kitchen and asked, "Are you by yourself this morning?" Usually there were a couple of ladies in the back, but this morning he didn't see anyone.

"Yes. Can you believe it?" she shouted from the kitchen. "Margie didn't show up so I guess that means she and Bubba had a big fight. Judy had a flat tire, but she'll be here soon."

Bubba was Anamarie's brother and he and Margie had an on-and-off-again relationship. Bubba owned the gas station and a wrecker service and he also helped the sheriff every now and then. He was well known around the town, and was a friend of the Rebel family. And of Jericho's.

After hooking his hat on an ornate wrought-iron hat rack made by Anamarie's father, he eased his tall frame into a chair at one of the small red tables in the eating area.

Anamarie returned with two steaming cups of coffee and a plate of fresh kolaches. The hairnet and apron were gone and her smile lit up his cold heart. Besides the Rebel family, she was the only one in town who hadn't snubbed him. Her blond hair was pulled back into a topknot and several strands were loose around her face. At forty, she had this idea in her head that she was overweight and she didn't think of herself as attractive. He'd told her before that she was just the right size. And she was to him. Time and time again she mentioned the weight thing. He couldn't convince her otherwise.

"Cherry kolaches," she said as he picked up the heavenly treat.

He took a bite and she picked up the cheese one. "I should just slather this on my hips." She made a face.

"Don't start. You're the perfect size and I don't know why you're always complaining about it. Look in the mirror for heaven sakes."

"You're just saying that to be nice."

"Do you think I come in here just for the kolaches?"

She shrugged, sipping coffee.

"Or to visit with an ugly overweight woman?"

She spit coffee all over the table and giggled. She quickly dabbed at her mouth, holding the laughter inside. But it showed on her face and he never saw anything more beautiful. Why couldn't she see that about herself?

"You're so good for me," she said, wiping coffee from the table with a napkin.

"You're good for me, too."

Their eyes met and there were so many emotions he saw there, but he could also see she wasn't ready to express them. He didn't know if she ever would be.

She leaned back in her chair. "It feels so good to sit and relax before all the madness starts." Her voice held a soft caring quality and he didn't know of anyone who cared more about people than she did.

"You work too hard." He wrapped his hands around his cup.

"Look who's talking. You put in long hours, just like I do."

"But I don't get up at two thirty in the morning."

"Yeah." She stared down into her coffee and he wished he could read her thoughts. "That is getting old, but it's my job. Mom's not as spry as she used to be, so it's up to me to run the bakery."

The Wiznowskis were one of the founding families of Horseshoe. Willard, Anamarie's dad, owned the blacksmith shop. Her twin sisters, Patsy and Peggy, ran Talk of the Town Beauty Shop. And, of course, Bubba had the gas station. The youngest, Angie, was married to Hardison Hollister, the district attorney. Angie also had an office connected to the bakery. She was an accountant and took care of the books for the bakery and several other businesses. There were another boy and girl, but they had moved away. The Wiznowskis were good people and Rico had to wonder if he would ever be allowed to see their daughter other than on Tuesday morning.

He had a good family, too, sort of. He had saved Egan Rebel's life in prison when Egan had been unjustly accused of a crime. Egan's mother, Kate Rebel, had hired a new attorney and had gotten her son out quickly. When Egan had told her about the incident in prison, Miss Kate had hired an attorney for Jericho and within three months he had been released. He had no family and nowhere to go. Miss Kate had offered him a job at Rebel Ranch and he had gladly accepted. Even though he had known nothing about cowboying, he'd been willing to learn. The family had accepted him wholeheartedly and without prejudice. That went a long way toward healing old wounds. There were seven Rebel sons: Falcon, Quincy, Egan, Elias, Jude, Paxton and Phoenix. At first, his loyalty had been to Egan, but now he was close to all the brothers and he would give his life for any one of them.

"Are you still building fences with Elias?"

He took a long sip of coffee. "Yep. Miss Kate and Falcon decided to clear some land to the north to run more cattle. It's overrun with bushes and scrub oaks. Elias and I are trying to get a cross fence up before hay season starts."

"They are so lucky to have you." She reached across the table and touched his hand around the cup. In a split second, she withdrew it and scooted back nervously in the chair.

He didn't want her to be nervous about touching him. It should be natural and easy, the way their conversations had been over the last few years. He wanted to reassure her, but she broke into his thoughts.

"I can't believe Maribel is pregnant. I saw her the other day at the bank and she's really showing now. Two kids, twenty years apart. That has to be a shock."

Talking about other people was more comfortable for her. He just wished he could turn the conversation back to them. But, as usual, he went with the flow.

"I think they miss Chase since he went off to college and they decided to have another child. Maribel really wants a girl. Elias, he's just happy."

"It's a true love story." Her eyes took on a faraway expression and Rico just stared at all the dreams he saw in them. Why she thought she could never have what other women had, he never understood. Maybe because of her mother, Doris, who was always putting her down. Always expecting things of her she didn't expect of her other children. He didn't like the way Anamarie was treated, but then again, it was his rule to stay out of family relationships. One day he might just have to break that rule.

Suddenly, a frown marred her face and he turned to see what had caused it. A little boy of about three or four stood at the front door with his face pressed against the glass. It was dark outside. Where had the kid come from? Rico got up and unlocked the door and the little boy stepped inside with a small mixed-breed black-and-white dog at his feet. The boy's jeans and T-shirt were filthy, as were his sneakers. He looked as if he hadn't had a bath in weeks. He had dark eyes and hair. One hand was clenched at his side and he raised it up and opened his hand. In the palm were a quarter, a nickel and two pennies.

"I'd like to buy some food, please." The dog barked as if to second the request.

"Ah...sure." Rico glanced toward Anamarie, but she was already in the kitchen. He guided the boy to a table and picked him up and sat him in a chair.

Anamarie brought a glass of milk and a plate of kolaches and cut-up sausage rolls and placed it in front of the little boy. He didn't take it. Instead he placed the money on the table.

"I have to pay for it," the little boy said. "My grandma said we have to pay for what we get."

"It's okay, sweetie. The food's on me. You don't have to pay me anything."

The little boy shook his head stubbornly. "No. My grandma said we have to pay for what we get."

Anamarie looked at Rico and he nodded.

She picked up a penny and said, "This pays for the food. You can keep the rest."

"Mickey's hungry, too." He glanced down at the dog. "He's a dog, not a mouse."

Anamarie smiled at Rico and his world felt complete when she did that. She then went to the kitchen and came back with a bowl of milk and some sausage rolls. As she placed it in front of the dog, the kid asked, "Do I owe you more money?"

"No, no," she replied. "You've paid for everything."

"'Kay." He slipped the rest of the money back into his pocket and picked up the glass of milk, guzzling it. Some ran down his chin.

"Hey, buddy, slow down." Rico reached for a napkin and dabbed at his chin. "Take it slow." The little boy did as he was told and Rico stepped over to Anamarie.

"Do you recognize him?"

"He's Wendy Miller's grandson. He's usually very neat. I can't imagine what he's doing out at this hour by himself."

"I'm going outside to check around. Maybe Mrs. Miller is outside and sent him in to get food. It's obvious he hasn't eaten in a while."

He couldn't see much through the darkness. The roar of cars on the highway hummed loudly. A delivery van pulled up to the diner and the sun strained to peep through the clouds—signs of a town slowly waking up to a new day. Nothing out of the ordinary. He went back inside.

"After he finishes eating, I'll talk to him," he told Anamarie.

The little boy wiped his mouth, and said, "Thank you. I gotta go home now." He slid from the chair, but Rico stopped him.

"Hold on, little guy." He pulled up a chair and sat in front of the boy. "What's your name?"

"Dustin," was the response. "But my grandma calls me Dusty."

"Do you know your last name?"

The boy nodded. "Dustin Miller. I can write it. Do you wanna see?"

"Maybe later. How old are you?"

Dustin held up four fingers.

"Do you go to school?"

The boy nodded again and made to walk around Rico. "I gotta go. My grandma will be mad if I'm not there when she wakes up."

"You live with your grandma?"

"Yeah. But she's sick and I can't wake her up."

That didn't sound good and Rico feared the worst. "Where does your grandma live?"

"Over there." The boy pointed toward the bakery's windows.

"Did you walk here by yourself?" Rico hated to ask so many questions, but he needed answers.

Dustin shook his head. "Mickey came with me 'cause we were hungry." The boy looked down at the dog and the dog licked his lips from the milk Anamarie had given him.

"Has your grandma been sick?"

"Yeah. She got moana."

Rico thought about that for a minute and asked, "You mean pneumonia?"

"Yeah. She has to rest. She made me a peanut butter and jelly sandwich and milk and told me to be good. She didn't wake up for supper so I made my own peanut butter jelly sandwich. Made one for Mickey, too. Grandma's still sleeping. She won't wake up and we don't have any more peanut butter and jelly."

Rico picked up the boy again and sat him in the chair. "Your grandma probably needs medical attention. I'm going to call someone to help her."

"'Kay." Dusty rubbed the side of his head and his eyelids fluttered. He was sleepy. He'd probably been up all night trying to wake his grandma.

There was a bench where customers could sit and wait for their orders. Rico turned to Anamarie. "Do you have any big jackets, a blanket or something?"

Rico laid Dusty on a big quilt Anamarie had provided. "Why don't you take a nap while I find out about your grandma."

"'Kay." His eyelids fluttered again and in a second he was sound asleep. The dog hopped up on the bench and snuggled against the boy.

Rico stared at the boy who seemed lost and alone, and a memory from his past wedged its way into his mind. He tried forcing it away but it was right there on the edge of his memory—a little boy, about the same age as Dusty, facing loss and an undetermined future. His mother had just died from a drug overdose. The boy was half Latino and half white and neither side of the family wanted him, so he was put into foster care. Then a miracle happened. His great-grandmother on the Latino side of the family came and got him and raised him. She lived in Houston and she taught him about love, faith and God. She also taught him about respect and manners. Every day she preached right from wrong and at night when she put him to bed, she always told him she loved him. His great-grandmother had been his whole world. Then the gangs had moved into the neighborhood and his happy world had been turned upside down. He promised his grandmother he would never do drugs and he fought those outside influences every step of the way. His hand unconsciously touched the scar on his face. His life was never the same again. But that boy got a second chance. The Rebel family said that Rico had saved Egan's life, but in truth Egan had saved Rico's life.

Rico was going to make sure this little boy had every chance available to him. He pulled out his phone and called the sheriff.

ANAMARIE WATCHED AS Rico dealt with the boy. He was gentle, loving and caring, and the boy responded to that. Dustin didn't even seem to notice the scar on Rico's face, as most kids did. People in town steered clear of the mysterious man who worked on Rebel Ranch. He was often given the cold shoulder. The first time Anamarie had met him he had come into the bakery to buy kolaches for Egan's dog. Any man who would take the time to buy kolaches for someone else's dog had to be special, that was her thought at the time. And that thought had never changed. He came into the shop many times and they talked about nonsensical things. Her mother scolded her for talking to him, but Anamarie never listened to her.

He stood staring at the little boy. Dustin was adorable and she knew the sheriff would find out what had happened to Wendy. It would get sorted out. She had to restrain herself from gobbling up the little boy like Mickey had gobbled his food. She was good at restraining herself around children. That was one area she knew she couldn't get involved. It would break her heart.

Her eyes rested on the man. Well over six feet tall, with broad shoulders, Rico had dark brown eyes and hair and a lean muscled body. His hair was long and tied into a ponytail at his neck, giving him a roguish sort of look. His face was all angles and planes, sharp and defined. The scar across his left cheek made him appear dark and intimidating to others, but never to her. Something in her was drawn to him. He had an air of inherent strength that came from life's lessons. He'd had a hard life and his persona spoke of that every time she saw him. When she looked into his dark eyes,

all she could feel was the warmth they radi-
ated and she knew there was a softer side to
Jericho Johnson—a soft pleasant side. But his
strength was always there.

About two years ago some boys who were
being bullied placed bombs in the school and
locked everyone inside the gym. Elias and
Jericho had gone in to get everyone out, not
knowing when the bombs would go off. Elias
had gotten all the credit for that, but Jericho
had also risked his life to save other people's
children. After that, the town's attitude toward Jericho had changed a little. Some people spoke to him when they met him on the
street, but not one of them would invite him
into their home or invite him to dinner. Her
mother was one of those people and some
days that was hard for Anamarie to stomach.

It was about that same time Miss Kate had
a problem with her heart and Jericho started
coming in to get kolaches for breakfast so
Miss Kate wouldn't have to cook. It turned
into a weekly thing and she couldn't bear to
think about not seeing him on Tuesday morning. They talked about many things, but they
shied away from the personal. There were
times she wanted to tell him about her past
just to see how he would react. She never had

that much courage, though. One rejection in her life was enough.

Earlier when she'd touched his hand, she just wanted to wrap her hand around his. And then she'd realized what she'd done and she was embarrassed. A woman her age was embarrassed at touching a man. How pathetic was that? Enough to give her cold feet. Since her fiancé had jilted her over twenty years ago she hadn't dated anyone. She was nervous as a teenager. And that was really pathetic.

Rico walked over to her and she quickly gathered her thoughts.

"The sheriff's going to Wendy Miller's house to check things out."

"If he's out this time in the morning, that means there's something really wrong with Wendy. She would never let him outside this early."

He glanced toward the boy. "Yeah. I'm taking him over to the sheriff's office until we find out. If something has happened to his grandmother, there has to be a relative who will take him."

"He's so adorable. I'm sure someone will want him." Rico reached down to gather the boy into his arms and she quickly added,

"Take the quilt. He's still asleep. Call me when you find out anything."

He frowned. "I don't have your number."

What! All the time she'd known Jericho amd she'd never given him her phone number. How stupid was that? Then it hit her. Maybe she was like the rest of the people in this town. She was willing to talk to him, but she would never invite him into her home. She would prove to him that she wasn't like everyone else.

She pulled his phone from his pocket and added her number and then reached for hers on the counter and added his to hers.

"Done. We should have done that a long time ago."

He settled Dustin on his shoulder and headed for the door.

"Rico…"

He glanced at her. "Hmm?"

She wanted to say something, but words failed her. Then she thought of the boxed kolaches on the counter. "What about the kolaches for Rebel Ranch?"

"I'll get Elias to pick them up."

"Okay. Call me about Dustin." As he went out the door, a deflated feeling came over her. After all these years, why hadn't she given him her phone number? Was she afraid her mother would find out? Was she a hypocrite like everyone else in this town?

CHAPTER TWO

THE BAKERY WAS on the east corner across the street from the courthouse, facing the main entrance. The sheriff's office and the jail were on the west side and connected to the courthouse by a covered walkway. Jericho walked instead of taking his truck. He called Elias on the way, telling him about the kolaches, the boy and that he would explain later.

It was after six in the morning and a steady line of people were going into the diner for breakfast. Another morning. Another day. Jericho looked down at the boy in his arms. But this one would be different.

He went through the sheriff's office door, but no one was at the front desk so he continued on into the office. Bubba was at a desk writing something in a file.

"Hey, Rico, what have you got there?" Bubba was a big guy, tall as Jericho, but he weighed close to three hundred pounds.

That never held Bubba back. There wasn't a friendlier person in Horseshoe, Texas.

"Dustin Miller. He walked into the bakery about five thirty this morning hungry and dirty. The sheriff is checking on his grandmother."

"What were you doing at the bakery that early?" There was an accusatory tone in his voice and Rico didn't like it. It was so unlike Bubba. But when it came to family, the Wiznowskis always pulled together. For a moment it crossed his mind that Bubba might think Rico wasn't good enough for his sister.

"I was picking up kolaches for the guys at Rebel Ranch. We go to work early, you know, and Anamarie always has them ready early." Rico laid Dustin on one of the cots in a cell and straightened to face Bubba, trying to ignore that feeling in his gut at the steel bars. "Do you have a problem with that?"

Bubba held up his hands. "No, man, no. You're taking this the wrong way."

"Which way should I take it?"

"Well, you know, my mom is…"

"She doesn't like me," Rico finished the sentence for him.

Bubba nodded. "Yeah. She's kind of out

there—" he made waves with his hand "—when it comes to Anamarie."

"Why is that? Or is it just with me?"

Bubba looked down at the floor and usually Rico wouldn't say another word. He'd already fought all his battles and he wasn't looking for another one. But this was about Anamarie and that was too important for him to walk away.

"You're judging me, Bubba, and your family is judging me without knowing the facts. You have no idea why I was in prison. You just know that I was and automatically that puts me on the outside of your righteous family."

"Come on, Rico, that's not true. The Rebel family accepted you and they mean a lot to me. They have been my friends all my life and that makes you my friend."

Rico shook his head. "Until you can accept me for me without the Rebels' approval, you're not my friend."

"Come on, Rico."

The sheriff came through the door and Rico walked out of the cell to talk to him. Some things were more important than the hypocrisy of the Wiznowski family.

"What did you find out?" he asked the sheriff, Wyatt Carson.

When Rico had first come to Horseshoe, he steered clear of the sheriff and his deputies. He just felt safer that way. But over the years Wyatt had begun to trust him and treated him as a person and not a convict. He appreciated that and today their relationship was based on trust, especially after rescuing the kids from the school before the bombing.

Wyatt removed his hat and sat in his chair. It squeaked from his weight. Wyatt had to be in his forties and he'd been sheriff for a long time. Everyone respected him, as did Rico.

Scooting forward, Wyatt asked, "I sensed a little tension when I came in. Is something going on with you and Bubba?"

Rico always tried to be honest and today he didn't shy away from that. "He and Miss Doris object to my friendship with Anamarie."

"Anamarie, huh? I didn't see that one coming and—" he held up a hand "—I'm not getting involved. But give Bubba a chance. He'll come around. That's the type of guy he is."

Rico didn't get a chance to respond as Bubba shouted from somewhere in the jail, "Wyatt, I'm clocking out."

"Okay," Wyatt called back. "But hang tight. I might need you some more today."

"Will do."

Rico was through with small talk. He needed to know what had happened at Mrs. Miller's.

"Wendy has passed away, probably night before last," Wyatt said before Rico could ask anything.

"That means Dustin was alone for two nights and a day."

"The funeral home is picking up the body and Stuart is over there getting all the information. I talked to Mrs. Waring, who lives next door, and she said Wendy had pneumonia and the doctor wanted to put her in the hospital, but she refused because she didn't have anywhere to leave Dustin."

"What kind of neighbor is she that she didn't offer to help?"

Wyatt glanced at Rico. "She's eighty-five years old and uses a walker. There's no way she could handle a four-year-old."

"Sorry, the thought of that little boy walking around during the night looking for food just gets to me."

"Mrs. Waring also said that Dustin's mother is still in prison for drug use. There is a sister, but as I recall Darlene and Connie are not on good terms. Connie didn't take Dustin when Darlene went to prison, so I'm guessing she's not going to want him now. I'll leave that up to CPS."

"A four-year-old couldn't have been easy for Mrs. Miller."

"She was fifty-two years old, Rico, but had a lot of health problems. She was a heavy smoker and had COPD and used an inhaler every day, so yeah it probably wasn't easy."

Another place. Another time. A great-grandmother had accepted a four-year-old into her life and it had changed that little boy forever. Would Dustin be that lucky?

"I have to call CPS to find a home for Dustin until they can locate the aunt or a relative who will take him."

"They'll put him in foster care." Rico's stomach clenched. The words created a bad taste in his mouth and he knew he had to do something. "Wyatt, can I ask a favor?"

"Sure."

"I'll take him until they find someone."

Wyatt leaned back his chair. "Rico, that's very admirable of you, but I have to be honest. CPS will do a thorough background check before they place Dustin in your care. And you know what that means."

"My record."

"Yeah."

"My record was supposed to be expunged. Will I have to pay for it the rest of my life? I'm a model citizen and you know that." Rico looked at his friend. "You would vouch for me, wouldn't you? To keep Dustin from being put into the system?"

"Rico." Wyatt sighed. "I'd trust you with my own kids, but this is CPS. They have rules and have to cross their *t*'s and dot their *i*'s. I'm sorry, that's just the way it is."

"Then why is there so much abuse and neglect in foster homes?"

Wyatt shrugged.

"I can offer Dustin a home for now. I never take any vacation and I know Miss Kate and Falcon will give me some days off. Dustin needs someone to be there for him. One-on-one. Not a household full of kids. I can help him through this. I've been through it." He stared into the sheriff's eyes. "Don't let me down. Don't let Dustin down."

"Rico…"

A loud wail sounded from the jail cell and Rico bounded for the door. Dusty was sitting up crying at the top of his lungs. Mickey barked just as loud. Rico quickly gathered the howling boy into his arms and said, "Hey,

hey, buddy. I'm here. Everything's going to be okay."

Dusty buried his face into Rico's chest. "I want my grandma. I want my grandma."

"You have to tell him," Wyatt whispered, standing in the doorway.

"I know."

"I can do it, if you'd rather."

"No, I just need a few minutes."

"I'm going to talk to CPS."

He held Dusty a little tighter and the boy drifted off to sleep again. Rico couldn't do this alone. He needed help. There was only one person he wanted with him. He fished his phone out of his pocket and sent a text to Anamarie:

I need help telling Dusty his grandmother has died. Do you have time?

In a second he got a text back: I'll be right there.

The weight on his shoulders lifted a little.

Dusty stirred and looked up at Rico. "What's your name?" he asked.

"My real name is Jericho, but everyone calls me Rico."

Dustin touched the scar on Rico's face. "How did you get that?"

"In a fight."

"Did you win?"

"Yeah." *Sort of.*

"Can you take me home now?"

"We need to talk first, buddy."

"Why?"

Rico heard the front door open and soon Anamarie was in the cell. Her face was slightly flushed, as if she'd run there.

She sat beside them. "Hi, Dusty. Look what I brought you." She handed him a sippy cup of milk.

"Thank you. I have to pay you for it."

"No, no, you don't. You've already paid me. Remember?"

Dusty sipped at the milk. "'Kay," he mumbled.

Rico looked at Anamarie for guidance. He didn't know how to start the conversation, but he knew he had to. Dusty took it out of his hands.

"I want my grandma."

Rico's arms wrapped around the boy and he struggled for words. The right words. "The sheriff checked on your grandmother and… she went home to Jesus."

Dusty sat up, his dark eyes wide. "Without me?" he cried.

Clearly the boy misunderstood and Rico was going to have to say the words out loud. "Buddy, can you be brave for me?"

Dusty nodded, taking another sip of milk, his eyes on Rico.

He took a deep breath. "Your grand-mother…died. That's why you couldn't wake her. She went to heaven to be with Jesus. Do you understand?"

"No!" Dusty shouted and threw the milk on the floor. "No!" Pitiful sounds erupted from his throat and then he laid his head on Rico's chest and sobbed until Rico thought his heart would break. At that moment he re-alized he had never had the chance to cry for his own mother when she had died. But he'd cried for his great-grandmother like Dusty was crying now. That pain he would never forget.

Anamarie moved closer and stroked the boy's hair. "It's okay, sweetie. Cry all you want. Rico and I are here for you."

"Rico," Wyatt called from his office. "Can we talk a minute?"

"Sure." With his thumb, he wiped a tear from Dusty's cheek. "Stay with Anamarie.

I'll be right back." He placed the boy in Anamarie's lap and she cuddled him close. Dusty seemed content.

"I just got off the phone with the CPS worker for this area. At the moment she doesn't have a foster home for the boy, but she said she would have one shortly just as soon as she could talk someone into it. All the foster homes are full."

"And…" He was hoping the next part would be what he wanted to hear.

"I told her there was someone here who would take the boy and give him a temporary home. She asked a lot of questions about you and I told her all she wanted to know."

"And…"

"She agreed to let you keep him temporarily, but she will be here at ten o'clock in the morning to visit with you and the boy at your home."

"No problem." The boulder on his chest eased. "Thank you, Wyatt."

"You might want to call Miss Kate. The caseworker will be calling her for a character reference."

"I don't need to call Miss Kate. I trust her to tell the truth and I have nothing to hide."

Wyatt seemed unsure as he shuffled papers on his desk. "I didn't mention anything about your prison record. I'll catch flak for that, but I'm willing to do it so the boy won't have to go into a foster home until they find a relative. And I think you're right. He needs to be with someone who cares about him." The sheriff looked at him. "And I believe you do."

"Yes, and I'll do anything to keep a kid out of foster care."

The sheriff eased back in his chair. "Sometimes the only place a kid has to go is foster homes, and some are really good. I sense you've had a bad experience with them. Would you like to talk about it?"

"No, but thanks for the offer." Rico glanced toward the cell. "Can I take him home now?"

"Sure. Let's see how Dustin feels about it."

Before they could reach the cell, Stuart, the chief deputy, came through the front door. He had a duffel bag in his hand.

Stuart was born and raised in Horseshoe and was a dedicated police officer. "I brought some of the boy's things," he said.

"Good," the sheriff replied. "Just leave it at my desk." Then he whispered to Rico, "Don't get too attached. They will find a home for him."

Rico tried to remember that as Dusty practically leapt into his arms. "Can we go to my house now?"

Rico sat with Dusty on his lap and was glad Anamarie was there to give him support. "You can't stay there by yourself, buddy."

The boy went limp against him. "Oh."

"Would you like to come home with me?"

Dusty raised up, his eyes bright. "My mommy's gonna come get me."

Rico was thrown for a moment. "What?"

"My grandma said she was sick and when she got better she would come and get me. She's probably better now."

Rico glanced at Wyatt, but he didn't offer any advice. "Buddy, we'll check on your mommy, but in the meantime you have to stay somewhere."

The boy's dark eyes grew thoughtful. "'Kay. I stay with you. Where do you live?"

"On a ranch."

"Can Mickey come, too?"

"You bet."

The little boy's eyes brightened. "You got a horse?"

"Sure do."

"Can I ride it?"

"You bet."

"Can Ann-a-ma… I can't say her name."

Anamarie touched his cheek. "You can call me Ana."

"Can Ana come, too?"

Rico looked into Anamarie's blue eyes. "You bet." He got to his feet, feeling a little unsure of what was ahead of him, but he could do no less.

"That's so nice of you to take him."

Rico placed Dustin on his feet. "Go tell the sheriff thank you for letting you stay with me. Then we'll go."

"'Kay."

Rico needed a minute to talk to Anamarie. She picked up the sippy cup, which hadn't broken or leaked onto the floor. "I might need your help. Are you available?"

She smiled one of her custom smiles. "You bet."

They walked back to the bakery with Dusty between them. Mickey trailed behind. Rico carried the duffel bag and quilt over his shoulder, and thought this was a slice of heaven being together with Anamarie and Dusty. It was almost like a family. It was almost real. The *almost* kept him from thinking any further. Happy ever after wasn't in his future. It never had been.

ANAMARIE WAVED GOODBYE and hurried into the bakery. People in line were waiting for kolaches. "Good morning," she said to everyone.

Margie was at the counter and mouthed, "Sorry." Anamarie thought it was about being late, but then she nodded toward the kitchen and she knew it was about something entirely different. Her mother was there.

All the wonderful feelings inside her vanished as she walked into the kitchen. Her mother's gray hair stuck out in all directions as if she hadn't taken time to comb it, and fury tightened every line on her sixty-seven-year-old face.

"Where have you been?" Her mother aimed the question at her like a dagger. "People are waiting to be served and there's only Judy and Margie here. It is your job to run this bakery."

Anamarie gritted her teeth and reached for her apron on a peg. *Don't react. Don't react,* she kept repeating to herself. "I'm well aware of my job description, but there was an unforeseen incident this morning that needed my attention. And it was more important than selling kolaches."

"I'm sorry about Wendy. She was a good

woman, but her grandson is none of your concern."

Anamarie fingered the cotton of the apron in her hand and fought to keep words from spewing out. "A little boy walking around in the dark looking for food is everyone's business. He didn't know his grandmother had passed away. He only knew she wasn't waking up. I went over to the jail to help tell him about his grandmother. If that offends you, then you have a problem."

"You were with *him*. Don't deny it."

"If you mean Rico, yes, I was with him."

"Bubba said he comes in here early before the store opens."

Anamarie took a long breath. *Thanks, Bubba.* "Yes, he comes in early to pick up kolaches for the Rebel family."

"Before six in the morning?"

"Yes."

"And you let him in?"

Anamarie nodded, getting tired of this conversation, but she wasn't going to lie to soothe her mother's judgmental attitude. "We have a cup of coffee and talk. He's a very nice man."

"You know nothing about him."

"I know everything that counts. He's warm and caring and wouldn't hurt a fly."

"I won't have this, Anamarie."

"Have what?"

"Have you getting involved with that man. He's an ex-con. Have you forgotten?"

"No. I see him as the man who risked his life to save all the kids in this town without thinking about himself."

"That was Elias. You're fantasizing about this man."

"Elias couldn't get all those kids out by himself. Rico was right there with him and if you can't see that, then I'm not talking to you anymore."

"I don't like your attitude. I own this bakery and you will do what I tell you. You will not let that man in this bakery before six. I'll call Miss Kate about it."

Anamarie waved a hand. "Call Miss Kate and you'll find out how much the Rebel family loves Rico. Once you make that call the Rebel family will not come back to the bakery, and do you remember Rachel, your daughter Angie's best friend? She's married to Egan and they will not be back in here, either. Miss Kate has a lot of power in this town and your customer list will dwindle. So please make that call."

Her mother's eyes narrowed to a steely

foreboding. "I forbid you to see this man. I will not have you getting involved with an ex-con. That's my last word. You will not bring disgrace to our family."

She turned to hang her apron on the peg and saw Rico standing in the doorway. He held the quilt she'd given him for Dusty in his hands. Without a word, he laid it on the counter and walked out.

No! No! No!

She ran after him but she wasn't quick enough. She saw his truck leaving the parking lot. Not a sound could be heard as people stood there watching and waiting for their orders. Anamarie didn't acknowledge anyone. She calmly walked back to the kitchen, seething.

The apron lay on the floor where she'd dropped it. She picked it up and hooked it over the peg. The moment she saw the hurt in his dark eyes she'd made a decision and she had to have the courage to follow through.

"It's better he heard it this way." Her mother went on as if nothing had happened. "There are a lot of men in this town who would go out with you. All you have to do is fix yourself up and lose some weight. You can find someone better than Jericho Johnson."

The seething turned to a full-blown rage, which threatened to explode right into her mother's face. But she was raised to respect her parents and she calmly reached for her purse and said. "As of this moment, I no longer work here. I quit. And I will not be coming back."

"What are you talking about? You run this bakery."

"But you own it, as you so rudely told me. Now run it." Turning on her heel, she headed for the back door.

"Anamarie, come back here. Don't you dare leave this bakery!"

Anamarie slammed the door so hard she was sure the customers at the front could feel it. She felt it, too. It was a release of all the anger inside her. But it would take a lot more than slamming a door to ease the pain in her.

For years she'd been on a treadmill of doing what her mother wanted and the sad part was she felt there wasn't anything else out there for her but to become the old maid of Horseshoe, Texas.

No one is ever going to want you. Fix yourself up. Lose some weight.

She'd heard those words for years and the criticisms eventually got to her. She believed them. Rico showed her she was still young, vibrant and attractive. She saw it in his eyes every Tuesday morning. He teased her, laughed with her and made her feel things she'd thought had died long ago. For once in her life she wasn't looking back or thinking the situation to death. There was only one option for her: she had to go forward to find herself, and to find the young girl she'd left behind with the heartache and the pain. And she had to embrace the woman she'd become to find the love she wanted. Because above all else she deserved it just like every other woman. And she saw her future in the dark, warm eyes of Jericho.

CHAPTER THREE

RICO DROVE STEADILY toward Rebel Ranch, trying to keep his thoughts at bay. He'd left this morning with hope and excitement in his chest. Now he was just numb with the words *ex-con* running through his brain. He knew Mrs. Wiznowski didn't like him, but this was the first time he'd heard her say it and with such venom that it shook his stony composure.

It was a brutal awakening he hadn't expected. He was letting himself dream about a life with Anamarie and he knew now that was never going to happen. The Wiznowskis were a tight-knit family and she would never go against them.

He'd never thought much about love until he came to live with the Rebel family. He'd loved his great-grandma. Familial love he was familiar with, but the man/woman thing eluded him. After what he'd been through, he never thought it would happen for him.

He saw all the Rebel boys fall in love and get married. As he watched all that happiness, he began to yearn for something of his own. A family of his own.

He was afraid he would never be able to feel the emotion. Or even recognize it. Not many women wanted to spend time with a man who had a scar across the side of his face, wore a long ponytail and had been in jail. He was used to that, until he'd met the lady at the bakery. She smiled at him, treated him nicely and made him want to go back just to spend a few moments with her.

Then one day he went in late to the bakery while Anamarie was closing up. She quickly pulled the shades down and locked the door. He was confused and thought he should leave until she said she'd saved some kolaches for Pete, Egan's dog. Then she offered him a glass of iced tea and they began to talk. As she was talking about her day, the rubber band around her topknot broke and her long hair had tumbled down around her. She'd laughed and immediately tried to put it back up, but he'd stopped her.

People tended to ignore her, but when he'd looked into her blue eyes that day, he received a jolt. The bright blue reminded him of the sky and what lay beyond. He figured God had checked out on him a long time ago, but that day he knew Anamarie was as close to heaven as he was ever going to get.

Love was that precarious thing all the Rebel boys talked about, but they had a hard time recognizing it. So he was surprised he could actually label his feelings: he loved her. Looking into her eyes, he saw it bright and clear. He had no idea how it had happened. He liked talking to her, being with her, but he never had the courage to tell her how he felt. And now he never would. Some things just weren't meant to be.

He glanced back at Dusty who was sound asleep in the car seat. Luckily Rico had two car seats in the back. He kept Egan's kids, Justin and Jordan, on date night.

He would weather this like all the other heartaches he'd been through. But he had to admit this cut a little deeper because it had taken a little piece of his heart.

ANAMARIE DROVE AROUND for a little while to cool down. If she went home, she was afraid her whole family would be there with their opinions of what she'd done. It was her decision and she wasn't backing down now even

if her family begged and pleaded, which she
knew they would do. No one wanted to go
in at three in the morning to make kolaches.
Since her mother had gotten older, the responsibility had fallen onto Anamarie's shoulders.
There was only so much Anamarie was willing to take, though.

Riding around she realized what she was
doing: avoiding a showdown. Time was up.
She had to stand strong. She drove into the
driveway of her home, her very own home.
When Angie had come home from Temple
with her daughter, Erin, she'd bought the
house to keep their mother from controlling
Angie's and Erin's every move, a decision
that had infuriated their mother.

Later Angie had married Erin's father,
Hardy Hollister, and she'd put the house on
the market. Anamarie had decided then it was
time for her to move out of her parents' home.
Of course, her mother had fought it all the
way and there was tension for several months
until her mother had accepted it. It had been
a lifesaver. She had her own space and peace
and quiet.

Parking in the garage, she made sure to
put the door down, and went inside to wait
for the onslaught. It didn't take long. Angie

was the first to arrive, then the twins, Patsy and Peggy, and then Bubba. Her dad was the last to trail in.

Everyone talked at once like angry birds chirping in her face and Anamarie wanted to scream. She raised her hands and said, "Let me make this clear. I am not going back. Someone else will have to make the kolaches from now on. I made this decision and I'm not changing my mind."

"Who's gonna do the baking then?" Patsy asked.

"How about you?" Anamarie countered.

"Me! Most mornings I have to be at the shop by eight. There's no way I'm going in to make kolaches. I didn't like it when I had to do it and I'm not doing it now."

"Don't look at me," Peggy said. "I have the same schedule as Patsy. And I do have a boyfriend, you know. I don't want to spend my extra time in the bakery."

Peggy was dating Stuart, the deputy. It was getting serious.

Everyone looked at Angie. "Oh, please." Angie rolled her eyes. "I'm not leaving my family before three in the morning to make kolaches."

Anamarie thought about her family and

how the situation would affect them. She hated that she had a soft heart, but she was well aware of how her family used her.

Her eyes centered on Bubba. "Do you realize how hard it is on me when Margie doesn't come into work? I have to do everything myself and it's really stressful."

Bubba shifted in his chair. "We were up late and she forgot to set the alarm clock. Sorry, sis."

"And that's okay?" She lifted an eyebrow, letting some of the anger show in her voice. "You're supposed to be a responsible adult, but I don't see much of it when you let your sister do double the work."

"Come on, sis. You know you love that bakery."

"That's a cop out, Bubba."

"Okay, I'll do better."

"I don't care if you do better. It's too late. I'm not going back." She looked around at their anxious faces. "Has Mom told you why I'm not going back?"

"She said you left the bakery with no one there to help the customers and when she called you on it, you were very rude and walked out." Patsy was very quick to quote their mother.

Anamarie shook her head. "Oh, no, that's not what happened." She told them about Dusty and Jericho. "She was upset because I was with Jericho and that I let Jericho into the bakery before six. She forbade me to see him or to let him into the bakery before opening. She said she owned it and I had to do what she wanted. That's what happened."

"You're seeing Jericho?" Patsy high-fived Peggy. "Now that's a story. When did this happen?"

"Don't encourage her," Bubba said. "Mom doesn't want her seeing him and it's causing trouble within the family."

Anamarie laughed. "A typical momma's boy. You won't marry Margie because she's been divorced and that's frowned on by the Catholic Church and your momma. You're weak, Bubba."

"Wait a minute." Bubba got to his feet with a scowl. "Why are you picking on me?"

"Because you're controlled by your mother. We all are," Anamarie told him. "Well, as of today, I'm not. I plan to see Jericho anytime I want and that means someone has to open the bakery and make the kolaches."

Willard, their father, stood. "Anamarie, why don't you come over to the house tonight and talk to your mom. Everyone else has jobs they need to go to and I'm sure you and your mother can work this out. You know she tends to say a lot of things she doesn't mean."

There it was. The guilt trip. This time it wasn't working. "You mean you want me to apologize. Like always."

"Well, you know how your mother is. She's bullheaded and overreacts about everything. Take some time to cool off and come talk to your mom."

She shook her head. "No. I'm not doing that this time. I'm serious."

"That bakery is your life," her father reminded her and that made her that much more determined.

"It shouldn't be. I deserve a life just like everyone else. You have a son and a daughter who moved away because Mom tried to manipulate their lives. And they rarely come home. We all deserve our own lives. So this time, Mom has to be the one to give. She has to realize she can't control us all the time. I've had enough."

"Good heavens. This is going to be like a category five hurricane." He picked up his baseball cap. "I guess I'll go home and look for shelter."

"Have you ever thought of telling her how you feel?" Anamarie asked.

"No, I gave up on that a long time ago. Peace is my goal every day and you kids are making it very hard by suddenly growing up."

As he walked out the door, the room became quiet. The siblings dealt with their own thoughts and Anamarie thought she should just give up. It was like beating her head against a wall. She was doing nothing but hurting herself. Then again, she could see Jericho's face and it gave her strength.

"Jericho, huh?" Patsy mused. "You go for the dark mysterious kind."

Peggy slapped her arm. "This is serious. Stop kidding around."

Patsy flung a hand toward Anamarie. "That's why she's leaving. Because of him, isn't it?"

"Do you know what it's like to hear every day that I can't run the bakery as well as she can, that I'm slow and incompetent and talk too much to the customers? And if I would just fix myself up and lose some weight, I could attract a decent man? Every day it's the same thing. Criticism after criticism. How in the world does anyone see that as love?"

"Anamarie…" Angie got up and sat on the arm of Anamarie's chair.

"When Jericho first started coming in, I spoke to him because no one else would. I found that he's a very nice man. He has the darkest, warmest eyes I've ever seen. Just looking into them I feel as if I'm sitting in front of a fire, all warm and cozy. He makes me feel good about myself and over the years we've grown closer. We talk a lot. He makes me laugh and he listens to what I have to say. He tells me I'm beautiful and I don't need to lose any weight. He tells me I'm perfect the way I am. Do you know what it's like to hear that after all the criticism?"

Again, there was silence in the room.

Anamarie cleared her throat. "I'm forty now and maybe I'm yearning for something I will never have, but I deserve a chance at love just like all of you. I know it's going to be hard and I regret that."

Angie rubbed her arm. "I'm sorry the responsibility for the bakery has landed on your shoulders. That's been very inconsiderate of us. Yes, you deserve a life and we'll all pitch in and help."

"I'd appreciate that, and Margie knows how to make the kolaches. She just needs someone there to help her. Judy is there, but we'd need another person, too. It can work."

"What about the family recipe Mom doesn't want anyone to know?" Peggy asked.

"Margie knows it. She watches me every morning and that secret has been out for a lot of years. Mom just doesn't know it."

"Mom will insist on going into the bakery if you're not there," Bubba said. "Margie has a hard time working with her."

"Welcome to my life," Anamarie quipped.

"Well, that's settled." Patsy raised a hand. "Who's in favor of Margie baking the ko-laches and hiring someone to help her?"

Everyone raised a hand.

"But we need someone there today to help," Peggy said.

"You guys work it out." Anamarie got to her feet. "I have things to do." She told them about Dusty and how she'd agreed to help.

"Have you told Jericho?" Patsy pressed.

A pain pierced her chest. "No. It's not something we've talked about."

"You're scared," Peggy said. "But if he's the man you say he is, it shouldn't be a prob-lem."

But it had always been a problem. The Wiznowski secret her mother wanted no one to know. But Anamarie carried it like a badge on her chest and every day it made her feel less of a woman. Less of a person. But no more. If she wanted a life with Jericho, she had to be honest and forthright and strong enough to handle his reaction.

After this morning, though, she had to wonder if he even wanted to see her.

RICO DROVE ACROSS the cattle guard to Rebel Ranch. It was one of the biggest ranches in Texas with miles and miles of ranchland. To the left was the big two-story log house John Rebel had built for his wife, Kate. About a hundred yards behind the house was a smaller log house which they called the homeplace. It had been the first Rebel home. Paxton and his wife, Remi, lived there now with their daughter, Annie. Not far from the house was an old white clapboard hosue that belonged to Grandpa Rebel. Grandpa didn't stay there much. He had a room at Elias's and slept there most of the time.

About half a mile to the right, through a coastal pasture filled with paint horses, was Quincy's house where he lived with his wife, Jenny, and their two daughters. Their third child was due in two months and this time it was a boy. A lot of babies had been born on the ranch recently. Jude's wife was expecting their third and it was a girl.

Jude, Phoenix and Egan had built homes for their families miles down Rebel Road. Falcon lived across the road from Miss Kate's house. He was the oldest and took over as head of the family when John Rebel had died. He and his mother ran the ranch together. Falcon had taken over completely when Miss Kate had health problems, but she was fine now and nothing was done without her approval.

The barns, office and cow pens were on the right. When Rico'd first come here, he'd been in awe of the big ranch and didn't know how he would fit in. But it had been easy as everyone accepted him without question. He'd learned to cowboy, herd and brand cattle, fix fences and bale hay. As much as he tried to stay to himself, the Rebels kept pulling him in, inviting him to family gatherings and on the holidays. After what Miss Kate had done for him, he would never refuse. But a part of him held back, not willing to believe they'd accepted him as one of the family.

Falcon and Miss Kate's trucks were at the office. He picked up his cell and called to tell them about Dusty. As he'd expected, they said to take all the time he needed.

When he stopped at the bunkhouse, Dusty woke up and looked around. Rico thought he might cry but he didn't. He pointed to the pasture where horses grazed. "Horse."

"Yeah. Are you hungry?"

"No. But I like hot dogs. You got some?"

"You bet." Rico got the boy out of the truck and carried him and the duffel bag into the house. Mickey trotted around looking at his new surroundings and occasionally barking at the horses.

"Toys!" Dusty shouted as they entered the bunkhouse, and ran to the toy box in the corner that Rico kept for Justin and Jordy. He grabbed a truck out of the box and pushed it around on the hardwood floor. Rico watched him for a moment. Dusty was happy for now, but he knew that wouldn't last long.

Rico set the duffel bag on the sofa and found some pull-up pants and a T-shirt. "Time for bath."

Dusty came without a murmur. The little boy was filthy from his hair to his shoes. Sand was even in his socks. Rico scrubbed his hair and had him clean in no time. After he was dressed, Dusty ran back to the toys.

He played for a little while and fell asleep on the floor. Rico picked him up and carried him to the bed. Mickey jumped on the bed and curled up by the boy. Rico watched them for a moment and then went back to the living room and sank into his chair.

He held his head in his hands and wondered what he'd gotten himself into. *Foster homes* were a dirty term to him and he couldn't let that little boy be put in one after losing his grandmother. Tomorrow CPS could take him away and do exactly that. Rico wouldn't be able to stop it, but for today he would be there for Dusty.

He got up and started making the hot dogs. He needed something healthy for the kid, but all he had was chips. And milk. That was healthy. He'd have to go to the grocery store to get food for tonight. As he poured milk into a glass, Dusty cried out. Rico made a dive for the bedroom.

Dusty sat up crying, holding on to Mickey.

"Hey, hey, little buddy, what's wrong?"

"I want my grandma."

Rico gathered him into his arms to comfort him and then carried him into the living room. Sitting in his recliner, Rico patted Dusty's back. "It's okay. I'm here."

Dusty wiped his face on Rico's shirt and looked at him. Rico realized for the first time that the boy's eyes were as dark as his.

"Where's my grandma?"

"She's in heaven."

Dusty twisted his hands, thinking. "With Jesus?"

"Yes."

"What she doing?"

Rico swallowed, trying to be patient. "She's looking down at you and hoping you're not sad. She wants you to be happy."

Dusty buried his face against Rico's chest.

To get the boy's mind on something else, Rico said, "Are you hungry?"

"'Kay."

Dusty ate a whole hot dog and drank a glass of milk. Rico also made Mickey a plate. Afterward Rico took Dusty back to the chair, trying to find a way to cheer him up.

"Were you scared walking around in the dark last night?"

"No." Dusty shook his head. "I had Mickey. He's a monster. He would protect me."

Rico looked down at the sleeping dog that looked more like a timid rabbit. But it was what Dusty thought that mattered.

"What made you leave the house?"

"Mickey and me were hungry and we walked to the grocery store where Grandma gets food. It's not far from our house and… I…I had my money in my pocket, but it was closed." As he talked he twisted his hands and his eyes were dark and serious. "Then we went where we get all the good stuff…and…and…" He seemed to run out of words and rested his head on Rico's chest once again. "Where's my grandma?" he mumbled.

Rico rubbed his back. "I told you, buddy."

"No!" Dusty's eyes grew darker as he looked toward the windows and the sky. "I don't mean there. I mean where is she now?"

Rico had no idea what he was talking about and was clueless about what to say. He wanted to console him and help him but his words were useless. Rubbing his back again, he said, "Tell me what you mean."

"I have to say goodbye to Grandma."

Rico searched for words once again. "Buddy…"

"When…when…" he twisted his hands in agitation "…when Mr. Kovar died, Grandma said we had to say goodbye. We…we…went to a place and Mr. Kovar was in a big box. Grandma lifted me up so I could say goodbye." His bottom lip trembled. "I have to say goodbye to Grandma."

Rico could do nothing but wrap his arms around the little boy who seemed more mature than a normal four-year-old. He didn't understand what was happening. He just knew he had to say goodbye like his grandmother had taught him. Rico now wondered if he should take Dusty to the funeral home. Would it help him? Or would it traumatize him?

He needed a woman's advice. He could call Miss Kate. She'd be more than willing to help, but another woman's face was in his mind. Anamarie. She would know what to do and she could help Dusty with his grieving. But did he call her? Or just let her go?

Dusty slid from his lap. He pulled a tractor from the box and started pushing it around on the floor.

Rico reached for his phone in his pocket. He had her number. All he had to do was call. But it was a lot more complicated than that. His goal ever since he stepped out of a Huntsville prison was to live a quiet and peaceful life. If he called Anamarie, it would be anything but peaceful. Mrs. Wiznowski would make Anamarie's life hell. And he would never do that to her. But then, there was Dusty, grieving, needing someone desperately. He shoved the phone back into his pocket just as a knock sounded at the door.

Dusty's head jerked up.

"We've got company," Rico said in as bright of a voice as he could manage. Bright wasn't in his nature. It was probably Miss Kate or one of the Rebels. It might do Dusty good to see other people. He stepped over toys to get to the door and opened it.

Anamarie stood there.

Several strands of her blond hair had come loose from her topknot and curled around her flushed face. Her eyes were hesitant and filled with worry. He had never wanted to hurt her, but that's exactly what had happened.

"May I come in?" Her anxiety showed in her voice and he had to be strong.

"I… I don't think that's a good idea."

CHAPTER FOUR

"PLEASE, RICO. We need to talk."

At the plea in her voice he opened the door wider.

"Ana." When Dusty saw her, he ran to her and pointed to the toys. "Rico got toys."

"I see," she replied. "I didn't know Rico still played with toys."

Beneath his sun-browned skin she noticed a slight flush to his cheeks. She didn't think it was possible to embarrass him.

He waved at the toys. "They're for Egan's kids. I keep them on date night."

"Ah." He loved kids. It was obvious by the handmade plywood toy box painted red and all the toys piled into it. Now it was going to be even harder to tell him what she needed to.

She sat on the sofa and Dusty placed a trac-tor in her lap. "See, you push this button and the tractor roars." He pushed the button and tractor sounds filled the room. Dusty giggled.

"I see. That's cool." She handed him the toy

and said, "Why don't you play with it while I talk to Rico."

"'Kay."

As she followed Jericho to the kitchen area she looked around at his home. From the hardwood floors to the leather furniture, stainless steel appliances and granite countertops, everything was pristine and clean. She knew that Paxton and Phoenix used to live here with him and it was definitely a bachelor pad, except for the toy box.

There were stools pulled up to a bar and a table in the center of the kitchen. She took a chair at the table, as did Rico. She wasn't sure how to start the conversation, but she'd never had a problem talking to him before.

"You don't believe I think the same way as my mother, do you?"

"No. I know you don't, but my relationship with you causes problems within your family and I don't want to cause you that kind of stress. It's best if we don't see each other anymore."

Her heart sank, but she wasn't giving up. At her age, shyness and embarrassment shouldn't affect her so much. She would be as bold and honest as possible. That was the only way they could have a good relationship.

"Why have you never asked me out on a date?"

He shifted uncomfortably in his seat. "Because your mother wouldn't like it and, again, I didn't want to put you in an awkward situation."

She clasped her hands in her lap. "Well, I'm asking you to go with me on a date to a nice restaurant where I can eat food that I don't have to cook. And we can talk freely and be with each other."

"Anamarie—"

"Why is it so important to you what my mother thinks? She's judgmental. Angie had a hard time when Erin found out that Hardy was her biological father because my mother disapproved strongly. But Angie lived her life the way she wanted and I'm going to do the same. So, do we have a date?"

He tapped his fingers on the wood table and then looked at her. "Yes."

She relaxed a little bit.

"Your mother's opinion matters because it affects you."

"I can take care of myself, Rico. I just don't want our relationship to end, and at our ages we should be able to say and do what we want within reason."

"I just don't want you to get hurt."

She smiled at him and Rico glanced over at Dusty. "The date will have to wait until they find a home for Dusty."

"That's fine with me. I'm here to help."

"What about the bakery?"

Her eyes locked with his. "I quit. I've had enough and I'm not going back."

"What?" One dark eyebrow almost disappeared into his hairline. "How are you going to make a living?"

"I'm very frugal and I've saved most of my salary. I can afford to take some time to help you with Dusty until I decide what I'm going to do. That starts with our first date." Her hands were numb as she stared at the salt and pepper shakers and napkin holder on the table. There were little blue flowers on them and she focused on that. "I want to tell you some things about myself."

"You don't have to tell me anything. I know everything I need to know."

She shook her head. "No. I need to tell you."

"Anamarie, there's nothing you could say that would change the way I feel about you." The warmth of his eyes said she didn't need to say a thing, but for her own peace of mind she had to.

"Just listen. Okay?"

He nodded.

"In high school I had a relationship with Greg Holmes. We fell in love and he asked me to marry him. He gave me a ring and as soon as we graduated we were going to get married. We made all kinds of plans. He was going to take over his dad's plumbing company and I was going to take over the bakery. But then I got sick."

She took a gulp of air. "When I had my period, I started bleeding and it wouldn't stop. I was in a lot of pain. It went on for weeks till my mom took me to the doctor. After a lot of tests, they discovered I had endometriosis, and they also found tumors on my ovaries. They did a biopsy and they were malignant and had to come out. The only solution was a partial hysterectomy." She paused and looked directly at him. "I'll never be able to have children."

The sadness on his face gave her the courage to continue. "Greg said it didn't matter. We'd get married anyway and adopt. Then rumors started to spread around town about Greg and Charlotte Carter. Finally, he came to see me and said he couldn't go through with the wedding. That he wanted children of his own. He was sorry, but that was the way he felt. I was devastated and depressed for a long time. I just poured myself into work. My only thought was that I would be the old maid of Horseshoe, Texas."

He reached across the table for her hand and held it between his warm palms. "No. You're a beautiful vibrant woman and Greg is a jerk."

His hands were rough. She could feel the calluses that indicated how hard he worked. At the understanding in his eyes, she kept talking. "It made me feel less of a woman." He made to speak and she stopped him with a raised hand. "I know it doesn't matter to you. You don't even have to tell me that. Somehow I know deep in my heart that you would never hurt me."

He stroked the back of her hand. "Do you ever see Greg?"

"Oh, sure. He comes into the bakery all the time with his three girls and Charlotte. At first I avoided them, but now it doesn't even matter. They're just another group of customers."

He continued to stroke her hand and she'd

never felt anything so good. "Let's see if I got this right. That's the reason your mother is so protective of you?"

"Yes. She doesn't want anyone to know I can't have children. It somehow diminishes me in her sight and she thinks it would in other people's eyes, too."

"Wow. You have some mother, but in a way I guess I can see that she's trying to keep you from getting hurt again."

"Oh, please." She rolled her eyes.

Rico's phone buzzed, interrupting them. He looked at his phone and said, "It's Wyatt. Maybe they've found a relative to take Dusty." He got up to answer it and she followed.

"Hey, Wyatt." Rico talked for a minute and then clicked off. "Wyatt wants me to bring Dusty into the office. The CPS worker will be there and she's going to talk to Dustin's mother in prison and let Dusty talk to her, too."

"Then we better go."

He stared at her for a moment and she wasn't sure what to read in his expression. "I said I would help you with him."

"Are you sure? Because, you know, we're going to have to give him back."

She did something she was never bold

enough to do. She wrapped her arms around his waist and rested her face on his solid chest. "I can handle it." She never met anyone who was so concerned about her feelings or about her. She got lost in the shuffle of her family. But with Rico, she came first. She felt it and she needed that. She needed him.

And she hoped he needed her, too.

THEY WENT IN Rico's truck and Dusty was full of questions.

"Why do we have to go back there?"

"We just do. Play with your truck and we'll be there in a few minutes." Rico glanced at Anamarie and he couldn't believe all the things she'd shared with him. He wanted to show her just how much of a woman she really was.

In the sheriff's office, he was introduced to Ms. Henshaw, the social worker. Dusty stayed with Anamarie in the outer office.

Ms. Henshaw adjusted her wire-rimmed glasses with the tip of her forefinger. "The sheriff failed to mention a big part of your past."

He met her eyes squarely. "If you're talking about prison, that's exactly what it is. My past."

"Still, I don't appreciate being given half-truths."

"We all want what's best for this little boy," Wyatt said. "So let's concentrate on that. I did what was best at the time and I'm sticking to my decision and I really don't care what CPS thinks, Ms. Henshaw."

"You don't have to get snippy."

"Then let's focus on what happens next."

Ms. Henshaw glanced at the watch on her arm. "The warden should be calling right about this time." As the words left her mouth, Wyatt's phone rang. He put it on speakerphone.

"Sheriff Carson."

"Sheriff, this is Della Riley, the warden at the woman's prison. I have Darlene Miller in my office and she would like to speak to her son."

"He'll be here in a second."

"Is this the sheriff?" A softer female voice came on the line.

"Yes, it is. I suppose the warden told you that your mother has passed away."

"Yes, I've been crying for hours. Where's my baby?"

Loud voices outside the door interrupted the conversation. Suddenly the door swung open and a blonde in a nice dress and heels stood in the doorway. She removed her sunglasses; bracelets jangled as she did. "I want to speak to Sheriff Carson."

"Is my sister there?" Darlene asked.

Wyatt got to his feet. "Yes, I suppose she is."

"Don't let her take my baby. I don't want her to have him."

The woman held out her hand to Wyatt and he shook it. "I'm Connie Grimes, Darlene's sister, and I'm here to help with my nephew."

"No!" Darlene shouted through the phone. "I don't want her to have him. She's wanted everything I've ever had and she's not getting Dustin!"

Rico didn't know what to think, but the conversation soon escalated into a shouting match until Wyatt put a stop to it.

There was quiet for a brief moment and then the social worker spoke to Darlene. "We have to find a home for Dustin. Your sister is willing…"

"No. She doesn't even like kids. That's why she doesn't have any of her own. She's mean and cruel. No, I refuse to let her have Dustin."

"Darlene." Ms. Henshaw sighed. "Dustin needs a home until you get out of prison."

"Who's keeping him now?"

Ms. Henshaw glanced at Rico. "Jericho Johnson."

"Who? I never heard of him. Is he from Horseshoe?"

Wyatt jumped back into the conversation. "Rico, as everyone calls him, works on Rebel Ranch. He's part of the Rebel family and he was the one who found Dusty looking for food and brought him to my office. He and Dusty have formed a connection."

"Is Mr. Johnson there?"

"Yes, ma'am. I'm right here and Dusty is outside the office."

"I'd like to talk to my son."

Rico went into the squad room, picked up Dusty and carried him into the sheriff's office. Anamarie waited for them. "He's here."

"Baby, it's Mommy."

Dustin's eyes flew wide. "Mommy, are you coming to get me? Grandma went to be with Jesus."

There was a long pause on the line and then they heard sniffling. "No, baby, I can't come right now. I still need more time, but I want to find a nice place for you to stay until I can get there."

"I can stay with Rico. He got horses and he got toys. I stay with Rico."

"Okay, baby, I needed to hear your voice. I love you and I'll see you soon."

"I love you, too, Mommy."

Rico took the boy to Anamarie and went back into the office. Connie was in full tirade. "You've always been stubborn thinking of yourself instead of others. Think of your son for once."

"Why do you want my son? You told Mom he should be in foster care."

"You needed to be taught a lesson, but what was I thinking? You never learn, not even when we were little. You defied Mom and Dad and did exactly what you wanted."

There was another long pause as they waited for Darlene to speak.

"Yeah, because you tattled on me so many times. Even when we were in school you tattled to teachers and got me in trouble. You ruined my whole school experience with your jealousy. You took a lot of things from me, but you will never take my son."

Darlene seemed to take a breath, and then asked, "Mr. Johnson?"

Rico leaned against the doorjamb, but at

the sound of his name he stood up straight. "Yes, ma'am?"

"Do you live on Rebel Ranch?"

"Yes."

"I remember how beautiful it was and I wanted to live in that big house with all those handsome cowboys. I want Dusty to be somewhere where he's happy. He wants to stay with you. Do you think you could keep him until I get out? My lawyer said I could probably get out in three months."

He saw this coming when Dusty had said he wanted to stay with Rico, but he didn't really believe Darlene would want him to take the boy. His heart was going to get involved, especially when he would have to give the boy back. So many questions rolled around in his head, but there was only one answer. For him. For Dusty.

"Sheriff," Darlene called. "Do you vouch for Mr. Johnson?"

"Yes, ma'am, I do. He's a good man. He was one of the guys who helped get our kids out of the gym when the bombs went off in our school."

"I remember reading about that. I was just glad my Dustin wasn't in school yet."

There was a short pause and then, "Ms.

Henshaw, I'd like for Mr. Johnson to take Dusty until I can get him. That is, if he's willing."

"You're so stupid!" Connie shouted to the phone. "You've always been stupid!"

Wyatt motioned for Stuart to get the woman out of his office, which he did. As Connie passed Rico, he got a whiff of cigarette smoke. She was a smoker. Even expensive perfume couldn't disguise that.

Wyatt took his seat. "Okay, Darlene, let's get this straight. You want Mr. Johnson to take care of Dusty until you can get out of prison."

"I do, but he never said anything. Dustin gets government assistance and Mr. Johnson can get that."

Rico cleared his throat. "I'll keep him, but I don't want any money."

"Now I know you're a good guy.

"The warden is indicating that I need to get off the phone. Take good care of my baby, Mr. Johnson. I trust you and when I get out this time I'm going to stay clean."

"For Dustin's sake, I hope you do."

The line went dead and the three people left in the room stared at each other. Ms. Henshaw was the first to speak. "Mr. Johnson, I'll be at your home tomorrow morning at nine to see where Dustin will be living. He's in school for most of the day and I expect you to get him there and pick him up."

"No problem. But nine o'clock in the morning isn't going to work. I have to get Dustin to school and go to work. I can meet you about six in the evening."

"I'll rearrange my schedule to make sure this little boy is placed where he will be happy and safe." Ms. Henshaw gathered her briefcase and purse and left the room.

Wyatt glanced at Rico. "You work long hours on the ranch. How are you going to make this work?"

"I know a pretty lady who's going to help me." He tried hard not to smile.

"Anamarie. You won't find anyone nicer than her and I hope it works out for you."

"Thanks, Wyatt." He paused for a moment. "What about arrangements for Wendy Miller?"

Wyatt shrugged. "Fred from the funeral home called and the body will be ready tomorrow morning. He's wondering how he's going to get his money. I told him he would have first claim after her estate is settled. There won't be much. The sale of the house will more than pay for her funeral and maybe some left over for Dustin."

"Maybe it would give Darlene a new start."

"We can hope. But with the sister in town I don't know what's going to happen." Wyatt waved a hand. "Anyway, that's another story. I'll have Stuart go through Mrs. Miller's papers. Maybe he can find a will and then everything will be simple."

"Yeah, right." He heard Wyatt laugh as he left the room.

It was refreshing to see Anamarie's pretty face, even if she was frowning.

"No, no, no!" Dusty shouted, burying his face in Anamarie's chest as Connie attempted to talk to him.

"I'm your aunt," Connie kept on. "I just want to get to know you."

"Nooo!" Dusty wailed.

"No means no, Ms. Grimes," Rico said with a bite in his voice.

"Now listen here—"

Dusty scrambled from Anamarie's lap and ran to Rico. With Dusty in his arms, they walked out of the office.

"I don't want to go with her!" Dusty cried.

Rico patted his back. "It's okay, buddy. You're going home with me...and Anamarie." He looked over at her and her smile was everything he wanted to see.

ANAMARIE MARVELED AT Rico's gentle nature with Dusty. He eased all of the little boy's fears. And somehow he eased hers, too.

He slid into the driver's seat, his hands on the steering wheel. "It's getting late so how about if we go to Temple and have supper?"

"Sounds great," she said with a slight smile. "I really don't mind cooking. I don't know why I said that."

"No cooking. Right, Dusty?"

"Uh-huh."

"Where do you want to go?" Rico asked her.

She had hoped that he would choose a place, but he probably didn't go out all that much and didn't know of any restaurants in Temple.

"Pizza," Dusty shouted from the back seat.

"Anamarie gets to choose."

"Why?" Dustin wanted to know.

"Because she's a girl and we always let girls go first."

"Oh." Clearly Dusty was baffled by the answer.

"There's a nice Italian restaurant that I used

to go to with Angie and Rachel and it has a kiddie menu. It was Angie's way of getting me out of the bakery and the food was delicious."

"Pizza it is then."

Excitement ran through her veins at the light in his dark eyes; her first date with a dark, mysterious stranger. Except he wasn't a stranger. He was the man of her dreams and the man she wanted to share her life with. They'd talked enough and it was time to take their relationship further. It was long overdue.

CHAPTER FIVE

EVEN THOUGH DUSTY was with them, the date was everything she imagined it would be, except for the stares that came their way. Everyone in the restaurant wore shorts and T-shirts. Rico had on his jeans, boots and a Stetson. He hooked his hat over the back of a chair and a little boy ran by and knocked it off. The boy stopped and picked it up and said he was sorry and then asked, "Are you a cowboy?"

"Yes, I guess I am."

"Cool." The boy ran back to his parents and Anamarie sensed Rico was a little nervous. He wasn't quite sure how people would react to his appearance, the scar on his face and the long ponytail down his back. He didn't have to worry. All the women were looking at a handsome cowboy, as was Anamarie.

Dusty fell asleep on the way home. He didn't even wake up when they put his pajamas on him.

As they walked back into the living room, Rico asked, "How about a cup of coffee?"

"Coffee? Doesn't it keep you awake?"

He shook his head. "No."

"Well, then. I'll have a cup," she replied. She was all for trying new things with him. She sat on the sofa while he made the coffee.

"Dusty is worn out," he said as he handed her a mug. "It's been a long day for him."

"Yes, and Darlene's sister didn't help." She took a sip of the coffee. It had cream and sugar. She glanced at him. "How do you know the way I like my coffee?"

"I've seen you make it at the bakery." He eased into a recliner, the swish of the leather soothing to her senses.

"You're very perceptive." She traced the handle of the cup with her forefinger. She was flirting with him and she felt a little naughty.

"When it comes to you, I am."

"Rico…" She had no idea what she was going to say, but she wanted to say something.

He spoke first. "We had a good time tonight, didn't we?"

"Considering everything that happened today, yes, we did. Dusty enjoyed himself, too. Next time I'm going to cook you supper at my house."

"You don't have to do that."

She lifted an eyebrow. "Why? Are you afraid of my cooking?"

"No. I know it would be as delicious as your kolaches."

The eyebrow darted higher. "You do?" He was so good for her. He made her feel special. But this day had to end and she was dreading that. She placed her mug on the coffee table. "I better go. It's getting late." She reached for her purse on the sofa.

"You could stay. There's an extra bedroom. I don't want to pressure you, but Dusty would be excited if you were here in the morning."

The offer was, oh, so tempting and she wasn't sure why she was holding back. She wanted to stay, but she also wanted to be free of all the guilt and insecurities that plagued her.

She stood, pushing the strap of her purse over her shoulder. "I'd like nothing better, but I have to get some things straight in my head first. I have to do this without feeling guilty or worrying about my mother."

"Take your time. No pressure." He stood also, his tall frame towering over her. "I was going to ask if you could pick Dusty up from school tomorrow. I missed work today and I know Elias is chomping at the bit to finish that fence."

"No problem. I'll pick him up."

They walked toward the door. "I'm going in early to introduce myself to his teacher and explain Dusty's situation. I'll let her know you'll be there for Dusty."

Rico opened the door and they stood facing each other as the warm night air embraced them. She didn't know what to say. It had been a long time since she'd been with a man and she wasn't sure how to take the lead. But she needn't have worried. Rico cupped her face with his hands and gently kissed her lips. She'd waited a long time and it was worth every minute. She rested her head on his chest.

"You're the most wonderful man, and I want our relationship to be honest and straightforward. I don't want to be sneaking around. I just need to be sure of what I'm doing. Right now I'm still upset with my mother, but I'm not going to let her control my life."

"Do what you have to," he whispered. She turned and walked to her car and drove away. She couldn't help but feel she was leaving the best part of her life behind.

Rico was up early the next morning, fixed breakfast and then woke up Dusty to get dressed for school. He had his backpack Stuart had sent with Dusty's things. It wasn't long before they were out the door. He put Dusty in the car seat and drove to the office, which was across from Miss Kate's house.

He didn't want to leave Dusty alone in the truck so he took him with him. He wanted to speak to Miss Kate. All the brothers were there and their voices ebbed away as they entered the room.

"Oh, my," Miss Kate said. "He's a cutie."

Miss Kate and Falcon were sitting at their desks and the brothers sat around in chairs. Grandpa Abe sat in the comfy chair.

"You're bringing the kid to work, Rico? What are you thinking? You can't work with a kid."

"I don't plan to, Elias. I just wanted to stop by to let you know I have to take Dusty to school, but I'll come right back to work on the fence."

"What do you know about kids?" Elias asked, leaning back in a chair.

"About as much as you do," Rico shot back, and everyone in the room laughed. Rico was used to Elias. They bantered all the time.

Soon all of the brothers filed out of the office to go to work, even Grandpa. But he didn't go to work. He'd go to his house and take a nap and then eat lunch with Miss Kate. For years they tolerated each other, both blaming the other for John Rebel's death. As they had grown older they'd found peace and they were all grateful for that.

Until now Dusty had his head buried in Rico's neck, a little shy with so many men around. After everyone had gone, except Miss Kate, Dusty raised his head.

"He's a handsome little boy," Miss Kate remarked. "And you'll do very well with him." With salt-and-pepper hair and a friendly smile, she was the personification of what a mother should be. Everything she did, she did for family.

"Thank you. And thank you for giving me a good character reference to Ms. Henshaw."

"I only told her the truth."

"I still appreciate it."

"Is something wrong, Rico?"

"Huh… I just wanted to let you know that Anamarie will be spending a lot of time at my house."

"You think I might disapprove?" She lifted an eyebrow.

"No, I know you're not that type. Since it's your house, though, I just wanted you to know."

She folded her hands on the desk. "Rico, the bunkhouse is your home. It's yours and what you do there is your business. I can't tell you the number of women who drove in and out of here when Phoenix and Paxton lived there. But as long as they kept it there and not in my home, I was okay with it. You're more than welcome to bring Anamarie into my home or anywhere else on this property. She's a very nice woman and I hope there's a little romance going on there, too."

"Maybe." He winked and walked out of the room.

As he was putting Dusty in his car seat, he said, "Ana."

"Yeah, Ana. She's going to pick you up from school today," Rico told him.

"Why you not picking me up?"

"I have to work, and I'll be there just as soon as I get off. You'll be okay with Ana."

Dusty twisted his hands in agitation. He was getting attached to Rico. He felt secure and safe around him. And now that security was a little shaky and he didn't know what to say or do. Rico didn't neither, other than to reassure him.

"I'm not going anywhere, buddy. I'll always be here. Do you understand?"

"Huh-hmm."

Rico drove to the school and helped Dusty with his backpack. He should've looked inside, but he hadn't had time. He hoped everything Dusty needed was in there. Inside the foyer, he paused for a moment, glancing at the wall on the left. A large glass case showcased photos of the bombing of the school. There was a photo of him carrying the principal out of the rubble and of Elias running toward safety as he'd gotten the last person out. There was also a photo of them on horses. How they'd gotten that photo he'd never know, but he suspected it was one of the Rebels' wives. At the bottom it read: Heroes of Horseshoe, Texas. Elias Rebel and Jericho Johnson.

Rico hated going to the principal's office. Every time he saw principal Gaston the man would shake his hand until Rico's arm grew numb. The man was thankful Rico had saved his life and Rico understood that, but it was time to forget and move on.

The visit was short. As usual the principal shook his hand and thanked him one more time, and then told him that he'd been notified by the sheriff about Dusty. Everything was okay and he could go to class.

Miss Phyllis Holt was all of twenty-five years old, blonde and pretty. She smiled sweetly at Rico, telling him how sorry she was about what Dusty was going through and she would handle it as carefully as possible.

"Thank you," he replied.

She glanced at Dusty's backpack. "Is his lunch in there? Mrs. Miller always fixed his lunch."

Damn! He'd forgotten about lunch. He wasn't used to this. "I'm sorry, I forgot about his lunch."

"Oh, no worry. He can get lunch in the cafeteria. I'll go with him and make sure he does."

"I'd appreciate that and tomorrow I'll pack his lunch."

"Don't worry about it. I admire you stepping up and taking care of Dusty. If you need any help…" A wealth of meaning that Rico understood coated every word.

"I have that covered, thank you. Anamarie Wiznowski will pick him up from school. If you can make sure he gets to her, I'd appreciate it."

"Oh…okay."

Clearly she didn't like his answer, but he wasn't getting involved with Dusty's teacher. There was only one woman for him. He squatted in front of Dusty.

"Have fun today. I'll see you tonight at the bunkhouse."

Dusty nodded his head and suddenly threw his arms around Rico's neck and squeezed tight. Rico patted his back. "You'll be okay." He stood and walked out of the room, resisting the urge to look back. He had to go and he couldn't be swayed by emotion. Dusty would do fine.

But he wondered if his life would ever be the same again.

ANAMARIE HAD A restless night. She was forty and trying to decide what to do with the rest of her life. It was an important decision and she wanted to make the right one for her and for Rico. She wasn't going to let guilt make her feel less than who she was. Once she had quit the bakery she'd found her wings and she wasn't going to be tied down anymore.

By morning she'd made a decision and she knew it was the right one. She packed a suitcase of everything she would need. She placed it in the car and drove to her parents' house. It was around lunchtime and she knew her mother always went home to fix her dad's lunch. She wanted to catch both of them.

She parked in front of the house and went through the front door. It was one of the older homes in Horseshoe. It had half brick columns along the front porch and her parents sat out there in the evenings and watched the traffic and the neighbors. It was a three-bedroom two-bath house, but it wasn't big enough for seven kids. They'd all survived, though.

Her parents sat at the kitchen table, eating lunch. Her mother glanced up and said, "I guess you've come to your senses."

Anamarie knew how this was going to go and she was prepared. She pulled out a chair. "No. I'm not coming back, but I wanted you to know what my plans are. I don't want you to hear it from someone else."

Her mother wiped her mouth with a napkin. "Most of the time I hear what my kids are doing from someone else anyway, so it wouldn't be anything new."

"That's because we can't talk to you."

"Oh, now it's my fault. It's always the

mother's fault." She pushed back her chair and carried her plate to the sink.

"For heaven's sakes, Doris," her dad spoke up. "Let the girl talk."

Her mother came back and sat with her arms folded across her chest, indicating that she wasn't going to listen with an open mind. But that didn't matter. Anamarie had to tell her anyway.

"Rico has asked me to help him with Dusty, Wendy Miller's grandson. He has nowhere to go and Dusty's mother has asked Rico to keep him until she can get out of prison. I've agreed to help. I've packed my things and will be moving into the bunkhouse with Rico. I'm sure he's cleared this with Miss Kate."

"You can't be serious." Her mother's eyes almost bugged out her head. "It will be the talk of the town. You're making yourself available for this man. Can't you see that?"

"No." Anamarie kept her cool. "I see a very nice man trying to help a little boy who has no home. That's the type of person he is. If you would just let down your guard and get to know him, you'd see that. He's not going to take advantage of me. He wouldn't do one thing unless I wanted it. And if people want to talk, let them. I'm sorry it bothers you, though."

Her dad laid his napkin in his plate. "Well, Anamarie, it's your life and I think you're old enough to make your own decisions. And I'm gonna do what every father does, I'm going to support you because I believe it's about time for you to get out from under your mother's wings."

"How dare you, Willard!" Her mother was furious.

"I'm more open-minded than you, Doris. You've been trying to protect her since the cancer scare and Greg breaking the engagement. It's time to let go and let her live her life the way she wants."

"By moving in with an ex-con?" Her mother's shrill voice scraped across her skin.

Her dad got up from his chair. "I'm sure there's a story behind his incarceration. I've heard the governor pardoned him, but that's just a rumor, and unlike you, Doris, I paid little attention to rumors. The Rebel family has accepted him as one of them and that's good enough for me." He walked toward his chair in the living room, but suddenly turned back. "Since you're up there on your high and mighty pedestal, you might want to tell your daughter why we got married."

"Willard!" Her mother's face turned red.

Her father could only mean one thing and Anamarie quickly counted the months from when her parents got married and her brother Frank was born. It didn't add up. Her parents were married in October and Frank was born the next August.

"If you're counting months," her dad added, "we didn't get married in October. We got married January fifteenth, the same year Frank was born. Your mom just told everybody we got married in October. When she discovered she was pregnant, her mother sent her to live with her aunt in Temple, so no one here really knew what was going on until we came home that summer with the baby."

Her mother stared at her husband with steely cold eyes. "I'll never forgive you for this. There was no need for her to know."

"Yes, there is. You're human, Doris. Just like everyone else. So cut the apron strings and let Anamarie go live her life. You've held on long enough. Give her your blessings. Bubba's already living with Margie so I don't see the difference."

"Bubba's a man. It's different."

Her dad shook his head. "No, it isn't. Now I'm going to watch the news and get back to work. I've said all I'm going to say."

"And it was more than enough," her mother snapped.

Silence filled the room and seemed to enclose Anamarie and her mother in a private capsule. What was said now would shape the rest of Anamarie's life. Today she would talk to her mother as an adult.

Her mother picked up a napkin from table and squeezed it in her hand, and kept squeezing it over and over. Her mother was embarrassed and didn't know what to say. But Anamarie did.

"Did you love Dad at the time?" There was no doubt in her mind that her parents loved each other. It was just hard to see that at times with her mother's judgmental attitude.

"What does a teenager know about love?" her mother mumbled.

"A lot. Those feelings last a lifetime."

Her mother's head shot up. "Are you still in love with Greg?"

"Heavens, no. But I remember what it felt like at the time. I thought he was the one and my feelings were real and he crushed them. I'll never forget that."

"This Rico thing, is it like your feelings for Greg?"

"No." She shook her head. "My feelings now are nothing compared to what I felt then. My feelings for Rico are much different. He makes me feel special. He tells me I'm beautiful and I'm perfect just the way I am. It feels good to hear that. He makes me feel like a woman and I needed that feeling to make me realize that I still am. Do you understand that?"

Her mother nodded. "I'm just so afraid he's going to hurt you."

Anamarie reached out and clasped her mother's hand. "Then let me feel the pain and the joy of loving someone."

"If that's what you want," her mother murmured so low she could barely hear it.

"Thank you." She got to her feet. "Now I have to go pick up a little boy who desperately needs someone and then we're going to the grocery store to buy food for supper."

"I still disapprove, Anamarie."

"I know, Mom." She patted her mother's hand. "If anyone asks you about me and Rico, you can tell them I'm having the time of my life."

"You go, girl," her dad said.

She had to resist the urge to skip all the way to her car. The meeting went better than she had ever imagined. Now she could go into this new relationship with Rico with her heart wide open.

With a smile on her face she waited for Dusty outside his classroom. All the kids came out, except Dusty. She glanced in and saw the teacher talking to him.

"Is something wrong?" she asked, holding out her hand. "I'm Anamarie Wiznowski and I'm here to pick up Dusty."

"Oh, yes," the teacher said, shaking her hand. "I'm Phyllis Holt and Mr. Johnson said you would be coming for him."

"Ana!" Dusty cried and ran to her.

"You ready to go home?"

"Yeah. To Rico's."

As they made to leave, the teacher asked, "May I speak to you for a minute?"

"Sure. Wait right here," she said to Dusty, and walked back to the teacher.

"Our lesson today was to draw a picture of our families and I pulled Dusty aside and asked if that would make him sad and he said no. I just wanted you to know that. I wouldn't want Mr. Johnson to be upset with me."

Anamarie caught that note in her voice.

She was interested in Rico. And, oh, she was young and beautiful. But she wasn't going to let that get to her. She was too happy and nothing was going to ruin this day.

As she strapped him into the car seat, Dusty said, holding up a piece of paper, "Look what I drew."

She took the paper and stared at it. Three stick figures were at the bottom. One was tall and had long brown hair. The other was a blonde woman standing next to the tall man. A little boy stood beside the woman. In the clouds was a gray-haired lady with wings. She had to look closely to figure that out. Darlene was nowhere in sight.

Dusty had drawn them as his family. She wasn't sure how to deal with this so she'd wait and let Rico handle it. They would probably just let it go, but she knew somewhere in their hearts they were becoming a family. There was no way to stop that.

CHAPTER SIX

AS THE SUN inched toward the west, Rico stopped nailing barbed wire to a post and pulled out his phone. It was five thirty. He wiped sweat from his brow with a sleeve of his chambray shirt. Ms. Henshaw would be at his house at six o'clock and he had to go.

He had already texted Anamarie that the woman was coming, but he needed to be there. Elias wasn't going to take this well. He was a workaholic.

"What's up?" Elias shouted. Elias pulled the wire with a wire stretcher and Rico always nailed it to the post. That was their pattern; the way they worked. "We need to keep working."

"I've got to go," Rico called back. "The CPS worker is coming to my house at six and I have to be there."

"Oh."

Rico had never said no to a Rebel and he didn't want to today, but he had to be there for Dusty. As words were about to leave his mouth, Elias's phone buzzed. There was only one person who could keep Elias from working and Rico hoped it was her.

It was. Elias talked for a few seconds and then clicked off. "I've got to go home, too. I guess this fence can wait."

"Is something wrong?" Elias's demeanor changed drastically and Rico wondered if anything was wrong with Maribel.

"I don't think so," Elias answered, picking up tools to put back into the Polaris Ranger. "Maribel's at home with her feet up. They're swollen and her back hurts so she's lying down and wants me to come home. I swear, that baby's going to weigh twelve pounds by the time it's born. She's only a little over four months and she's huge."

They crawled into the Ranger and headed for the barn. Rico jumped out as soon as the ATV stopped. He had to go, but he hesitated. He was the hired hand and did what the Rebels told him, but today he had to take a stand and he wasn't sure how Elias would react. "I'll help you tomorrow and a half a day Friday, but I'm taking some time off to help Dusty adjust. And I got a call from

Wyatt that Mrs. Miller's funeral is on Saturday at ten. I have to take Dusty to that."

"Good luck, man."

That was easier than Rico had anticipated. In that moment he realized the problem wasn't with the Rebels. It was with him. He felt obligated and didn't want to ever let the Rebels down. It was his mindset and he didn't know if he could ever change that. He shook off the thoughts.

"Thanks." Rico waved to Elias and got in his truck and headed for the bunkhouse. He noticed a car at the big house and he assumed it was Ms. Henshaw talking to Miss Kate. He had a few minutes.

He opened the front door and two things hit him at once. The delicious smell and a little tornado barreled into him. Mickey barked his head off. Rico picked up Dusty and glanced at the woman in the kitchen who looked at him with the most beautiful smile. For the first time he knew what it was like to really feel at home.

"Hey," he said. "It smells heavenly in here."

"Ana made sghetti for us." Dusty pointed to the counter. "And a chocolate pie. I helped her."

Rico patted his small chest. "Good for you."

Dusty wiggled down and went back to his coloring book on the coffee table.

"Ms. Henshaw is at Miss Kate's," he said to Anamarie. "I'm dirty and sweaty, but I don't have time to change."

"It doesn't matter," she told him, laying a dish towel on the counter. "She just wants to see where Dusty will be living."

A knock sounded at the door and he went to answer it. Ms. Henshaw stood there with a purse over her shoulder and a briefcase in her hand. They shook hands and he invited her inside.

"I just saw you drive up, but I didn't see Dusty. Was he here by himself?"

"Of course not," Rico told her with grit in his voice. "I wouldn't leave him by himself." He glanced toward Anamarie in the kitchen. "I have some help."

At the sound of Ms. Henshaw's voice, Dusty jumped up and ran to Rico and practically climbed up his body. "Don't let her take me, Rico. Don't let her take me."

Rico patted his back. "Hey, buddy, no one's going to take you. You're staying with me until your mom can come get you. Ms. Henshaw is here to see where you live. Can you show her where you sleep and where you take a bath?"

Dusty was hesitant at first. Rico set him on his feet and he ran to his bedroom and Ms. Henshaw followed, as did Rico.

"This is my bed and that's Elmo," Dusty said, pointing to the stuffed doll. "He sleeps with me." Mickey jumped up on the bed and Dusty added, "Mickey sleeps with me, too." Mickey licked his face and Dusty giggled, running into the bathroom. "This is where I take a bath." He darted to the kitchen. "And this is where I eat." He went to Anamaria and she picked him up. "Ana makes good food."

As if sensing that Ms. Henshaw wanted to ask questions, Anamarie said to Dusty, "Why don't you color me a picture?"

"'Kay." Dusty dashed back to the living room.

Ms. Henshaw frowned. "Don't you work at the bakery in town?" she asked Anamarie.

"Yes, but I've taken some time off to help Rico with Dusty."

"That's nice. I think it's good to have a woman's influence." Ms. Henshaw looked around and Rico expected her to ask more questions, instead she said, "This isn't what I expected."

"What did you expect?"

"When Miss Kate said you lived in the bunkhouse, I pictured something very sparse and primitive." She glanced around again. "But this is obviously a nice home and he seems very happy."

"He is. Later in the week I'm taking him to his grandmother's funeral and things might change. If he gets upset, we'll just bring him home."

Ms. Henshaw glanced at Anamarie. "Will you be there?"

"Yes."

Ms. Henshaw nodded. "That's good. Kids react better with women. No offense, Mr. Johnson. That's just a known fact."

"No offense taken. Anamarie will be with me all the way."

Ms. Henshaw held out her hand and Rico shook it. "Everything seems in order. I'll check in with you in a couple weeks or if I hear from Darlene before then. Her lawyer is working very hard to get her out and the parole board tends to be lenient when there's a child involved."

Ms. Henshaw left and Rico sank into his

chair. He was tired and dirty and needed a break. Anamarie handed him a glass of tea. He took it and caught her hand with his other one and pulled her down on the arm of his chair. "Thank you for being here."

"No problem, Mr. Johnson."

He looked into her eyes. "You know that song 'You Light Up My Life'?"

"Yes."

"That's what you do for me. Every time I look at you."

Anamarie held a hand to her chest. "Oh, my goodness, you're making me blush."

Dusty spoiled the moment by crawling into Rico's lap. He sensed they were having fun and he wanted to be a part of it. Anamarie plucked him from Rico's lap. "Rico is tired and we have to let him rest. You can help me in the kitchen."

"Why is he tired?"

"He's been working all day."

"Oh…"

Their voices trailed away and Rico thought this was what it was like to have family. A real family. A woman he loved and a child he adored. Except the child wasn't theirs. They had to give him back. At that moment, Rico realized just how hard that was going to be. For him. And Anamarie.

AFTER SUPPER AND getting Dusty to bed, Rico took a shower and Anamarie curled up on the sofa, sipping coffee. In worn jeans, a T-shirt and no shoes, Rico sank into his recliner with his feet propped up. His feet were white and she laughed.

"They're in my boots all day and never see the light of day."

His long damp hair hung down his back and reminded her of a fierce warrior coming to right a wrong. She was happy to just be around him. After Greg's rejection, she had shut down her emotions and her mother's over protectiveness had reinforced the way she felt about herself, ugly, unattractive and unfeminine. Rico had changed all that.

"I thought Ms. Henshaw was going to ask questions about your presence here," Rico said, sipping his coffee.

"Me, too. But she seemed okay with it."

"Yeah. I think she trusts us to do the right thing by Dusty."

"And she would be right," Anamaria replied, tracing the handle on her coffee mug.

She had to tell him her decision. She placed her cup on the coffee table.

"You don't have to leave this early, do you?" he asked.

"No." She leaned back on the sofa. "I don't plan to leave at all."

That got his attention. He removed his feet from the rest and sat up straight. "Does that mean…?"

She told him about her visit with her parents and he listened intently. "I put my things in the spare room."

He reached out and grabbed her arm and pulled her onto his lap. "Let's go over this again. You told your parents you're moving in with me and they're okay with that?"

She tilted her head to look into his dark eyes. "My dad is fine with it. My mother is my mother and she disapproves. I think we've come to mutual agreement and she won't interfere in my life anymore."

He rested his forehead against hers. "Wow. I didn't expect this to happen so soon, but I'm happy about it. Dusty needs you here too, just as Ms. Henshaw had said." He kissed the side of her face. "We need to take this slow so you're sure about this arrangement."

She nestled against him. "I'm sure, Rico."

He was right, though. They needed to take things slow, especially with a kid in the house. "But we need to take care of Dusty and then we'll see where this relationship goes."

He kissed her lightly. "Sounds like a good plan."

She scrambled up from the chair, feeling cool after his warm touch. "I'll check on Dusty, take a shower and go to bed."

Dusty was curled up with Elmo and Mickey. When Anamarie came out of the shower, she noticed Rico was sound asleep in his chair. He probably slept there a lot. Unable to resist she walked over and kissed his brow. He stirred and touched her face.

"Shouldn't you go to bed?" she whispered.

"I will, in a minute," he replied sleepily.

She walked toward her bedroom, leaving him asleep. He was totally exhausted from the day's work. Surely the Rebels didn't expect him to work that hard. From what she'd heard he'd worked that way for a long time. Maybe he did it to fit in with the Rebels. He had no family and maybe it was his way of becoming a part of the family. She was sure Miss Kate didn't expect that of him though.

She drifted off to sleep and hoped that one day she and Rico could have their own home.

Their own family. She could prove to him how much she loved him just the way he was; scar, long hair, prison record and all. And he would never have to work himself to death for her. That was the wish of her heart. A fairy tale. But fairy tales were known to come true.

ON SATURDAY THEY scrambled to get ready for the funeral. Rico sat with Dusty in the living room trying to explain what was going to happen today.

"You remember you wanted to say good-bye to your grandma."

"Yeah. When we gonna do that?"

"This morning."

"Oh... I gotta wear my good pants." Dusty darted to his room and suddenly came back. "Where's my good pants?"

Rico had no idea where his good pants were, so he spent ten minutes sorting through Dusty's clothes before he found them with a white shirt.

"That's them!" Dusty shouted, looking at the wrinkled pants and shirt. "They got wrinkles."

"Do you have an iron and ironing board?" Anamaria asked.

Rico turned around and stared at the

woman in the doorway. She wore a black dress with high heels that made her appear more sophisticated and more out of his league.

"Whoa." He took a step toward her, holding out his hand. "I don't believe we've met."

She smiled, but before she could say anything, Dusty intervened, "That's Ana."

With a shy grin, she took the shirt and pants from Rico.

"The ironing board is in the utility room," he told her.

Within minutes they were all dressed and in the truck ready to go. They were quiet on the way into town. Rico was trying to figure out what would be easier for Dusty. He just had to walk him through it and do the best he could. Anamarie was there to help him.

They were early because Rico wanted Dusty to have private time with his grandmother alone. He released Dusty's seat belt and asked, "Are you ready for this, buddy?"

Dusty nodded his head. "I have to say goodbye to Grandma."

Rico lifted him out of the seat. "Okay, then, let's do this."

He took Dusty's hand and then Dusty reached out his other hand to Anamarie. He walked between them into the funeral home. Rico had called ahead to let the funeral director know they were coming. Red carpet led to the front where the casket rested on a platform. The top of the silver casket was open and an arrangement of white roses rested on the bottom half.

Rico had called Lacey, Miss Kate's sister-in-law, who was the only florist in town, and had asked if Connie Grimes had ordered flowers for the casket. She'd said no and he had ordered flowers. He might have been out of line, but he'd done it for Dusty. A big pink spray on the right was from the Rebel family and there were two more sprays on the left and some potted plants.

When they reached the casket, Dusty held up his arms to Rico and he lifted the boy up so he could see his grandmother. It surprised him that the woman had gray hair. A serene face showed the passing of the years. She looked at peace. Dusty stared down at her for a minute and then he leaned over to kiss her. "Goodbye, Grandma. I live with Rico now. I…" Dusty started to cry, big tears running down his cheeks and Rico gathered him into his arms and patted his back.

"Are you ready to go, buddy?"

Dusty nodded with his head buried into Rico's shoulder.

Before they could leave the pastor came up and tried to speak to Dusty. "I'm so sorry about your grandma," the man said.

"No, no, no!" Dusty cried.

"I don't think he's ready for this," he told the pastor and carried Dusty out of the funeral home with Anamarie by his side.

Dusty continued to cry as Rico strapped him into the car seat. Anamarie sat in the back with him, wedged between two car seats, stroking his hair and kissing him, telling him everything was going to be okay. Rico wasn't sure where to go, but he knew Dusty needed a break. He had to grieve and he had to do that in private. There was a newly updated park in Horseshoe and Rico drove there, hoping the slides and rides would get his attention on something else.

They got out and sat at a picnic table. Dusty wiped tears from his face. "I said goodbye to Grandma."

Anamarie hugged him. "Yes, you did. You were very brave. I'm so proud of you."

"She's in heaven with Jesus."

"Yes, she is," Anamarie replied, staring at Rico over Dusty's head. There was quiet for

a moment as Rico and Anamarie tried to figure out what to do next. How to help Dusty?

Anamarie pointed to a slide in the distance.
"If I got on that slide, would you come with
me?"

Dusty nodded vigorously and she took his
hand and walked to the slide. Rico followed
wondering if Anamarie was going down that
slide in the nice black dress. She kicked off
her heels and started up the ladder. Dusty
followed. When she got to the top, she took
Dusty in her arms, sat down and pushed them
off. They came down, down, down. Rico hurried to catch them before they hit the ground.

Giggles filled the morning air. Dusty
jumped up and down laughing. "Let's do it
again, Ana. Let's do it again." He grabbed her
hand and led her toward the ladder.

Up the ladder they went and down they
came, over and over until Anamarie said,
"Enough. I need to take a breath." She sat
beside Rico on the bench and he stared at her.

"What?" she asked.

"You're getting your nice dress dirty."

She looked at the smudges on it. "It can be
cleaned."

"I've never seen you like this."

"You didn't think I had a fun side?"

"I'm enjoying seeing all the sides of Anamarie."

Dusty interrupted the moment. "Look." He pointed to a swing set. "I wanna go there."

Anamarie took his hand and they walked to the swing set. Rico followed more slowly. She put him in the kiddie swing and then she sat on another one. They both stared at him.

"What?"

She lifted an eyebrow.

"Oh. You want me to push?"

"Now he gets it." Anamarie laughed.

He pushed Dusty off and then Anamarie.

"Higher!" Dusty squealed.

"Higher!" Anamarie yelled.

He pushed until they both were squealing. If he didn't already love her, he'd be head over heels by now.

"We're having fun, Rico."

"I see, buddy."

Finally they made their way back to the truck. The playing had lifted Dusty's spirits and that's what they'd wanted.

"Take us home, Mr. Wonderful," she said, leaning her head against the seat. "I'm exhausted."

Dusty was happy for the rest of the day and so was Rico. Just being with Anamarie made him happy. They watched a children's movie and Dusty laughed and giggled all the way through it. With his arms outstretched, he zoomed around the house as an airplane, making airplane noises. He zoomed all the way into bed. They kissed him good-night and left the room. At the doorway they heard him say, "'Nite, Grandma. I love you."

"Oh, that breaks my heart," Anamarie said.

"I think he's fine, though. This morning in the park did the trick."

"Yeah, he had lots of fun." Anamarie gathered toys from the floor and then suddenly caught her back. "Oh, I'm getting too old to play on slides and swings."

Rico slid into his recliner. "I read in a fortune cookie one time that said age is just a state of mind, and your state of mind was young today. I enjoyed watching you turn into a five-year-old."

She sat on the coffee table facing him. "It was a good day for all of us." She turned a wheel on the tractor she was holding. "We're good at this."

"Yeah, but I couldn't do it without you."

"Mmm, but I have to start thinking about getting a job soon."

"You'll eventually go back to the bakery."

She shook her head. "No, I have to get out from under my mother's thumb and live my own life."

"While we have Dusty I'll pay you to take care of him."

Her eyes narrowed. "You're kidding, right? I wouldn't take one dime to care for that little boy." She tossed the tractor into the toy box and got to her feet. "But you owe me big, mister. At least every Saturday night out for a year."

"Deal."

He'd do just about anything to keep her with him.

CHAPTER SEVEN

ANAMARIE WOKE UP at three in the morning and couldn't go back to sleep. Old habits were hard to break. She tossed and turned until about four and then got up and quietly made her way to the kitchen, not wanting to wake Rico. She made coffee and was about to sit at the table when Rico appeared in the doorway in pajama bottoms and a T-shirt. His long hair was all around him and she could sense his frown from where she was standing.

"I'm sorry. I didn't mean to wake you."

"Is something wrong?" he asked.

"No. I just woke up early." She shrugged. "Force of habit."

"Oh." He stepped toward Dusty's room. "Is the kid okay?"

That's what she loved most about him; his loving nature.

"He's sound asleep."

Rico glanced around at the dark house. "You didn't turn on any lights."

"I didn't want to wake anyone and the moon is bright." She glanced toward the kitchen window. "I was just going to drink a cup of coffee and relax. Would you like a cup?"

"Mmm…yeah…sure."

She handed him a mug.

"Thanks, Ana."

She was startled when he called her by her nickname. "You called me Ana."

"If it's okay, I think I'll call you Ana from now on. When I say Anamarie, I can hear your mother's voice saying your name in that critical tone. I'd rather not hear her voice in my head."

Laughter erupted from her throat. "Okay." She had no problem with that. Sometimes she could hear her mother's voice, too. It was time now to be the woman she should have been years ago.

They sat at the kitchen table and it was comfortable and nice. It was even nicer to share the early morning with him, especially in the dark room where they could talk freely without the intimidation of the light.

"May I ask you a question?"

"Anything."

"Why do you wear your hair so long? It's not that I don't like it, I do. I just wonder why. It has to be hot in the summertime."

He pushed his hair away from his face. "When I was about fourteen, Dominic Santiago, leader of a Houston gang, recruited me to peddle his drugs. I refused, but he threatened to kill my great-grandmother. I had no choice. He made me cut my hair short so I'd appear like an all-American boy and the cops wouldn't notice me. I swore then I would never wear my hair short again. It's my statement of freedom."

With the tip of her forefinger, she touched the scar on his face. "Did he do that?"

He nodded. "When I was eighteen, I graduated high school and I'd had enough. I wanted out. Two of his guys jumped me, but it took six of them to bring me down. Santi got on top of me and told me the only way I was leaving was in a pine box. He tried to slit my throat, but I turned my head and he split my cheek. Blood gushed everywhere and then they stuck a needle in my arm. I woke up in an alley with a homeless man looking at me. I told him where to take me and my grandmother gave him five dollars for his troubles."

She was sickened at what they had done to him and could only imagine what he'd been through as a teenager. Her heart ached for that young boy who had no other choices.

"My grandmother couldn't take me to the ER because the drugs were still in my system and I would be arrested. She nursed me back to health, but Santi still wouldn't leave us alone. One day a cop stopped me because a taillight was out on my car and there was Santi's poison on my passenger seat to be delivered. I went down for dealing and manufacturing. And I was just the delivery boy."

"I'm so sorry for all you've been through." She looked directly into his dark eyes. "You've been in Horseshoe for years and you've had no contact with this Santi person. You've been free for a long time."

He moved restlessly. "Sometimes I feel as if I can see him in my peripheral vision. All I have to do is turn my head and he's there. I'm not free and I never will be."

"Rico." She touched his hand, feeling his pain as if it were her own. "He can't hurt you anymore. Do you even know where he is?"

"As part of the deal for my pardon from the governor I had to tell where I had gotten the drugs. Santi was already in prison as was most of his gang. Miss Kate and the governor's representative came to prison for my statement. Three days later I was released. Egan was waiting for me."

"Rico, you don't have to say anything else."

He finished his coffee and got to his feet. "I'll get dressed before the kid wakes up."

Anamarie now understood why he worked so hard for the Rebels—out of gratitude. He was grateful for what they had done for him. They'd given him a life and he would never forget that. She just wished he would understand that everyone loved him for the person he was and not for the person he'd been. They were probably one and the same, though. To love Rico now she had to love the man he'd been years ago. She had no problem with that. Love was love any way you turned it. She loved Rico and she would prove it every day she was with him.

WHEN RICO CAME out of the bedroom, Ana showed him the drawing. "I forgot to show you this. Dusty drew it in school."

"Whoa."

"Yeah. I wasn't sure what to say about it so I didn't say anything. He just handed it to me. What should we do?"

"He's forming a bond with us and..."

"I know, it's not good, but what can we do? We want him to be happy and to be able to adjust to everything that's going on in his life. We can handle this, can't we?"

He reached into a drawer and pulled out a heart-shaped magnet. "Justin was about two when he started drawing pictures for my refrigerator. Rachel bought colorful magnets to put them up. But there were so many they started falling off and Rachel suggested that Justin put the pictures in a scrapbook-type thing."

"You really are a part of the Rebel family."

"Sort of."

"Sort of?" She shook her head at him.

To keep from discussing his family status he took the drawing from her and attached it to the refrigerator. "Now we can see it and he can see it and nothing else needs to be said."

He stood for a moment, enjoying the feeling of happiness she brought to him. A life without her, he couldn't imagine. She seemed to be a part of him now. She understood him and accepted him the way he was.

With a smile on his face, he went to get coffee. But he had to wonder if there was a time limit on happiness.

THE MORNING WENT smoothly. Dusty woke up and Anamarie fixed breakfast, and then Dusty wanted to watch cartoons. He was happy. No sign of sadness on his face. Anamarie got his pillow and a blanket and he lay in front of the TV completely engrossed in it.

Her phone buzzed as she was putting dishes in the dishwasher. She frowned. "It's my mother."

Rico closed the dishwasher. "Answer it. We said we would be honest and straightforward."

She clicked on. "Hi, Mom."

"Anamarie, you weren't in church this morning." Her mother's critical tone jerked the bow off her present of happiness.

"I know." She kept her voice as civil as possible.

"At the funeral yesterday, the pastor said the little boy got upset and y'all took him home. Is he okay?"

"He's fine now. He just needs a lot of attention to help him get through this."

"I don't like you missing church, Anamarie."

Her hand tightened on the phone and she chose her words carefully. "I feel God has me right where He wants me, helping Rico take care of this little boy who has no one. I'm happy. Please be happy for me. That's all I'm asking."

"I'm trying."

"Thank you." She hung up with a long sigh.

"Painful, huh?" Rico leaned against the counter with his arms folded across his chest, watching her.

"Yes. My mother is so obsessive about certain things and at times it drives us all crazy."

"Like religion."

"Yeah." She reached for the dish towel and wadded it into a ball. She squeezed it. She wondered about Rico and she wanted to ask, but she didn't want to hurt his feelings. "Can... Can I ask you a personal question?"

"Sure," he replied, and there was a crooked grin on his face that she didn't understand.

"You said your great-grandmother raised you. Did she ever take you to church?"

The grin broadened. "Are you asking if I'm an atheist?"

"Well..." She tilted her head, searching for an answer but one wasn't there. "I guess... And it doesn't matter. I would just like to know."

"With your family's history of Catholicism, I think it would matter a great deal."

She placed the dish towel on the counter and took a deep breath. "So you have no religion?"

He straightened from the counter. "You have to wait for this one. I mean really wait."

"What are you talking about?"

"My great-grandmother was a devout Catholic. Her name was Mary and she took me to church every Sunday morning. We took the bus. Sometimes if my grandmother had enough money, we would stop at this little bakery not far from the bus stop and she would buy me macaroon cookies. She knew I loved them. But I couldn't eat them until after lunch. That's one of the good memories."

"Your grandmother was Catholic." She could barely get the words out of her mouth. She waited a moment and then asked, "Are you Catholic, too? And don't make me wait for the answer."

He came toward her and backed her against the counter, one hand on each side of her. "I was baptized and confirmed into the Catholic Church. Now, doesn't that make me more appealing?"

"No. That will never change whether you go to church or not."

He pushed away from her, the scar on his

face pronounced. "It was hard to keep that faith when the gang members held my grandmother's arms behind her back and Santi threatened to cut her throat if I didn't do what he wanted. I knew he was heartless and he would do it in front of me so I did his dirty work. We had no one and my grandmother never did anything but good in her life. She didn't deserve that and she didn't deserve to see me go to prison. She…" He walked around the counter and out the front door.

Dusty jumped up. "Where Rico going?"

"He'll be back in a minute," she answered, and realized she was shaking. She took a deep breath and wished she'd never brought up the subject of religion. It proved to be a hot topic for Rico and she understood that completely.

"I wanna go with Rico." Dusty ran to the door, but Anamarie caught him before he could open it.

"We have to wait for Rico. Let's read a book or something." They knelt at the toy box and Dusty started pulling out stuff and found a remote control truck.

"Look, Ana." He held up the truck and pushed the remote control and the truck flew across the room.

"Wow!" Dusty shouted, and continued to

push the button as the truck darted from room to room. Mickey chased it, barking.

Ana looked up at the ceiling and mouthed, "Thank you." Dusty was occupied and now she could concentrate on Rico. Sitting on the sofa, she looked out the window toward the barn, hoping to see him strolling toward the house. An hour later she was still watching.

Dusty fell asleep on the floor, pushing the button on the remote control. Lifting him into her arms, she took one last look out the window and then carried Dusty to his bed for a nap. She went back to the window and waited. And waited.

Where was Rico?

As the thought left her mind, she saw him walking from the barn, his head bent. He'd forgotten his hat. His long hair was tied, as usual, at his neck. He didn't seem angry anymore. She wiped her clammy hands on her jeans.

Rico came in and sat in his recliner, his forearms on his thighs and his hands clasped between his knees.

"I'm sorry I brought up religion. I didn't know." She sat on the sofa as close to him as possible.

"It's okay," he replied, tightening his clasped

hands. "Like I told you most of the time my past is in my peripheral vision, but when I was talking about my grandma it was right there in front of my face. I could see the fear in her eyes and the evil on Santi's face, and as always I'm powerless to change it or do anything about it."

She wanted to ask a question, but she didn't want to upset him any more than he was. Swallowing back all her doubts, she asked, "What happened to your grandmother?"

Rico kept staring at his hands. "She continued to live in the apartment. Santi paid me one last visit in the jail. He said if I squealed on him, my grandmother was a dead woman, so I kept my mouth shut."

He took a breath and she waited for him to continue.

"When I was released from prison, Egan asked me where I wanted to go and I said to see my grandma. After I was arrested, my grandmother's younger sister moved into the apartment with her and they took care of each other. I was happy about that. About a year before I was released my grandma fell and broke her hip. My aunt couldn't take care of her anymore so she had to put her in a home. That made me angry and sad. I needed to be there for her, but I was locked away for a very long time."

His hands tightened until his knuckles turned white. "When I was released, she was very old and frail, but she was still alive. The doctor said she told him she wasn't dying until she saw her great-grandson. When I walked into that room, she started to cry. I cried. Egan cried. It was very emotional for all of us. I held her hand during the night and we talked about the past and the present. She told me I had my freedom now and I had to thank Kate Rebel for what she'd done for me. I had a chance for a new life and she said she knew I would turn out to be the fine young man I was meant to be. She died holding on to my hand."

She slid onto the arm of the chair and wrapped her arm around his neck. "Rico. I'm so sorry."

As if she hadn't spoken, he added, "I had no money to pay for her burial. The lady at the home said the county would bury her in a pine box in a county cemetery. That hurt more than all the pain I've been through. Suddenly Egan was there. I thought he'd gone home, but he was still in Houston. He told me the funeral had been taken care of. He handed me a card with the funeral home's name on it. Miss Kate paid for my grandmother's funeral. I was speechless. I'd never met people like that before and I kept wondering what they were going to expect from me in return. Those first few weeks I was very cautious, but I soon learned that there are really good people in this world."

That's why he worked so hard. Everything he did he did for the Rebels. She kissed his brow. "Miss Kate is a cut above the rest."

"I tried to pay her back over the years, but she either leaves the room or walks away from me. I just make sure if Miss Kate needs anything that I'm there."

"Do you have any memories of your grandmother or your mother?"

"Sometimes I hear this lullaby in my head and I know it's my mother. I think she tried to be a good mother, but the drugs had taken over her life."

"And your grandmother?"

"She died before I was born. My grandfather died in a work-related accident and my grandmother received a large sum of money. She bought a big house in Austin and moved there with my mother to start a new life. My great-grandmother didn't drive and had to take the bus to see them."

He leaned his head against her arm. "My grandmother met a man who went through her money quickly. She was left penniless with a teenage daughter. To get her daughter straightened out my great-grandmother went to Austin and stayed with them for a while. My grandmother found a job at a large insurance company and was soon promoted. One night she was working late and had to walk to her car in the dark. She was mugged. A man tried to take her purse and she fought him. She fought for her life and lost. He stabbed her and she died in the parking lot."

He drew a deep breath. "My mother was sixteen at the time and when she heard the news, my great-grandmother said she fell apart and had to be hospitalized. My great-grandmother went to Austin to be with her and to bring her back to Houston. She planned to raise my mother, but my mother didn't like Houston. It was too boring and my great-grandmother was too strict. She ran away and the cops brought her back. She ran away again and the cops brought her back. The third time the cops couldn't find her and my great-grandmother never saw her again."

He paused for a moment. "My mother called when she discovered she was pregnant and asked for money. My great-grandmother sent her a hundred dollars and a bus ticket to Houston. She didn't come. She called when I was born and told my great-grandmother she'd had a boy and she wanted to come home. My great-grandmother sent her another hundred dollars and a bus ticket, but my mother never came."

He swallowed hard. "The next call she got was from the police to inform her of my mother's death from a drug overdose. She asked about me and they told her I was put into foster care. She immediately contacted CPS. When she came to the foster home to get me, I saw this little old lady with white hair and I thought she was an angel. And she was. She saved my life by getting me out of that home with eight kids. No one got any attention. But with my great-grandmother I got hugs and kisses and I knew I was loved. That means everything to a kid."

Now she knew why he connected with Dusty. Almost the same backstory. Almost identical. Rico had to see a lot of himself in Dusty and he would do everything he could to make him happy until Darlene could come get him. But would their hearts ever be the same?

CHAPTER EIGHT

MICKEY BARKED, SIGNALING that the little guy was awake. Ana went to get him and Rico took a moment to catch his breath. He'd never talked so much in his whole life, but it was easy with her. She listened with an open heart.

The moment Dusty saw Rico he held out his arms for him. "Mickey woke me up," he mumbled, still half-asleep.

Rico patted his back. "But weren't you already awake?"

Dusty rubbed his eyes. "I don't know."

Rico thought it was time to lighten the mood and to get out of the house. "Have you ever been to a carnival?" he asked Dusty.

Dusty raised his head. "No. What's that?"

Rico looked at Ana. "Are you game? I saw in the paper there was one in the mall in Temple. I think we need to have some fun."

She smiled that smile he loved. "I'm game."

It wasn't long before they were in the truck

and on the way to Temple. Dusty's eyes lit up when he saw all the lights, but he was scared. He held on to Rico. When he tried to put him on a ride, Dusty always pulled back. Maybe this wasn't such a good idea after all.

But then Ana walked to a ride with twirling teacups and went to sit in one, holding out her arms for Dusty. She held him as the teacup spun round and round and round. Dusty giggled and shouted to Rico, "Watch us!" He rode the pony carousel with Rico and Ana on both sides of him. A big smile split his face.

They ate cotton candy and had hot dogs for lunch. Rico won a teddy bear for Ana and a stuffed dog for Dusty. At one of the games, he broke the target with the baseball and the man wasn't pleased. Sometimes he didn't know his own strength. At the back of his mind, though, he knew there was still a lot of anger in him. He glanced at Ana and Dusty. But that was changing.

Dusty was antsy. He wanted to go on another ride. They found the kiddie bumper cars and Dusty wanted Rico to ride with him. Rico couldn't get his long legs into the small car and Ana had to take him. After a moment, Dusty wanted to ride by himself.

Smiling, Ana said, "That hurt my feelings.

I'll show him." She got on a separate car and she and Dusty bumped into each other over and over and over. Giggles erupted through the noise on the warm afternoon. And it wasn't just Dusty's giggles. Ana was having the time of her life. Rico stood and watched them. He never knew Ana was such a big kid. He loved it.

As he stood there, he thought back to his childhood and couldn't remember a time his great-grandmother had taken him to anything like a carnival. At church there was a children's playground and she often let him play on the swings and slides. But he never laughed like they were laughing now. The clip on Ana's ponytail broke and her hair tumbled around her. She didn't bother with it. She kept playing with Dusty.

"Watch us!" Dusty shouted to Rico.

"I'm watching!" he shouted back. He couldn't stand it. He pulled out his wallet and paid the man for a ride and for Ana and Dusty another ride.

"I thought you couldn't get into the car," the man said.

"I think I needed a little motivation," Rico replied as he stepped on to the ride and then into a car. Other people got off the ride, but

Ana and Dusty sat watching him. It wasn't easy, but he managed to wedge inside the small car, drawing his knees almost up to his chin. The steering wheel was between his legs and he could drive the car. First thing he did was bump into Ana and she came right back at him. Then Dusty bumped into him and he turned around and went after Dusty. Then Ana got his car against the rail and he couldn't move it.

She laughed. "Hey, I really drive like this. I'm good at it."

"We'll see." He went after her once again. On and on they played with the bumper cars. Rico paid for another round and they went at it again.

Finally, he said, "Enough." His chest hurt from laughing so much. Ana and Dusty climbed out of their cars, but Rico had a problem. He was wedged in and couldn't move.

Ana leaned over his car. "Do you have a problem, Mr. Johnson?"

He met the humor in her voice. "Maybe."

"Maybe?" She glanced at the man who took money for the rides. "Could you help us please?"

"I told him he was too big for these cars,"

the man grumbled, "but I let him ride 'cause the kid was having so much fun."

Rico would be embarrassed if he wasn't so darned amused. The man took one arm and Ana took the other. They pulled and he was able to get out of the car. He rubbed his knees. "I'll never be the same again."

"Getting old, are you?" Her eyes twinkled at him.

"I'll show you old." He grabbed her around the waist and tickled her rib cage. She threw back her head and laughed uncontrollably. The sound was infectious and he swung her around laughing with her. Dusty jumped up and down with excitement.

This was real happiness and he never wanted it to end.

THE NEXT MORNING they overslept and were in a rush to get Dusty to school and Rico to work. Anamarie took Dusty to school, but she didn't have time to make his lunch. She told perky Ms. Holt she would bring his lunch later. She hurried to the grocery store to buy stuff Dusty said he liked and then went to her house to fix it and to check on things since she'd been away. The closed-up house was lonely and depressing and she could see clearly what had been missing in her life—a man to love her just the way she was.

They'd had so much fun yesterday. It was a time out of the time for her as she saw Rico as someone who could laugh and play and enjoy life. It would be a long day without seeing him. She hurried back to the school to drop off Dusty's lunch and then she stopped by Angie's office to chat.

"Wow!" Angie said when she saw her sister. "You're absolutely glowing."

Anamarie sank into the chair across from Angie's desk. "That's because I've been running all morning. We overslept and I barely got Dusty to school in time and then I had to go to the grocery store to get things for his lunch."

"Whatever you're doing is working."

She leaned forward and whispered, "It's called love."

"Yeah, the four-letter word that makes women do crazy things."

"I don't know what's going to happen when we have to give Dusty back, but I know one thing. I will never regret this time with Rico. He's the most wonderful man and I could sit here all day and talk about him, but I don't want to sound foolish and insecure."

"Ana, you're the most mature person I know, and I'm so happy you're enjoying yourself." Angie glanced over her shoulder. "Have you been to the bakery?" Angie's office was next to the bakery and the scent of kolaches baking wafted through the door.

Anamarie shook her head. "No."

"Please go and just say hi," Angie urged. "It would help ease the tension."

Angie was sweet and loving and she wanted everyone to get along. She loved everything and everybody, but sometimes things just didn't work that way.

"I've spoken to Mom and Dad and they know what I'm doing. Other than that I don't feel the need to go into the bakery. I talked to Margie. She's doing great and doesn't need me looking over her shoulder."

"Mom does seem rather calm about all this."

The connecting door suddenly opened and their mother stood there. "I thought I heard Anamarie's voice."

Anamarie gritted her teeth, a normal reaction around her mother. "I just stopped by to visit with Angie."

"Why?" Her mother was instantly on the

alert. "What's going on? You girls never tell me anything."

Anamarie picked up her purse. "I think I'll go. I have a lot to do today. I have to run some errands and then do laundry and…"

"Are you his maid now?" Her mother's irate words burned her skin like a bull nettle.

Trying not to overreact, she replied, "No, Mom, I'm a lot more than that."

"I don't want to hear it," her mother snapped.

"I'll see y'all later," she said, going out the door.

As she drove home, she thought about what her mother had said and tried not to let it get to her. She and Rico were together because of Dusty, but they loved each other. Didn't they? He'd never said the words and he had never mentioned marriage. Was she getting in over her head once again?

IT WAS THE first time Rico was late for the morning meeting. The guys razzed him about it and it didn't bother him. He was happier than he'd ever been in his whole life and he could take a little ribbing.

"C'mon, Rico," Elias said. "We're burning daylight."

"Would you let him get a cup of coffee first?" Falcon spoke up.

Paxton handed Rico a cup and he gladly took it. He'd only had time for one cup this morning.

"We'll finish that fence today and tomorrow then Rico and I will start cutting hay in the north pasture. We're going into hay season and everyone has to pull their weight." Elias was in full work mode.

Rico glanced at his friend. "Don't you find out the sex of the baby tomorrow? It's circled on the calendar in the barn and it's circled there." He pointed to the calendar on the wall.

Elias sank into a chair. "How could I forget that?"

"Take a deep breath, Elias," Falcon told him. "Quincy and Egan will start cutting in the north pasture tomorrow. You take care of Maribel."

"Ah, you can't talk to him," Grandpa said. "He's wound up like an eight-day clock."

Everyone chuckled.

After they all filed out to go to work, Rico held back.

"Miss Kate, could I talk to you for a minute?"

"Sure, Rico. You can talk to me anytime you want. Is the little boy okay?"

"He had a rough day Saturday, but he seems fine now. That's what I wanted to ask you about. Could I have more time off this weekend to spend with him?"

"Take all the time you need."

"Rico." Falcon leaned back in his chair. "You haven't had any vacation since you've been here. Take a couple of weeks or more if you need it. This ranch will survive for a few weeks without you. Although, I don't know if Elias will."

"Thank you. The weekend will be fine."

"You've been with us for a long time and you've become a part of this family. I hope you know that."

Rico nodded and walked out with Falcon's words ringing in his head. Sometimes he felt like family and sometimes he felt out of place. That was from all the bad things that had happened in his life. He was eternally grateful to the Rebels and maybe one day he would feel like he was one of them instead of the hired hand. But he wasn't there yet.

The fence building didn't go according to plan. They broke the wire stretcher and had to make a trip to the barn to get another one. Then they ran out of barbed wire and there wasn't any in the supply shed. That called for a trip into town. It was four o'clock in the afternoon when they finally finished the fence. Elias called it a day. Rico was eager to go home, too. Ana and Dusty were waiting for him.

Since he was early, they weren't expecting him. He quietly opened the door and saw them sitting at the coffee table playing with dominoes. Dusty was counting the white spots on the black dominoes.

Ana was the first to notice him and then Dusty jumped up and ran to him. "I'm counting, Rico. I can count all the way—" he lifted his arms toward the ceiling "—to a hundred. Wanna hear me?"

Dusty started to count and Rico sank down by Ana on the sofa. "How was your day?"

"Good." She smiled at him. "And it's even better now."

It was for him, too. Dusty continued to count loudly and he watched her face as she stared at Dusty. She was falling in love with the kid, as he was. At that moment a doubt entered his head and he hated himself for it. But he had to wonder if she was here just because of Dusty. The kid satisfied all her motherly instincts. Where did that leave him when they had to let Dusty go?

He pushed the doubt away as he helped her prepare supper. Their time together was too good to do otherwise. After supper he got a call from Wyatt. He clicked on immediately wondering if Darlene was going to get out early.

"Hey, Wyatt. What's going on?"

"Stuart found a will in Wendy's papers."

"And?"

"She left everything to Dusty."

"That's good. It will give Darlene and Dusty a new start." Ana was giving Dusty a bath and he couldn't hear Rico on the phone.

"There's nothing to inherit. Stuart also found two bank loans with the house as collateral. Wendy borrowed twenty thousand six years ago to pay for Connie's wedding and then another twenty thousand a year ago so Connie wouldn't lose her expensive home in Austin. To make this short, the bank owns the house. I talked to the banker today and they will be taking ownership tomorrow. You think there's anything in the house that Dusty might want? Stuart said he got everything that belonged to the boy. I went over there today and looked around. There were pictures of the Millers, Connie, Darlene and Dusty in Wendy's bedroom. I took them down and put them in a box. There is also a baby book of Dusty. I put that in the box, too. After tomorrow, you won't be able to get anything out of there."

"I don't want to take him back there."

"There's nothing much in the house. Very little furniture. There was a can of corn and a can of green beans in the cabinet and a half a stick of butter, two eggs and an empty milk carton in the refrigerator. Also there was an empty jar of peanut butter and jelly on the counter. They were living at the poverty level here in Horseshoe, Texas. That gets to me."

Things like that got to him, too. It reminded him of his childhood. Although, they had never gone hungry.

Rico cleared his throat. "He's well taken care of now and hopefully we can ensure that for the future."

"Yeah, thanks to you. By stepping up you've become a big part of this community."

Had he? It didn't feel like it. People still shied away from him.

"Connie has gone back to Austin. Now I have to deal with the bank."

"Good luck."

"Do you want to come by and pick up this stuff?"

"No, I don't think so. Just keep it for when Darlene gets released. I'm sure she would want it."

He placed his phone on the counter and stood there for a moment. The walls started to close in on him. He'd had that feeling in prison. There were walls and bars and no place to go. He was trapped. Why did he feel that way now?

"Hey, what's wrong?" Ana asked.

"Nothing."

There was a whole lot going on inside him. For the first time he realized he was trapped in the middle of a little boy's life. He had to remain detached. How was he supposed to do that?

THE NEXT MORNING Jericho made sure he was on time. It was a long day. He'd already told Ana he would be late and he was pleasantly surprised when Quincy called a halt at six o'clock.

Rico stopped the Polaris Ranger at the barn. He got out and stretched his muscles and paused at the sight at the north end of the barn. Elias sat on a bale of hay; his forearms rested on his thighs and his hands dangled as if he didn't know what to do with them.

Oh, man, he thought. Something must be wrong with the baby. He wasn't sure whether to approach him or not. But then they'd been friends for a long time. If Elias needed someone to listen, he'd be there.

"Hey, Elias, what are you doing here? I thought you took the day off."

"You know life never turns out the way you plan."

"I can testify to that." Rico took a moment and then asked, "Is the baby okay?"

"Yeah." Elias rubbed his hands together. "Maribel's fine, too."

That was a relief. "So what are you having? A girl or a boy?"

Elias held up two fingers.

"What does that mean?"

"We're having twins."

"Oh."

"I can't even imagine it," Elias said. "Now we have to buy two of everything."

"What are they?"

"Boys. Maribel is heartbroken. She wanted one of them to be a girl."

"Why are you so down? Why aren't you jumping for joy?"

"Well, Rico, I built the house in town for Maribel and Chase so they'd have a place to call home. It has three bedrooms, one for Chase, one for Grandpa and one for us. Where are we going to put two babies?"

"You can add on."

Elias shook his head. "Mom has been after me for a while to move into the big house. It sits on my share of the land."

Rico frowned. "Miss Kate's giving up her house?"

"No, we'll all be living together, Mom, Grandpa, Chase, the new babies and us. There's room for all of us. Doesn't that just warm the cockles of your heart?"

"At the expression on your face, I just want to laugh."

Elias's eyes narrowed. "You better not."

"Your mom will be a lot of help with the babies and you'll be living on the property again."

"Yeah, there's that." Elias stood and patted Rico on the shoulder. "See you tomorrow."

Rico stared after his friend. Married life wasn't easy and he witnessed that today in Elias. He was strong and tough, but two little babies had sidetracked him. The Rebel family was stronger, though, and there would be lots of help from family members. That's what family was about.

THE WEEK WENT smoothly and on Saturday they took Dusty to a mall in Temple to buy new clothes. Mrs. Miller had patched his underwear and socks but his clothes were threadbare. His sneakers were also worn. They spent most of the day looking at boys' clothes. Dusty was excited. He'd never had new clothes.

As they were leaving, they noticed a large trampoline and kids were jumping on it. The kid had to wear a harness and then he could jump almost to the ceiling. Squeals of laughter echoed around them.

Dusty stopped walking and watched the kids. Anamarie squatted by him. "Do you like that?"

Dusty nodded vigorously. She looked at Rico.

"He might be too small."

She went over and asked the man if Dusty could jump on the trampoline.

"Sure, but little kids usually get scared."

"If he does, we'll take him off."

The man strapped Dusty into the harness and Rico placed him on the trampoline.

"Jump," the man instructed.

Dusty jumped and his eyes opened wide

as the harness took him up and down again. He jumped over and over and over, giggling.

They sat on a bench watching him. She linked her arm through Rico's. "He's having so much fun."

"Yeah."

Something was wrong. She could feel it. He seemed uncomfortable and she didn't know what to do to get him to talk.

After they had put Dusty to bed that night, Rico sat in his recliner with a sad expression on his face. It twisted her heart. She slid onto his lap and rested her head in the crook of his neck.

"What is it?" she asked softly.

"We have to give him back and I don't know how I'm going to do that. I'm attached to him and he's attached to me. How did I get myself into this mess?"

She rubbed her hand over his heart. "Because there's nothing but good in there and a little boy desperately needed you."

"I should have let him go into foster care."

"No, you made the right decision and we can handle this."

He wrapped his arms around her. "I couldn't do this without you. I have to work and my first loyalty is to the Rebels."

"I'm here and I don't plan on going anywhere." But she had worries too, but in a different way. After Dusty left, would she still be a part of Rico's life?

CHAPTER NINE

THEY SETTLED INTO an easy comfortable routine. He worked on the ranch and Ana took care of Dusty. It was working for them, but he knew she was taking most of the load. They had started hay season and he worked from sunup to sundown and had very little time for Dusty. That bothered him, but it was a way to detach. And he needed that, too. He kept waiting for news that Darlene was getting out. He was still waiting.

On Friday that week they stopped working at six. The tractors needed oil and they planned to do that first thing in the morning while dew was still on the hay. He was dog tired but deep inside a spark of energy ignited at the thought of seeing Ana. She'd have something good cooked and she'd be playing with Dusty. That allowed him to rest for a moment and drink a glass of iced tea.

After supper, Dusty leaned on the arm of Rico's chair, smiling at him.

"What's up, buddy?"

"I'm gonna take a bath."

"You want me to help?"

Dusty shook his head. "No. Ana lets me play in the water."

"Okay." There was a stack of new coloring books on the coffee table and a big box of crayons. "Did you get new coloring books?"

Dusty straightened, his mouth a big O. "I forgot." He ran to his room.

He had no idea what that was about, but soon Dusty came back with a penny in his hand. He gave it to Ana. "I forgot to pay you for my stuff."

Ana looked at Rico and he shrugged. He didn't know how to handle the situation but he knew someone had to. As words rolled around in his head, Ana knelt in front of Dusty.

"Did your grandma ever buy you a gift like on your birthday or Christmas?"

"Yeah." Dusty twisted his fingers. "She bought me a tractor for my birthday and a big truck for Christmas."

"Did you pay her for them?"

"No."

Ana pulled Dusty to her. "Because it was a gift. You don't pay for a gift. You say thank you and give the person a hug or a kiss. The coloring books and colors were a gift from me."

"Oh." He took the penny out of Ana's hand. "Thank you." Then he gave her a big hug.

The look on Ana's face said it all. There were tears in her eyes and she quickly fought against them. She pushed Dusty slightly back. "But if you go somewhere like a store, like Walmart, you have to pay for what you get in there. Do you understand?"

He nodded.

"How much money did your grandma give you a week?" Rico asked, wondering where he got his money since they seemed to be penniless.

"I show you." Dusty ran to his room again and came back with a quarter in his hand.

Rico fished in his jeans and found a quarter. He handed it to Dusty. "As long as you're with me, this will be your allowance each week."

"Oh, boy, now I have lots of money." Dusty ran to his room to put it on his nightstand where he kept his money.

Ana looked at him with her hands on her hips. "What's my allowance?"

"This." He stood and kissed her forehead. How had he ever lived without her?

The buzz of his phone interrupted them.

Ana drew back. "Someone's calling you."

"Yeah. It might be Miss Kate or Falcon. I have to get it."

Ana handed him his phone from the counter.

"It's Wyatt." He tapped his phone. "Hey, Wyatt, what's going on?"

"I need you to come into the office. I know it's late, but this is important."

"I'll be right there."

"What's wrong?" Ana asked.

Rico went into his bedroom and slipped on his boots. "I don't know. He just said he needs to talk to me. I guess Darlene is getting out and he wants to tell me in person."

"Oh." Her face crumbled like a heated marshmallow.

He paused for a moment. "It's time to let go."

"Rico." She went into his arms and he held her, trying not to show any sign of weakness when inside he felt like someone had rammed a bowling ball into his gut.

"It's okay. We can get through this." He reached for his hat on the dresser.

ANAMARIE GATHERED HERSELF and gave Dusty
a bath, determined to keep all those shaky
emotions inside. She poured bubble bath into
the water and bubbles came up over the tub.
There was a small boat and he played with it
in the water.

"Look, Ana. We have to get through the
snow." He called the bubbles snow and sailed
the boat across the bubbles, giggling.

She sat back on her heels, watching him.
Until that moment, she never realized how
hard letting go would be. She choked back
a sob. She had gone into this with her heart
wide open and... Getting up, she managed to
brush away a tear before Dusty could see it.
She hoped and prayed Darlene Miller gave
her son the home he deserved.

RICO MADE IT to the sheriff's office in record
time. He wasn't thinking. He was just trying to get through it. Bubba sat in the office,
working on a file.

"Hey," Bubba called as he made to walk
into Wyatt's office. "I was out of line the
other day. I apologize for that."

"Thank you."

"You're my friend just like the Rebel guys
are."

Rico didn't want to get into it with Bubba. He had other things on his mind. But he appreciated the apology. Walking into Wyatt's office, he stopped short. Ms. Henshaw was there. Darlene was getting out. There could be the only reason she was here—to take Dusty.

"Sit down, Rico," Wyatt said.

Taking a seat, he looked from Wyatt to Ms. Henshaw. "What's going on? Is Darlene getting out early?"

Ms. Henshaw shook her head. "Darlene's not getting out anytime soon."

His eyes narrowed. "What?"

"She got into a fight with another inmate over drugs. The other girl had a knife and she tried to stab Darlene. She has a big cut on her arm."

"What?" He had expected a lot of things, but this wasn't one of them. "She said she was going to stay clean for Dusty. He's waiting on her. What am I supposed to tell him?"

Ms. Henshaw didn't answer the question. Instead she said, "Dusty is the reason I'm here. I found a foster home for him. The couple has five other children. He will be number six. It's a nice home and the couple takes good care of the kids." She glanced at her watch. "The warden is going to call here in a few minutes and she's taking Darlene out of lockdown and allowing her five minutes on the phone so we can settle Dusty's future."

After all he had done, Dusty was still going into foster care. That was all he could think. The letting go would be even harder now. Rico had to push down all his feelings about foster homes. How could Darlene do this to her kid?

Wyatt's landline rang and he put it on speakerphone.

"Sheriff Carson, are you there?"

"Yes, Darlene. I'm here and so is Ms. Henshaw." Wyatt glanced at him and he must've left out his name for a reason so Rico stayed quiet.

"Where's Mr. Johnson?"

"Why do you need to know that?" Wyatt asked.

"I want to know how my baby is."

"Dusty is fine. He's waiting for you to come get him."

There was a pause on the line. "Sorry. I screwed up but it wasn't my fault. I didn't have the pills. The other girl did and she tried to force them on me. She said if she wasn't getting out, I wasn't either and then she pulled a knife. No one will listen to me and I'm taking the fall for this. I didn't do anything but defend myself. I was staying clean for Dusty."

"The authorities will sort that out," Ms. Henshaw told her. "Right now my main concern is your son. We have to decide what to do with him."

"Doesn't Mr. Johnson have him?"

"Yes, but that was for short-term. There will be several years tacked onto your sentence. A judge will decide that, but in the meantime I have found a foster home for Dusty. The couple has five other children, but it's nice and so is the couple."

"No!" Darlene cried. "I don't want my kid in foster care. I want my kid to have a better life. Why isn't Mr. Johnson there?"

Wyatt glanced at Rico. "I'm here," Rico said.

"Oh, Mr. Johnson, how is my baby?"

"He's doing great. He's a good kid with good manners and I'm trying to figure out what possessed you to get into a fight when you're so close to getting out."

"I didn't, but no one will believe me."

"Because you're a drug addict and addicts are notorious for getting drugs any way they can." He didn't pull any punches.

"I know," she said softly. "It was there and I wanted it, but I fought her off."

"Darlene, we're getting off topic here," Ms. Henshaw cut in. "We have to make a decision about Dusty."

"I want him to stay with Mr. Johnson."

"Mr. Johnson works long hours and doesn't have time to raise Dusty. It was very nice of him to keep him for a short time, but…"

"Mr. Johnson, please, take him—" Darlene broke in. "I'll sign over my maternal rights to you. I want him to grow up in a place like Rebel Ranch where he will be happy and with good people. Please, Mr. Johnson."

Everyone in the room was stunned and it took a moment for Rico to find words to answer her. "You're giving me your kid?"

"Yes. I'm a screwup and I'll be in here for a long time. By the time I get out Dusty won't know me."

"You don't even know me. I'm a stranger. An ex-con." Saying the words brought bile into his throat and he forced it back. That's who he was, though.

"Ms. Henshaw and the sheriff say you're a very nice man. That's good enough for me. Please keep Dusty. My lawyer will draw up the papers."

"Darlene, you better think about this," Ms. Henshaw said. "You're giving away your child and if you change your mind down the road, it will be very hard to get him back. I wouldn't want to put Mr. Johnson through that…or Dusty."

"I won't change my mind. Dusty deserves better than being put in a foster home and if I can make that happen, I'm going to do it. Mr. Johnson, please."

"Let's get this straight, Darlene," Wyatt said. "You're going to sign over your rights as a parent to Mr. Johnson. What guarantee does he have later down the road you won't change your mind?"

"My lawyer said I'll probably get four years tacked onto my sentence. Dusty will be almost nine when I get out. I wouldn't take him out of a happy home. He deserves to be loved and a part of a family. I want that for him. When I sign my name to that paper, it will be forever. And though it will break my heart, I will do it for Dusty."

"What am I supposed to tell him about his mother?" Rico asked.

"Mom always told him I was sick and you can use the same gimmick. I just won't ever come back."

There it was. A gift. A child. What he and Ana wanted more than anything—to be a family. Then why were there doubts in his head? Why wasn't he grabbing this with both hands? They loved Dusty and Dusty loved them. He should be excited, but something held him back.

"I need to think about this," he finally said.

"Thank you, Mr. Johnson. Take good care of my son." The phone went dead and Rico felt a little dead inside, too. She was giving away her son. What type of mother gives away her child?

Ms. Henshaw closed her laptop and gathered her things. "I need an answer by ten o'clock tomorrow morning, Mr. Johnson. If Darlene signs away her rights, the state will allow you to keep Dusty. You have to go before a judge to make it legal. But if you say no, I'll pick Dusty up in the morning to take him to the foster home. Please have his things ready." She walked out the door as if she was making a deal for a car and not a little boy's life.

Rico sat with his hands clenched between his legs, trying to figure out what to do. He worked long hours and had no time for a kid. Ana took care of Dusty, but soon she would go back to the bakery. She'd built that business into what it was today. She was angry with her mother over him. In time that would pass. He didn't want to hold her back from doing what she wanted. Where did that leave him? Where did that leave Dusty? In a foster home, probably.

"Rico." Wyatt's voice broke through his thoughts. "Don't feel obligated to take Dusty. He will do fine in foster care."

He glanced up. "Will he, Wyatt? I've been in foster care and look how I turned out."

"You're one of the finest men I've ever met." Wyatt leaned forward in his chair. "You said your great-grandmother raised you. She did a bang-up job. As for Darlene I think she's sincere about wanting what's best for Dusty."

"Yeah." He stood up. "I'll talk to you later."

As he drove home he searched for answers but they eluded him at every turn. It was either yes or no and he had to choose. But which choice was right for him? And Dusty? And Ana?

ANA PUT DUSTY to bed and waited and waited. She couldn't understand what was taking so long. She heard his truck and ran to the front door. He came in looking haggard. His face was tight and his skin pale. What had happened? She had coffee made and brought him a cup.

He sat in his chair and wrapped his hands around the mug, staring into the dark liquid.

"When is Darlene getting out?" That could be the only reason he looked so dejected.

"She isn't." He took a sip of the coffee.

"What?"

He told her what had happened in Wyatt's office.

"She's giving you Dusty?"

"That's what it amounts to."

Her legs felt shaky and she sat on the coffee table. "What did you say?"

"I told her I had to think about it." His hand tightened on the cup. "I mean, I work all day, sometimes long hours. How can I raise a child? But if I don't take him, they have a foster home ready that will. How do I let him go into a foster home? I've been there and I know how it feels. It feels as if the world has forgotten about you. I don't want Dusty to feel that way. I…"

"I'm here, Rico. I will help you."

He raised his head. "But for how long? Aren't you going back to the bakery? The bakery has been your life since you were a teenager."

Anger sparked in her stomach. "I wish everyone would stop telling me that the bakery is my life. It isn't. I have other dreams, too."

"What kind of dreams?"

"You know that I bake cakes for anniversaries, weddings and birthdays. That is separate from the bakery and my own money. Last year was very profitable because news has gotten out and people from other small towns have called wanting cakes."

"So you'll make wedding cakes at the bakery?"

"No. I want a separate business without my mother looking over my shoulder. There's a big office space next to Angie's office that's for sale. It used to be a dress shop and then later a resale shop. But it's vacant now. I thought about buying it and opening up my own place. I think I'll call it The Cake Shop or Cakes, etc. or maybe Bite Me. The place is big enough to have a party room for kids. There's no place for kids to have birthday parties in Horseshoe except the park. I'd put games and stuff in there and they could have a good time. And, of course, I'd make the birthday cake."

"I never knew you wanted to do that."

"You're the first person I've told and I've been thinking about it since I've been living with you. I'm tired of my mother complaining about the cakes getting in the way of making kolaches."

"So you'll be busy."

"Not so busy that I can't take care of Dusty." Why wasn't he asking her to marry him? They loved each other, didn't they?

"Well, then." He placed his hands on his knees. "I guess we should get married. We can go to the courthouse or Wyatt can marry us."

In all the years she dreamed about someone asking her to marry them, it wasn't like this. She stood up, anger in every part of her body. "I'm not getting married at the courthouse or by Wyatt Carson."

"Why not?" He was genuinely puzzled and that eased the anger inside her.

"Ever since I was a little girl I dreamed of walking down the aisle on my dad's arm in a white dress. My sisters and I used to play 'bride.' We'd walk down the hall with a pillowcase over our heads holding some fake flowers of our mom's. Sometimes Bubba played dad. I want to get married in the church."

He frowned. "Anamarie, I'm not into big weddings."

"It would be just my family and your family."

"I don't have a family."

"Excuse me. Who are the Rebels?"

"They're my employers."

He was putting up walls and she had to go at this another way. "Where do you spend your holidays?"

"At Miss Kate's and on Christmas morning I go to Egan's first and then to Miss Kate's."

"Really? I don't know many people who go to their employers' house on Christmas."

"They're good to me, but we're not blood."

"And that matters to you? Because I don't see it mattering to the Rebels." Why was it so hard for him to admit that he was a part of the Rebel family? The walls he had built around himself were getting thicker and she didn't know if she could get through to make him understand how much she loved him and how much the Rebels loved him.

She sat on the coffee table again, giving him a few minutes. As the clock ticked away, he said nothing. She finally asked, "What are you going to do about Dusty?"

"I can't let him go into foster care."

"Then do something about it."

After a moment, he said, "Okay, I guess we'll do the wedding thing you want." His voice held a tinge of resentment that didn't sit well with her.

She got up from the coffee table. "I'm going to pack my things, but I won't leave until the morning. I want to say goodbye to Dusty."

"What? Wait?" As she walked by his chair, he caught her hand. "What are you talking about?"

"I don't want to feel as if I'm forcing you into marriage. It has to be something you want, too, and clearly you don't."

"I'm just trying to get this right."

"Well, you got it wrong." She took a deep breath. "Rico, when a man proposes to a woman, she wants to hear more than *we should get married*. I need more if I'm going to spend my life with you. And you seem very hesitant to offer that."

"What do you mean? You know I love you. I've been crazy about you for years."

The magic words would have been wonderful if he hadn't tacked on *you know*.

She placed her hand over her heart. "I love you, Rico, and I want to spend the rest of my life with you."

He got to his feet, still holding her hand. "The only person I've ever loved is my great-grandmother and it's hard for me to recognize those emotions after everything that has happened to me. But I know that I love you. I love you more than I've loved anyone in my whole life. Will you marry me and help me make a home for Dusty?"

"Yes," she replied through shining tears.

He cupped her face in his hands. The calluses felt like cashmere. He kissed her then in a slow drugging kiss and then rested his forehead against hers. "Remember you told Dusty that when he receives a gift he should say thank you and accept it. That's what I'm going to do. I'm going to accept Darlene's gift and we're going to raise Dusty as our child."

"Okay." She was in full agreement.

"When I was in Wyatt's office listening to Darlene, I kept wondering why I wasn't excited. I didn't want to let Dusty go, but I was so conflicted about my time and your participation. But as you were walking away, it hit me. I want to keep Dusty because I want him to be the child you can never have. I want him to be our child."

"Oh, Rico."

He held her as if she was the most precious thing in his life. She now understood him better than anyone. Somewhere inside him was a little boy who felt unloved and unwanted and he was never going to open himself up to that kind of pain again. But he had. He'd taken the risk and shared his feelings and she would love him to the day she died and beyond.

CHAPTER TEN

THE NEXT TWO weeks passed by quickly. Darlene signed away her parental rights and Rico went before a judge seven days later and he became legal guardian of Dusty. The judge suggested that he adopt Dusty to prevent problems down the road. He then went to see Gabe Garrison, Miss Kate's younger brother, who was a lawyer in Horseshoe, to start adoption proceedings. Rico told Gabe that he and Anamarie were getting married and he wanted her name on the adoption papers, too.

They told the Rebels and everyone was excited for them. But no way was he going to the Wiznowski house. Ana didn't push him and she told her parents on her own. And as he had expected Miss Doris said she didn't approve of the marriage. Ana seemed to be fine with that and she was busy making plans for the wedding. There was one problem. They couldn't get the church until the first Saturday in September. Ana still wanted a church wedding so they would wait until September. In the meantime, they settled into family life.

School let out and hay season was in full swing. He didn't have much time for Dusty, but Ana always kept him up until Rico could get home. That bothered Rico. He needed to spend more time with Dusty, but he couldn't let the Rebels down.

The first Monday in June, Falcon surprised them. "Everyone sit down. I want to talk to y'all."

Everyone took seats and Rico leaned against the doorjamb.

"We're all getting older and we all have families that we neglect during hay season. I want to change that up a bit. Eden helped me and we've come up with a program that I think is going to work. It's on my laptop."

Eden was Falcon's daughter and she was in vet school at Texas A&M.

Falcon turned his laptop around so everyone could see. "This is how it works. Everyone will work three days from sunup to sundown, then they'll have three regular days and one day off."

"You've already typed in our names," Phoenix pointed out.

"Yes, son," Miss Kate answered, "but you're free to switch days with your brothers if you need to."

"No, I think this is great."

"Elias, Quincy and Jude have babies coming," Falcon commented. "I know everyone will pitch in to help during that time." He patted a stack of papers. "Here's a copy for everyone."

Rico thought this was the best thing that could have happened. Now he would have more time with Dusty.

"I have Monday, Tuesday and Wednesday from sunup to sundown. Who's working with me?" Elias asked.

"I am," Rico replied.

"Wow, Falcon, you do know what you're doing."

Rico seconded that and he couldn't wait to get home to tell Ana.

ON FRIDAY RICO had a regular day and he was home by five o'clock. As always Dusty was at the front door. When he reached the barn, he would text Ana to let her know he was coming. He swung Dusty up and gave him a hug and then Dusty ran to his room.

Rico walked around the counter and took

Ana into his arms. This was the best part of his day. After a sweet kiss, he asked, "What's Dusty doing in his room?"

"Counting his money."

"Can he count?"

"Money, no." She kissed his cheek. "Just be prepared for something."

Dusty charged back into the room and held out his hand with four quarters in it. "Is that enough money to buy boots? I want boots like yours."

Rico squatted in front of him. "I think that's just about the right amount."

"Oh, boy." Dusty carefully handed each quarter to Rico. "When can we get them?"

"I have tomorrow off and we'll go and buy new boots."

"Oh, boy! Did you hear, Ana?"

He turned his head to look at her and saw tears in her eyes. He'd gotten the marriage proposal thing all wrong, but he'd gotten it wrong with the right woman. He couldn't imagine coming home and not finding her here. She'd become a part of him in a short period of time. Dusty ran to the living room and he stood and took her into his arms again.

"He's just so precious," she mumbled into his shoulder.

He stroked her hair. "And so are you."

He never imagined he would have a family. He just thought he would always be the hired hand on Rebel Ranch. After his troubled past, that was okay with him. But things had changed and now he had his own family. And soon he would have to start looking for a home because above everything else he wanted them to have their own home.

On Saturday they got up late and went to buy boots for Dusty. He was one excited little boy, especially since Rico bought him a hat, too. He wanted to sleep in the boots so they let him. After he fell asleep, Ana took them off and placed them on the floor beside his bed.

SUNDAY WAS A long day without Rico. It was one of his full days and they wouldn't see him until about nine or ten o'clock that night. Ana had bought a couple of bridal magazines and Dusty was trying to help her pick out a dress. He fell asleep in her arms and she held him tight. Through the years she had wondered what it would feel like to hold her own child and it was unlike anything she had ever envisioned. Even though Dusty wasn't biologically hers, he was her child in every other way.

LIFE WAS BETTER than Rico could ever remember. Falcon's schedule worked out great for everyone. The more time he spent with Ana and Dusty the more he knew he had it all—a wonderful woman and a happy kid.

Ana was busy with wedding plans, making the deal for the cake shop and entertaining Dusty. Every day was a new adventure with her.

By the end of June the heat became a factor with hay hauling, but the guys were used to it. Near the end of one of his regular days, Falcon gave him a list of errands to run. He left the hayfield about three thirty and he hoped to be home by five. With his truck loaded down with supplies, he headed home.

The McGregor place was across the road from Rebel Ranch. The entrance was directly across from where Rico had to turn on to Rebel Road. Mr. McGregor was in his nineties and Rico noticed him standing by his mailbox in pajamas and a T-shirt. Mr. McGregor was a tall thin man with a balding head and it was too hot for him to be out this time of day. Rico supposed he was getting his mail.

He turned on to Rebel Road but something made him look back. Taking a second look, he realized the man was holding onto the mailbox. Rico turned around and went back and pulled into the bar ditch next to the mailbox. Cars whizzed by and he was afraid Mr. McGregor was going to get hit.

He got out and ran to the man. "Mr. McGregor, do you need any help?"

"No, I don't need any help." His knuckles were white from his grip on the box.

A Mexican lady in scrubs came from the house pushing a wheelchair. She was out of breath when she reached them. "I've been looking for him everywhere. Mr. McGregor, you know you're not supposed to go to the mailbox. Your grandson takes care of that."

"Don't tell me what to do," Mr. McGregor growled at her.

Clearly there was a problem here and Rico just wanted to go home. "Let me help you into the chair, Mr. McGregor."

"I don't need anybody's help." His voice was rough and angry.

"Then sit in the chair."

"I'm trying to find my sea legs."

The old man was being difficult and probably rightly so. Old age was a bitter pill to swallow and being a strong man he probably had never needed help in his whole life.

"I'll help you," Rico told him. "Just hold on to me."

But the old man couldn't move and his body trembled from weakness. Rico did the only thing he could. He lifted the man into his arms and placed him in the chair.

"Take me to the house," Mr. McGregor ordered. "I don't want her touching me."

"He's like this all the time," the woman muttered.

Rico had no choice but to roll the man to the house. It was an old house, probably built in the 1800s and Rico admired it every time he drove by. With its long veranda and white columns, it was a showplace of days gone by.

"There's a ramp at the back of the house," the woman told him.

He rolled the man through a screened-in back porch and into the house. "My bedroom is down the hall to the right." The old man waved a hand at the woman. "Go back to watching TV like you always do."

Rico felt he had to say something. "Mr. McGregor, you're being very rude to someone who takes care of you."

"Ah, my grandson hired her. I can take care of myself. My son want to put me in a home and sell this property. I've lived here my whole life, as have my ancestors, and I'm not going anywhere. But that fancy gal who has her hooks in my son calls the shots."

If Mr. McGregor was in his nineties, that meant his son had to be somewhere in his seventies and fancy gal probably wasn't too fancy anymore, either. The old man was just mad at the world and life and what it could do to a person.

"I'll help you into bed," Rico said. He really had to get home.

"Hand me that walker. I can get in bed by myself."

Rico found the walker against the wall and placed it in front of him. It took Mr. McGregor a moment but he got to his feet and shuffled to the bed and sat on it. He peered at Jericho through his round wire-rim glasses.

"Who are you?"

"Jericho Johnson."

"Yeah, you're that mysterious guy who works on Rebel Ranch."

"That's me."

The old man looked him up and down. "You're a big strong fella."

"That comes from throwing eighty-pound bales of hay onto a trailer."

"Yeah, I used to do that. I used to do a lot

of things. Now I'm just waiting for the good Lord to call me home so I can be with my wife again." The man lay down and pulled the covers over him. "You have any kids, Mr. Johnson?"

"I have a son," he replied. It was the first time he'd said the words out loud and it made his situation that much more real. *He had a son.*

"Love him while you can because when he grows up, he'll grow away from you or meet some fancy gal who puts all kinds of nonsense in his head. You'll never get your son back."

On that note, Mr. McGregor went to sleep. The Mexican lady hovered in the doorway and he walked over to her. "I know he's difficult, just hang in there."

"Thanks for your help," she called as he walked out the door.

Outside, he took a moment to look around. An old wood barn stood not far from the house. The tin roof had rusted away in spots. The adjoining corral was also wood and needed work. Several of the boards had fallen off and others had rotted away. In the distance was a smaller barn. Most likely used for hay. The pasture hadn't been mowed in years and it grew wild with weeds. The rolling hills nestled under towering oak trees. There wasn't a fence in the distance or to the side of him. Mr. McGregor owned a lot of land.

He'd talk to Falcon tomorrow about Mr. McGregor. If his grandson was going to sell, he wanted to be the first to make an offer. This could be his and Ana's home—their very own home.

LATER THAT NIGHT, after Dusty was in bed, he told Ana about the McGregor property.

"The McGregor place?" One eyebrow lifted sharply as she settled onto the sofa with a cup of coffee.

"Yeah. I know it's old, but I can fix it up any way you want. I just don't know how much land goes with the place. It might be out of my price range."

"Horseshoe is high-tech now and I can look it up on the Horseshoe website tomorrow. We have a new tax assessor and she has updated everything. I looked the shop up and it gave me the tax value and information I needed. We can do the same for the McGregor place."

"Let's do it now." Their future was together and he wanted to get it started as soon as possible. He wanted the place for Ana and

Dusty—a place where Dusty could grow up and call home.

She made to get up and then sat down again. "I can look it up on my phone." Leaning over, she grabbed her phone from the coffee table. Her thumbs went to work. "I'll use McGregor as a keyword and it should bring it up." After a moment, she said. "Okay, here it is. Oh."

"What?"

She handed him her phone and he glanced at the acreage. As he'd thought, Mr. McGregor owned a lot of land. A sinking feeling crashed into his stomach. All his hopes of buying that house and land were gone. He would never be able to afford it.

"We'll find another house," Ana tried to reassure him. "We have lots of time and the bunkhouse is fine for what we need right now."

He had his heart set on the house and now he had to let go like he had to do so many times in his life. One thing he was never letting go of was Ana.

THE NEXT DAY Rico had another regular workday. As they filed out of the office to go do their jobs, Falcon said, "Rico, can I talk to you for a moment?"

He had no idea what Falcon wanted, but he stayed as he was asked to do.

"I got a call early this morning from Mr. McGregor."

Mr. McGregor?

"Obviously you helped him yesterday and he's very grateful for that."

He told Falcon about the mailbox incident. "He's just a very old and angry man."

"Yeah, everybody knows that and no one can get along with him."

"Is that it?" Rico asked. "I need to get to work."

"No, that's not all. He asked if you would pick up his mail every day. He wants to pay you twenty dollars a month to do that."

Rico gave a chuckle. "You're kidding."

"Nope. That's the message he gave me."

"Then, I guess I'll go over and pick up his mail every day, but I don't want his money."

"You'll have to tell him that."

Before he could leave, Falcon asked, "Did you notice what kind of shape that land is in?"

"It's bad. It hasn't been cultivated or fertilized in years."

"I talked to his grandson in town not too

long ago and he said they were trying to put Mr. McGregor in a home, but he was refusing to go. If the grandson is planning on selling that land, I was thinking about extending Rebel Ranch across the road."

Rico was good at keeping his emotions hidden, but that morning disappointment must have shown on his face.

"What?"

"Nothing."

"It's not nothing, Rico. Your face changed when I mentioned it."

He could do this. He could talk to Falcon. "Yesterday, as I looked around the place I thought it would make a good home for Ana and Dusty. I thought I would make an offer when the place came up for sale, but then I found out how much land there is and there's no way I could afford that house and land."

"You want that place? I'll help you get it."

"No. It will be a good addition to Rebel Ranch." He swung toward the door.

"Rico!" Falcon called, getting to his feet. "Come back here!"

As always, when a Rebel gave him an order, he did it.

"Now, I'm going to talk to the grandson again and tell him when he puts that land on the market I want to be the first to offer a bid. And I'm going to make that bid for you. You want that place? I'll make sure you get it. Understood?"

"Falcon—"

"Don't worry about financing. Mom or I will go with you to the bank. We'll help you make this happen. Whether that land is Rebel Ranch or in your name, it's all the same thing. You're a part of this family."

Part of the family. He'd heard that so many times. They just didn't understand that he wasn't. Everything in him was pulling back, but then he thought about Ana and Dusty. He really wanted that house for them, but he wanted to be able to buy it himself.

But he had to be realistic. There was no way a bank was going to loan an ex-con, that amount of money. He needed the Rebels if he wanted that house for his family.

Once again he would be indebted to the Rebels.

As SOON AS he got in his truck he called Ana and told her what had happened. She was excited, but they both were cautious about going into that much debt. He also told her about

Mr. McGregor and that he would be a little late getting home tonight.

That afternoon around four thirty he pulled up to Mr. McGregor's mailbox and took out a brochure from a car dealership in Temple. A driveway went around to the back of the house and that's where he parked. He knocked on the back door and the Mexican lady let him in.

Mr. McGregor was in his bedroom sitting in a wheelchair, watching television. It was turned up loud. The old man turned it off with Rico entered the room.

"Jericho, come on in," Mr. McGregor said. "Did you get my mail?"

He handed him the brochure.

"That's it?" The wrinkles on the old man's forehead deepened. He pointed toward the door. "She's stealing my mail. I don't even get my bank statements anymore. She's looking at them."

Going on what the Mexican lady had told him, he replied, "Mr. McGregor, I think your grandson has had your mail rerouted to his house so you don't have to worry with it anymore."

"What?" The old man shook his hand. "No. He wouldn't do that."

"You need to ask him."

"Hand me that phone by my bedside."

Rico handed him the portable phone, wondering how he had gotten mixed up in the McGregor family. Every time he helped someone it snowballed into much more. He really didn't have time for this.

"You had no right," Mr. McGregor screamed into the phone. "You're an ungrateful grandson taking away all my rights. I'm not dead yet."

The grandson had to be talking because Mr. McGregor sat in silence listening. Rico just wanted to leave, but he waited for some reason.

Finally, Mr. McGregor said, "Yeah. Yeah." Then he clicked off and handed Rico the phone. "My mail goes to his house just like you said. Ungrateful brat."

There was an antique chair not far from where Mr. McGregor was sitting. "Mind if I sit?"

"Go ahead."

"Your grandson loves you. That's why he's trying to make your life a little easier by taking care of your business. Do you really want to pay a lot of bills?"

Mr. McGregor looked down at his wrinkled arthritic hands. "I know, Jericho, but it's hard being old and useless."

"If you let people help you, maybe that feeling would go away." As he said the words it resonated with him. He did the same thing. He was always pushing people away, not letting them get too close. He could see himself in Mr. McGregor.

"I don't need help," the old man grumbled.

"You do need help."

The old man hung his head. Suddenly, he asked, "How old is your son?"

"He's four."

"I was twenty-one years old when my boy was born right here in this house in this bedroom. Sadly, my wife was unable to have any more children. So we spoiled him. I raised him as a cowboy because I'm a cowboy. I've always been a cowboy and I'll die a cowboy. Now my boy is citified. He calls, but we have nothing to say. This land will be passed down to him and he will sell it. It has no meaning to him."

"I'm sorry, Mr. McGregor." Rico didn't know what else to say. He knew the old man had been hurt deeply and there weren't enough words in the dictionary to comfort him.

"Were you always a cowboy?"

For some odd reason Rico started to tell the old man about his life. He never opened up to anyone but Miss Kate and Ana so it felt a little odd talking to a stranger. The words came pouring out and the old man just listened.

"I heard you were an ex-con," Mr. McGregor said.

"I have a lot of anger inside for what happened to me, but I try not to let it show."

"How do you do that?"

"By being grateful for what I have now. The Rebels accepted me for who I am when no one else would take a chance on me." Rico got to his feet. He really needed to get home. "Be grateful for what you have, Mr. McGregor, and be grateful for the good life you had. You've had a lot of good years with your son and now your grandson. Just accept them for who they are. It's clear they care about you."

"Yeah," the old man admitted. "They could've put me in a home a long time ago and I wouldn't've been able to do anything about it."

He patted the old man's shoulder. "Grandpa Rebel always says you can catch more flies with honey than with vinegar. Think about it." He walked toward the door. "I'll check in from time to time to see how you're doing."

"Thank you, Jericho. Stop by anytime you want."

As he drove away he hoped Mr. McGregor made the right decisions for himself. Being lonely and angry never did anyone any good. Rico knew that for a fact. He would be more accepting and open when people tried to help him, especially the Rebels.

CHAPTER ELEVEN

ANAMARIE HAD HER doubts about opening the cake shop. She was spending a lot of money and they needed every dime if they were going to make an offer on the McGregor place. That night she talked to Rico about it.

"No, that's your dream," he said. "We can make that work. I'm just not sure about the land and the house."

They were sitting in the living room talking like they always did.

"Okay, and I can sell my house. That should help with the down payment."

He leaned forward in his chair. "As you know I had coffee with Mr. McGregor early this morning for a few minutes. And every time I talk with him I want to bring up the sale of the land to let him know that I'd like to make an offer, but I can't do it. It just seems like ill-gotten gains. For me to make an offer Mr. McGregor has to die and..."

"Rico." She reached out and touched his

arm. "Let's not think about it anymore. Just enjoy your visits with Mr. McGregor. When it happens, we'll deal with it then."

He caught her hand and pulled her onto his lap. She rested against him, enjoying the closeness that bonded them together.

"Mr. McGregor's son and fancy gal, as he calls the wife, are coming for the weekend. He has Esther, that's the Mexican woman's name, cleaning out a bedroom for them. He's excited like a kid at Christmastime." His hand splayed across her waistline. "Are you losing weight?"

She sat up, running her hands down her body. "Yes. It's all that running around with Dusty. I get a lot of exercise and I'm not at the bakery stuffing my face with kolaches."

"You mean playing with Dusty. You're one big kid yourself and I love that part of you."

"Aw, you're sweet, too."

Happiness wasn't a state of mind. It was something she felt all the way to her toes.

In July there was a lot of hay to get off the fields. Monday was one of Rico's full days and he was eager to get to work. He and Elias would be hauling hay all day. Before he could leave the office, Miss Kate called him back.

She stood up and came around her desk to talk to him. "I got a call this morning. Mr. McGregor passed away peacefully late yesterday."

That bowling ball slammed into his gut again and sadness gnawed at his throat like it had so many other times. The last time Rico had seen him was Friday and Mr. McGregor was excited that his son and daughter-in-law were coming again for the weekend.

He swallowed hard. "When's the funeral?"

"Rico, it's okay to be sad. You befriended an old man who no one else wanted anything to do with."

"He was very lonely and I know how that feels."

She patted his arm. "But you're not lonely anymore. You have us."

"Yes, ma'am."

"You're part of this family."

There it was again. Part of the family. Why didn't he feel like he was?

"The funeral is Wednesday at ten in the morning."

"I'd like the morning off."

"Take the whole day and say goodbye to your friend. Paxton will be working that day for you and then he'll take Thursday which is your day off. Is that okay with you?"

"Yes, ma'am."

That day he threw bales of hay onto the trailer a little harder, needing to release some of the sadness and frustration inside him. He wouldn't let himself think about the land and the house. That didn't matter anymore.

On Wednesday he put on his starched jeans and white shirt and went to the funeral. Ana wanted to go, but she had to take care of Dusty. He had to do this alone.

A small crowd gathered at the Horseshoe Cemetery. Rico held back, waiting for the service to be over. When everyone walked away, he went to the grave and laid a small bouquet of flowers on it.

"Rest in peace, Mr. McGregor. You've earned it."

He turned around and came face-to-face with Mr. McGregor's son. Rico knew who he was because he looked just like his father. Tall and thin, he had a thatch of balding gray hair.

He held out his hand. "You're Jericho, aren't you?"

"Yes." He shook the man's hand.

"Thank you for what you did for my dad."

"I didn't do anything."

"Oh, but you did. My dad has been mad at me for a lot of years and he would barely speak to me when I would visit him. That broke my heart and I didn't know how to change it. I lived with the fear that he was going to die being mad at me. Then all of a sudden he's calling and he hasn't called me in forty years. I'm the one who does all the calling. He wants us to come visit. When we get here, he's all nice and talking about old times. He's even talking to my wife and I don't think he's ever said two words to her. He calls her fancy gal to her face."

"Yeah. He told me that."

"I asked him why the big change and he said a wise man named Jericho told him to be grateful for what he had. I kind of thought he made this character up, but Esther said you were a real person. So, Jericho, my dad died a happy man. And not mad at me anymore. Thank you."

He shook Rico's hand vigorously and walked away to a black car parked at the curb.

Rico drew a deep breath and went home to Ana.

ON MONDAY MORNING Miss Kate called him back again as he was about to go out the office door.

"Rico, I talked to Robert McGregor, Mr. McGregor's son, last night about the McGregor property and he said they'd already made plans for the land. I'm sorry. We weren't quick enough."

He felt a pang of regret that he hadn't mentioned the land to Mr. McGregor, but Rico wouldn't have done it any other way. He would've never been disrespectful to the old man.

"I guess it wasn't meant to be, but thanks, Miss Kate, for trying."

He called Ana as soon as he could and told her what Miss Kate had said.

"I'm sorry, Rico. I know how much you wanted that land."

"Yeah. But it was out of our price range."

"We'll find something else. Hopefully by the time the wedding comes around. You know, we can always move into my house."

"I don't want to live in town. I've been countrified for a long time."

"Then we'll find something."

"I'll be home by five."

Everything he had ever wanted seemed to

be just within his reach, but then it was always snatched away and he was left feeling a loss he couldn't explain.

But he had Ana and Dusty. They would always be a constant in his life.

ON HIS NEXT day off, Rico wanted to start on the cake shop, but Anamarie wanted him to rest. So they compromised. They slept in and had a late breakfast and then they packed their things to go to the office space.

They heard a car drive up and then another. "Wonder who that could be?" Ana asked Rico as he slipped into his boots.

Rico got up and opened the door and was surprised to see Wyatt, Gabe, Rachel and Egan standing there.

"What's going on?" Rico asked.

"Can we come in?" Wyatt countered.

Rachel slipped past them and went to Dusty. "Come with me," Rachel said and picked up Dusty and left the room.

Rico let him go because he knew something was wrong. Since Gabe was here that meant it had something to do with the adoption. Maybe he'd been denied. But then, why were Wyatt, Rachel and Egan here?

Ana came and stood beside him, taking his hand. He squeezed it tightly.

"What is it?" he asked in a steady voice.

Silence filled the room like a bad smell and everyone seemed to step away from what was happening. Finally, Wyatt said, "Darlene Miller is out of prison."

A new kind of fear gripped Rico. "What? How did that happen?"

Wyatt cleared his throat. "A pro bono eager-beaver attorney who wants to make a name for herself got the other girl to admit she was the one with the drugs. Two other inmates backed her up on that. Then she got the parole board to listen to Darlene's story and they believed her. She's out."

"Well, she's not getting anywhere near Dusty." Rico was firm on that. She'd given up her rights and now she had no rights.

Wyatt cleared his throat again. "There's more. She got that same lawyer to file a petition in Family Court here in Horseshoe. Judge Carvel heard the case and listened to Darlene. He gave her back her maternal rights due to the stress she'd been under hearing about her mother's death. He granted her full custody of Dusty."

"No! Don't do this, Wyatt."

"Rico—" Ana clutched his hand and turned to Gabe. "They can't do this. He's our baby."

"How is she going to take care of him?" Rico asked.

"The state got her an apartment and a job in Austin and CPS will check on them regularly."

"Well, isn't that great?"

"Darlene and Ms. Henshaw are waiting at the courthouse. You have to bring Dusty in. Pack his things."

"No, I don't. Just give me five minutes and we can be gone and you'll never find us." Fear echoed with every beat of his heart. They couldn't take his kid. He couldn't let them do that to him and Ana.

"I can't do that, Rico. I have to uphold the law. And the law says Darlene Miller gets her kid back. I'm sorry."

"I thought you were my friend."

"I am. That's why I don't want you to go back to prison."

Egan rubbed Rico's shoulder. "I know this is hard, but you have to do this. I'm right here if you need me."

Egan was the best friend he'd ever had in his whole life and Rico knew he was looking out for Rico's best interest. How did he let go of a little kid he loved?

"It would kill me if you had to go back to prison. Please, just pack Dusty's things and we'll get through this."

Ana silently cried beside him and like always he felt the walls closing in. There weren't any other choices for him. He had to let go. And in doing so it would take a part of his heart that he would never get back.

With a resolve that was as strong as he was supposed to be, he packed Dusty's things in a carryall. He left his boots and hat. He wouldn't need them where he was going. And then he loaded Dusty into his car seat and drove to the courthouse. Ana wiped away tears all the way and he was powerless to ease her pain. He was powerless to ease his own.

At the courthouse, he got out and unbuckled Dusty's seat belt. He had no idea what he was going to say. This was goodbye forever and words mixed with the bile in his throat.

"Hey, buddy," he said as he lifted the boy out of his car seat. "Remember how we were waiting for your mommy to get well?"

Dusty nodded.

"She's all better...and she's here to take you with her."

Dusty didn't say anything, just twisted his hands nervously.

Ana reached up and kissed him, stroking his hair. "Good…bye… I love you."

"Why you crying?" Dusty wanted to know.

There were no good answers they could give him so Rico walked toward Darlene and Ms. Henshaw who were standing in front of the courthouse. Of medium height with blond hair, Darlene Miller was thin—painfully thin. He couldn't see her eyes because she wore sunglasses.

He squatted on the lawn and pointed to Darlene. "There's your mother."

Dusty stood, but he made no move to go toward her.

Darlene ran to them. "Hey, baby, it's Mommy." She grabbed his hands. "Look at you. You've gotten so tall and big."

"I'm like Rico," Dusty replied.

"Yes, well." She lifted Dusty into her arms and Rico noticed her hands shook. She was nervous. "Now you're going to live with Mommy. I have an apartment and a job and we're going to live together. Isn't that wonderful?"

"Can Rico and Ana come with us?"

"No, baby, Rico stays here."

"No!" Dusty shouted. "I stay with Rico." Dusty tried to get down, but Darlene held on to him.

"Let's go," Ms. Henshaw said. She glanced at Rico, but he had nothing to say to the woman.

"Rico! Rico!" Dusty cried all the way to the car. "Rico, come get me! Come get me!" He fought as they put them in the car seat and he was banging on the window as they drove away.

Rico stood frozen in place with Dusty's words ringing in his ears. He would hear that frantic voice for the rest of his life. He drew a heavy breath and marched to his truck, shutting down his emotions.

Egan and Wyatt called his name, but he ignored them. He got in his truck and Ana slid into the passenger seat, tears streaming down her face. He ignored that, too. There was no way to go back and there was no way to go forward. He was back in that cell waiting to be released, waiting for freedom, but this time the freedom from the pain would take more courage than he could muster.

They say that strong men don't cry and not one tear had left his eyes. Maybe they were right.

ANA WIPED AWAY tears and fought for a measure of control. They'd lost their baby, but they could get through this. She just had to reach Rico.

"Rico…"

"I don't want to talk," he said shortly and with each mile she could feel him moving away from her, shutting her out.

When they reached the bunkhouse, he went inside and she slowly followed. He sat in his chair, hunched forward, his forearms resting on his thighs and his hands clasped between his knees. He stared at his hands.

"Rico, we need to talk."

"No, we don't."

She took a deep breath and tried again. "We can get through this together."

"No, we can't."

"How can you say that?"

He stood up, anger in every line of his body. "I came into that bakery for two years—" he held up two fingers "—and you never took one step to take our relationship further. You were afraid of what your mother would say about you talking to an ex-con, so I came in early so she wouldn't see me. Two years, Anamarie, and nothing. Then Dusty comes onto the scene and suddenly I'm more attractive. You come and stay here in the bunkhouse with me, defying your mother. It was never about me. Or us. It was always about Dusty and your need for a child."

"That's not true."

"It is!" he shouted. "And the sooner you realize that, the better it will be."

"Rico—" Her voice cracked and she had to stop.

Rico drew a ragged breath. "Our relationship was all about Dusty. Now that he's gone we have nothing left. It's over. Pack your things and leave."

He walked past her and out the door.

Trembling from head to toe, she tried to stop the tears, but gave up. Nothing mattered anymore. Rico wasn't going to believe her. She'd lost her baby and she'd lost Rico. How did she find her way back from that?

The sound of a car penetrated her numb mind and Rachel rushed into the house.

"Are you okay?" Rachel asked.

Ana shook her head. "I'll never be the same again."

Egan stood behind Rachel. "Where's Rico?"

"He went toward the barn."

Egan hurried out and Rachel said, "Sit down and let's talk."

Ana shook her head again. "I don't need to talk. I just need to be alone. Please leave." She didn't need words of solace. What she needed was her baby and no one could give her that.

"Anamarie…"

"Please, Rachel, let me grieve in peace."

Rachel hesitated and then said, "Okay, but if you need anything, just call."

Ana closed the door and went to her bedroom. Getting her suitcase out of the closet, she drew a hot tear-soaked breath and started to pack her clothes. And then she went to the refrigerator and took down the drawing Dusty had drawn of them. She placed it carefully in the suitcase so as not to crush it.

The teddy bear Rico had won for her at the carnival was on the bed and she tucked it under her arm. She couldn't leave it behind. It had a lot of good memories and she would need those in the days ahead.

She stopped in Dusty's doorway and a sob rose up in her throat. His cowboy boots were at the foot of the bed and his hat lay on the bed. She remembered the day he'd gotten them and how excited he'd been. Her precious baby. The only baby she would ever have. Now she had to go on. Without Rico. Without Dusty. Somewhere inside she would find the strength to do that. She just didn't know when that would happen.

After closing Dusty's door, she looked around at the place where she'd found love and happiness; cooking with Dusty in the kitchen, sitting in Rico's lap, talking, laughing and kissing until she couldn't think. And just like a puff of smoke it was all gone. But the memories remained. Wonderful memories she would treasure forever.

She got in her car and drove away, refusing to look back at everything she would never have again.

CHAPTER TWELVE

"Rico!" Egan shouted, but Rico kept walking. He didn't want to talk to anyone, not even
Egan.

He whistled for his horse, Brown Patch, a
brown-and-white paint that Quincy had given
him. The horse galloped toward the barn and
Rico quickly put a bridle on her and slid on
bareback. He didn't have time for a saddle.

"Rico—"

He kneed the horse and they flew out of
the barn, leaving Egan behind. They flew
over fences and through pastures of round
bales of hay and square bales of hay. On they
went through herds of cattle that hurried to
get out of their way. That's when he realized
that Patch was breathing heavily.

Pulling her up, he slid from her back to the
grass and stared up at the bright noonday sun.
It was blinding and he blinked several times
to shut it out. But like the pain it was right
there. They'd taken his kid. They'd taken

Dusty away from him. A tear slipped from his eyes and then another and he made no move to wipe them away. Soon sobs racked his body and he turned onto his side and curled into a ball, letting the grief take its toll.

Afterward, he got up and tied the reins on Patch's neck. He slapped her on the rump. "Go home, girl. Go home." Then he took out his phone and dropped it in the grass, not even looking at the many messages on it. Staring at the blue horizon, he started walking. Heavy woods and scrub brush didn't slow him down. He walked until he could no longer see then he fell down into a bed of leaves and tried to sleep. But Dusty's words kept pounding in his ears.

Rico, come get me! Rico, Rico, Rico...

He got up and started walking again, feeling his way around trees. Finally his knees gave way and he sank down beside a big oak tree. The darkness of the night trapped him in his own private hell. He was in a place where no one would ever find him and that's exactly where he wanted to be. *Nowhere.* Away from the Rebels and away from people who wanted to comfort him. He didn't need comfort. He needed his kid back. And he had to find a way to let go on his own.

It could prove to be the hardest thing he would ever have to do.

ANAMARIE WENT HOME and stuffed her wedding dress into the closet. She then lay on her bed and stared at the ceiling fan making endless circles. Her insides churned and she fought the nausea rising in her. Tears burned her eyes and she desperately needed someone to hold her, to comfort her. Not someone. Just Rico. But he was locked inside himself—a place she couldn't reach.

She tried not to think about Dusty, but his little voice screaming for Rico would be with her for a long time. Pushing it away, she turned onto her side and thought about Rico. He'd said their relationship was based on Dusty. She would never believe that. She'd been crazy about Rico for a long time, but she was afraid to take the relationship further. Of course, it had a lot to do with her mother and her mother's power over her.

After Greg, she'd hidden behind her mother's protection. It was safe, secure. She never wanted to be hurt like that again so she avoided men and she avoided living. Her life was the bakery just like everyone had said. She'd worked long hours so she wouldn't have to think about her dismal life. Then she started talking to Rico and he came back and came back. It excited her that he had taken an interest in her when no one else had.

So why hadn't she taken the first step? Fear of rejection was her immediate answer. Dusty gave her a way to get around that. She opened up her heart and went with her feelings to get closer to Rico. Their relationship wasn't just about Dusty and someday Rico would believe that. It would take time for both of them to get over losing Dusty. She was good at waiting.

A knock sounded at her door and she groaned. She got up and went to answer it. Angie and Rachel stood on the doorstep.

"Hey, sis. We thought we would visit for a while."

Anamarie shook her head. "No, I'm not in the mood to visit. Please. I just want to be alone."

"Sis…"

"Thanks. I'll talk to y'all later." She closed the door and made it almost to her bedroom when another knock sounded.

She marched back and yanked open the door. "I'm…" Her voice trailed away as she saw her mother and dad standing there.

"Can we come in?" her mother asked.

214 A CHILD'S GIFT

No! But she stepped aside and let them in. She had to face her mother's scorn so she might as well do it now.

Her mother sat on the blue tweed sofa with her purse in her lap.

"We heard what happened," her mother said. "How could they take that little boy? I know how much you loved him."

Ana was speechless. It wasn't like her mother to be kind and conciliatory.

"Wyatt should have done something to stop it," her mother went on.

"The judge ordered Dusty to be returned to his mother," Ana stated flatly. "There was nothing Wyatt could do."

Her mother looked around. "Is that man here with you?"

She bit her lip. "No. And his name is Rico."

"Why not?" her mother wanted to know.

She searched for words to explain in a way that her mother would understand. There weren't any so she went with the truth. "Rico is taking this hard and he asked me to leave."

Her mother jumped up, sliding the strap of her purse up her arm. "How dare he! After all you did for him."

Her dad got to his feet. "Doris, I think you've said enough. Let's go home."

"I'm not through, Willard."

"You're through." Her dad took her mother's arm and tugged her toward the door.

"Anamarie, please come home. Just come home," her mother called over her shoulder. "We'll get through this just like we did before."

"I'm not coming home. I have a house and this is where I'm going to stay. I'm not eighteen years old anymore and I don't need my mother to baby me."

"You don't need to be alone."

"That's exactly what I need. And for the record I still love Rico and I believe he still loves me. We're both hurting and trying to find ways to deal with life after Dusty. I'll be fine. It'll just take time."

"Come back to the bakery. That's where you belong."

Ana shook her head. "I'm not coming back to the bakery."

"You can't just sit here and grieve."

"She can do whatever she pleases," her father said. "I think she's old enough and strong enough to handle whatever life gives her."

"Willard, you never support me when we deal with our children."

"Go figure." Her father opened the door and had to pull her mother through it.

Ana went back to her bedroom and changed into an old T-shirt. Curling up in the bed, she clutched the teddy bear Rico had won for her. Tonight she wouldn't give Dusty his bath and watch him play in the bubbles. She wouldn't wrap him in a big towel and carry him to his bedroom and help with his pajamas. She wouldn't hear screeching as he would run and jump into Rico's lap. Their laughter tonight would be silent. She was alone again and that's when the tears came, so many she couldn't stop them.

She must have fallen asleep because the next thing she knew someone was pounding on her front door. Slipping out of bed, she realized it was completely dark outside. She hurried to the front door to find Rachel there.

"I'm sorry to bother you," Rachel said, holding her phone in her hand. She had Mickey in her other arm. "But I thought you'd like to know that Rico is missing. And I brought Mickey because I don't want my boys to get too attached to him. I'm not sure what Rico's plans are for him." Rachel placed the dog on the porch and he ran to Ana, barking.

She picked him up and cuddled him, but

her mind was on one thing. "Missing? What do you mean? Isn't he at the ranch?"

"No." Rachel glanced at her phone. "May I come in?"

Anamarie opened the door wider and they sat on the sofa. By Rachel's nervousness she knew something was really wrong.

"What happened?" she asked.

"Rico rode off on his horse and Egan couldn't stop him. Later, the horse came back without Rico. The Rebels have shut down hay season and they are all searching for him. They found his phone miles from the house."

Anamarie tried not to overreact, tried not to let her fears get the best of her. She knew deep inside that Rico wouldn't hurt himself. He was too strong. "He's just hurt and doesn't want to speak to anyone. He's hiding and grieving and he has to do that alone. We just have to give him time."

Rachel laid her phone on the sofa and kept staring at it. "I'm just worried about Egan."

"Why?"

Rachel blinked away a tear. "He and Rico have a special connection and Egan wants to help him like Rico helped Egan, but Rico keeps shutting him out."

"That's Rico. He's built this wall of protection around himself to keep anyone from getting too close. It's all connected to his past and the pain he had to go through. He let down his guard and allowed Dusty in and he allowed me in and we thought we would be together always. That ended abruptly and Rico isn't dealing with it very well. Egan just has to be patient. I have to be patient."

Mickey jumped into her lap and she stroked him, feeling a closeness to Dusty. Tears welled in her eyes again.

"But you'll get back together and you'll have your own family. Please tell me that." Rachel seemed to need reassurance.

Anamarie shook her head. "No. I'll never have a child." And for the first time she told another person besides Rico about what had happened to her as a teenager.

"Oh, Anamarie, I'm so sorry." Rachel threw her arms around Anamarie's neck and hugged her. Mickey yelped and jumped to the floor. "Angie has never mentioned any of this."

She drew back. "It's a Wiznowski family secret. Somehow that made me tainted in my mother's eyes and she didn't want anyone to know that her daughter couldn't have children."

"That's terrible."

"Yeah. It made me feel hopeless."

"But Rico made you feel otherwise?" Rachel asked.

A smile dented her sad expression. "Yes." *And so much more.* She took a deep breath. "When Dusty first came in to the bakery, I tried to keep my distance because I knew if I let my heart get involved, I would get hurt. Dusty was such a precious little boy and there was no way I could *not* get involved with him. He became our little boy. And it gave me a chance to get closer to Rico, something I was afraid to do on my own. Now Rico and I don't know how to move forward without him."

"But you will," Rachel insisted. "I've never seen Rico as happy as he was with you."

Anamarie played with the hem of her T-shirt. "He said our relationship was based on Dusty."

"Was it?" Rachel asked softly.

Ana raised her head and tears threatened again. "No. I'll never believe that."

Rachel's phone buzzed and she immediately grabbed it and talked for a minute to Egan. "The others are stopping for the night, but Egan is continuing on. He says he's not stopping until he finds Rico." Rachel stood.

"I better go. I left the boys at my dad's so Justin wouldn't hear that Rico's missing. I don't know how to tell Justin about Rico or that his dad won't be coming home tonight."

Ana got to her feet. "You'll find a way."

Rachel hugged Anamarie. "I'm so sorry for everything you've been through."

"Thank you. Please call me if you hear anything about Rico."

Ana closed the door and went back to bed. Mickey followed and curled up next to her. She clutched the dog, knowing they both missed Dusty. After the events of the day, her mind was supercharged and sleep eluded her. She just kept wondering where Rico was and if he was okay.

Her last thought was: *Come home, Rico. Just come home.*

THE BRIGHT MORNING sun woke Rico. He lay between two trees in a pile of leaves. He got to his feet and brushed the dirt and leaves from his clothes. For a moment he wondered where he was and what he was doing here in the woods. Then it all came rushing back and it brought him to his knees.

Dusty was gone.

Rico didn't cry. He was through shedding

tears over something he couldn't change. Getting to his feet, he reached for his hat and realized it was gone. He had no idea where it was. All he could see in front of him were tree trunks, some small and some big. He started walking through the tree maze and he knew he was on the property the Rebels hadn't cleared. It was miles away from the ranch. Sweat poured from his face and soaked his clothes. His long hair was hot and heavy. The July heat took its toll. Thirst gnawed at his dry throat.

Suddenly, he walked out of the woods into a low valley. The grass was brown, except for one spot which could mean only one thing; a natural spring. He ran toward it and fell onto his belly and crawled the rest of the way until he reached water. Cupping his hands, he scooped up water and brought it to his parched mouth over and over. Then he rolled onto his back, letting the mud cool his heated body.

He rose to a sitting position and froze. A huge bobcat was on the other side of the spring. The cat edged closer with a low growl in his throat, his eyes on Rico. There were a lot of wild animals out here and he didn't have a weapon, except for the knife on his belt.

All the Rebels carried a knife on the ranch. He reached for it and slid it out of its sheath in one easy movement so as not to startle the animal.

The cat drank and never took his eyes off Rico. He kept waiting for the animal to lunge toward him, but instead the cat turned and bounded into the woods. Rico sank back with a sigh of relief. After a while, he drank more water, but he knew he had to keep moving. The sun bore down on him and he had to reach shade. He kept walking until his legs would no longer hold him. He came upon another spring and bedded down for the night.

He sat some distance away and watched as deer drank from the spring. A squirrel chased a blackbird away and then night fell like a shade on a window shutting out everything but his thoughts. Crickets serenaded loudly, but all he could hear was Dusty.

Rico, come get me! Rico, Rico, Rico...

He wasn't ever going to get that out of his head. Not until he accepted that Dusty wasn't his kid. Dusty wasn't his blood, but in every other way he and Dusty had connected. And then Ana... No, he couldn't think about her. It was just too much.

A growl distracted him and he reached

for his knife. The bushes rustled and Rico tensed, but soon the growl faded into the distance. He dozed on and off and when the sun peeked through the blue clouds he walked to the spring and drank water. Then he set off walking again. He had no idea where he was going. He just had to keep moving to keep the pain at bay.

ANAMARIE SPENT HER days crying and watching her phone, waiting for Rachel to call. Rico was still missing and Egan was still looking for him. Ana called her whole family and told them she needed time and surprisingly they stayed away.

Finally she realized she had to stop wallowing in her misery. She had to do something. So she decided to clean her house from top to bottom. Getting rid of the dust and cobwebs was cathartic, releasing all her pent-up energy. By the evening she was tired and every muscle in her body ached. That night she welcomed the sleep that claimed her. Sleep without precious memories.

THE NOONDAY SUN was a killer and Rico removed his mud-caked shirt to hold over his head. He was in a clearing of tall dried weeds that scraped against his mud-caked jeans. Thirst once again gnawed at his throat, but there was no spring in sight. Then he saw it—a makeshift road that went into the hills. He knew that road. He'd helped Egan make it. It led to the Rebel cabin on Crooked Creek. The cabin was the first home of the Rebels who had settled here in the 1800s. When Egan and Rachel had first married, they'd camp out on weekends. They needed an easier way to get there so Rico helped Egan make a road so a Polaris Ranger could get through.

Rico hurried up the road, but thirst was about to get him. His mouth and throat were dry and it was hard to produce saliva. He needed water fast. He kept walking. Using every ounce of strength he had, he climbed the hill. Water was at the cabin. He just had to get there.

By the time he made it, his body was bathed in sweat and it ran from his hair, his forehead. His breathing was labored, but once he saw the tin roof of the old cabin he got a burst of renewed energy. He fell down by the old well then got up and pumped the well handle trying to bring up the water. He pumped until his muscles ached. The first trickle of water he caught in his mouth. Then he pumped more and drank until he was revived. He sat on the ground and drew long breaths. That's when he realized he smelled and he was filthy.

He found a bar of soap in the one-room log cabin and grabbed a towel Rachel had left there. With those two items in his hand, he made his way down to Crooked Creek. Stripping out of his clothes, he glanced around and didn't understand why because there was no one out here for miles. He picked up the bar of soap and stepped into the clear waters of the creek and scrubbed the dirt from his body and hair. The water cooled his sunburned skin.

After he finished, he wrapped the towel around his waist and made his way back to the cabin. There he washed his clothes and hung them in a tree. That's when hunger growled in his stomach. Rico knew that Egan kept SpaghettiOs here and it didn't take him long to find them. He sat on the stoop and ate and then grabbed a quilt to bed down on the porch. It was too stifling in the cabin. Soon he would have to make his way home to a life without Dusty and Ana. Although the thought stirred up the pain again, he was strong enough now to at least think about it.

ANA COULDN'T SIT in the house any longer with the memories. She started work on her shop. Rico was going to put up the wall to separate the party room from the cake shop, but now she would have to hire someone. She really needed to go back to work.

She was sweeping the floor for the second time when her dad walked in. "Hey, I saw your car outside. How you doing?"

She waffled her hand back and forth. "So-so."

"You look good."

"Thank you, Dad." She leaned on the broom. "Do you know a good carpenter who could put up a wall?" She pointed to where Rico had marked it. "And cabinets? And flooring?"

"Yeah." He thumbed toward his chest. "Me."

"No, I didn't mean…" She didn't want her dad to do that. He had enough work to do in his welding shop.

Her dad looked around at the empty building. "I can come over here every afternoon and get quite a bit done. If I need help, I'll just call Bubba."

"I'll be here to help, Dad. You won't need Bubba."

Her dad pulled off his baseball cap and scratched his head. "Well…"

She let the broom drop to the floor with a thudding sound that echoed in the empty space. Placing her hands on her hips, she said, "I can do anything Bubba can do and probably faster and better."

"Okay, okay." He pulled a pencil out of the front pocket of his overalls. "I'll make a list of everything you'll need."

"Rico has already made a list. I just have to order it and pick it up in Temple."

"Oh." He slid his pencil back into the pocket, the lines on his face deepened.

"It's okay, Dad. We can talk about Rico."

"I just hate that he hurt you."

"He's hurting too."

"Yeah." Her dad nodded. "It's just a sad situation."

"Yes, it is, but I plan to stay busy and open this business by Christmas. What do you think? Can we do it?"

"You bet."

At her dad's words, her stomach cramped. Rico used to say that all the time, but she wasn't going to wallow in any more pain. She had to move forward.

RICO SAT ON the porch in his jeans watching the deer at the creek when he heard the pounding of hooves. Someone was approaching on a horse. He didn't move. He just watched as the rider came into view. Egan. A very different Egan with a growth of beard and a haggard look pulled at his face.

"Rico!" Egan shouted and made his way to him. "Man, am I glad I found you."

"I didn't know I was lost."

Egan sank down beside him. "We've been looking for you for days."

"Why? I told you I needed some time alone."

Egan removed his hat and swiped a hand through his sweaty hair. "You're a part of this family and we're all worried about you. We've searched everywhere."

"We've?"

"All of us, even Mom and Grandpa were on horseback. We shut down hay season until we could find you."

"What?" He was shocked. He never meant for that to happen. Hay was a big part of Rebel income. He just assumed they'd go on with their lives until he got his act together. "Y'all shouldn't have done that."

"Rico, we all have kids and know what it's like when something happens to one of them. We just wanted to make sure you were okay and to be there if you needed us. The same as we would do for anyone in this family."

Family. They kept throwing that word at him and he ducked every time. He wasn't a Rebel. He wasn't blood, but Dusty wasn't his blood either and he'd loved him as if he was his own. That was a sobering thought.

There was silence for a moment and then he said, "I don't know what to say."

"You don't have to say anything," Egan told him. "You just have to come home."

"I… I'm not ready just yet."

"Okay. I'll stay until you're ready because I'm not leaving until you do."

Rico looked at his friend. He had never realized that when gang members in prison were cruelly taunting Egan and Rico had stepped in that he would have a friend for life. But then, he was friends with all the Rebels and maybe he was trying to deny something that he already was. A part of the family.

"You look like hell," Rico told him.

"Says the man who looks scarier than I've

ever seen him. What's up with your hair? It's everywhere."

"I washed it in the creek. I got a minnow in it, but I think I got it out. I'm not sure."

Egan chuckled and it relieved the tension that had welled up in Rico.

Rico glanced toward Egan's horse. "You don't by any chance have a steak in those saddlebags, do you?"

"Nah, but something that will help." Egan got up and went to rummage in his saddlebags. He came back with protein bars and beef jerky and dumped them into Rico's lap.

"Thanks," Rico said, tearing into a package of beef jerky.

Egan went to the well and came back with a bucket of water. They sat eating in silence.

"Tastes like steak," Rico said with a touch of humor.

"Yeah, anything would at this point." Egan chuckled.

Rico looked down at Crooked Creek and so many emotions erupted inside him. But for the first time he was able to look at his situation and not feel like his insides were caving in.

"She played me."

"What?" Egan's head jerked up. "Who?"

"Darlene Miller played me like a pro. She needed Dusty somewhere safe so her sister couldn't get him and she unknowingly hit on my weakness."

"Foster care."

"Yeah. I should have let Dusty go into foster care. He would've done fine and Anamarie and I wouldn't be going through our own private hell now. And Dusty would have been glad to see his mother. Instead, he's hurting just like us. Hindsight is twenty-twenty."

"You know Anamarie…"

"I don't want to talk about her," he snapped.

Egan held up his hands. "Okay, but we *will* talk about her later."

"Maybe. Depends on who's the strongest."

"Don't pull that on me. As Elias is always saying you could tie me into a pretzel."

"Just remember that."

"I'm sorry for everything you had to go through," Egan said softly.

"I know. Let's just leave it at that."

"Okay." Egan brushed dirt from his jeans. "Yesterday or was it the day before? I can't remember. Falcon said that you didn't want to be found. We had looked everywhere, except for the hills around the cabin. I told him it was time for everyone to go back to work and I would search the hills. I got a fresh horse and picked up Patch and headed this way. Patch is tied to a tree at the bottom of the hill. When you're ready, we can go."

It was time. It was time to go back to a life without Dusty and Anamarie. He could do that now and still maintain his dignity and some sort of strength to face the future. He got to his feet. "I have to find my shirt and some string to tie back my hair."

"You get the shirt and I'll get the string."

In less than five minutes they both were on Egan's horse headed down the hill to Patch. Then they rode for home. They were far far away from the ranch. As night fell on the second day they could see the roof of Miss Kate's house. They rode hard, but it was still late when they rode into the barn.

After taking care of the horses, Egan said, "Now I'm going home and hug my wife and kids." He glanced at Rico. "Don't worry about anyone bothering you. I'll tell everyone to stay away until you're ready."

"Thanks."

Rico stared out at the black night and the

millions of stars that twinkled above. He hoped that Dusty was doing well and adjusting to his environment. Crickets entertained him with their constant chirping as he slowly made his way toward the bunkhouse to deal with the memories.

CHAPTER THIRTEEN

ANAMARIE GAVE UP trying to sleep and got up and made coffee. Rachel had called late last night and said that Egan had found Rico and had brought him home. She had lain in bed with her cell in her hand, hoping he would call. He didn't.

Mickey whined at her feet and she made him a bowl of biscuits, bacon and milk. He gobbled it up, wagging his tail.

"Happy now?" Mickey didn't even take time to bark. He was too busy eating.

A knock at the door startled her. It was a little after five in the morning and she wasn't expecting anyone. Unless… She hurried to the door and peeked through the glass on the door. It was Rico.

She opened the door uncaring that she was in her old T-shirt. "Rico…are you okay?"

He held his hat in his hand and his face, neck and hands were sunburned. Her heart sank at the set stern expression on his face. The scar stood out against his red skin.

"I'm fine," he replied in a stiff voice she'd never heard before and she knew he hadn't come to say he was sorry and that he still loved her. She clutched the door for support as her last hope died.

"Sorry to bother you so early, but Egan said you had Mickey. I came to get him before I go to work."

At the sound of his name Mickey trotted to the door and circled Rico, sniffing at his boots. Then he trotted to Anamarie and sat on his haunches staring at Rico. He barked at Rico several times.

"He does that a lot. I think he's asking about Dusty," Ana said.

"Yeah." Rico said the word almost to himself as he appeared deep in thought. "Listen, about the other day... I don't remember what I said, but I know it was hurtful and that's the last thing I wanted to do."

"Yes, it was hurtful." She took a deep breath. "To me, our relationship was not based on Dusty."

"I don't have time to get into that."

"Well, I do and we're going to talk about it." She wasn't going to let him get away by saying their relationship was over. "If you remember correctly, I did not get involved with Dusty when he came into the bakery that morning. You did, but I held back. I only got involved when you asked me to. I saw it as a way to get closer to you. That's the only reason I helped you. For two years I've been searching for a way to take our relationship further and Dusty gave me the chance. Of course, I fell in love with him and..."

"I'm not talking about this."

"Why not?" she pressed. "I don't regret the time I spent with you and Dusty. He was our little boy and I couldn't have loved him more even if I'd given birth to him. I hope he remembers the lady who loved him with all her heart and who cooks good, as he used to say. I..." She had to take a breath as emotions jammed her throat. "But after all the tears and the sadness, I realized one thing. Dusty wasn't ours to keep. He had a mother."

Rico remained silent, staring at Mickey.

"You said our relationship was based on Dusty. It wasn't. Dusty wasn't there on all those Tuesday mornings when we laughed, talked, shared our lives and fell in love. That was us. Just us and our feelings."

He slapped his leg with his hand. "Come on, Mickey. Let's go. I have to go to work."

Mickey didn't move. "I'm guessing from sunup to sundown, right? To make up for the days you've lost. The Rebels don't expect that of you. What I don't understand is why you do."

When he didn't speak, she reached out her hand and said, "I can almost touch that steel wall you've erected around yourself. For a brief moment in time you let down your guard and allowed Dusty and me in. Now you're shutting everyone else out again. Loving someone means you open your heart and you open yourself up for pain. That's a risk that comes with everything, even love. That's what life is about, Rico. You get hurt but you learn to survive and go on."

He stared straight ahead as if he was in a trance and that made her angry. Why couldn't he talk to her? They never had a problem talking. That anger drove her to add, "Until you can admit that what we shared was real, I'm not talking to you anymore." She reached down and picked up Mickey. "And I'm keeping Mickey."

She closed the door in his face.

Rico shut out Anamarie's voice as he traveled toward the ranch. He refused to think about what she'd said. He couldn't let himself get involved anymore. Living by himself and being alone was his future. He'd known that from the start, but he'd gotten sidetracked. He wouldn't again.

It was just as well she'd kept Mickey. He didn't need any reminders. He just needed to work until he couldn't think.

Instead of turning left to Rebel Road, he turned right and drove over the cattle guard onto the McGregor property. Foggy dew danced in the beam of his headlights, but he could see the old McGregor house clearly. The house was closed up; not a light anywhere. Dark shadows loomed over the house mingling with the early morning dawn with an eerie ghost-like feel. Mr. McGregor's life was this ranch and Rico thought it sad his only son had no interest in being a rancher. But Robert McGregor had a right to live his own life. Rico understood that. He only hoped that the people who'd bought the land would treat it as kindly as Mr. McGregor had.

As much as he tried to shut out Ana's words, they followed him into the office.

Until you admit what we had was real, I'm not talking to you.

Dusty wasn't ours to keep.

He was so into his own feelings that it startled him when everyone jumped to their feet and shouted, "Rico, welcome home."

"You could've taken the day off," Falcon said.

"I've had too many days off," Rico replied, fighting to maintain his composure. "I'm ready to go to work. I just don't know where I'm supposed to be today."

"With me." Elias slapped him on the back. "We have five hundred square bales on the ground and we need to get them into the barn. Let's go."

Elias's phone buzzed and he immediately reached for it in his pocket. "Calm down. I'll be right there." Headed toward the door, Elias shouted over his shoulder, "Maribel's water broke and Chase is having a meltdown. It's too early. The boys are coming too early. I've got to go."

There was silence for a moment and then Miss Kate got to her feet. "I better go check on Maribel and make sure everything's okay." As she passed Rico she hugged him around the waist. "I'm glad you're home. I sleep better when I know where my boys are."

He tried not to stiffen, but he feared he failed. He wasn't one of her boys. Once again he was ducking all those family ties.

"That leaves us short on manpower today." Falcon's words penetrated the numbness of his mind. "Jude and Quincy's babies have arrived and they'll be out for a couple days."

"Rico and I will get the hay off the field," Egan said.

"I'll drive for y'all and we can switch around." Falcon looked at the ledger he always kept beside him. "Mr. Higbee is coming at nine for fifty round bales of hay."

"Paxton and I will handle that," Phoenix said.

Rico threw bales of hay onto the trailer with more energy than ever. He just wanted to block out the world.

"Are you okay?" Egan asked.

"I'm fine."

"Did you get the dog back?"

"No, she kept it."

Egan paused in picking up a bale of hay. "Is that going to be a problem?"

"Nope." Rico jumped onto the trailer and

stacked bales, shutting out Egan's voice and shutting out everything but the work.

Paxton joined them at noon and they worked steadily until nine o'clock that night. With the last bale in the barn, Rico made his way to the bunkhouse. Hay stung his skin and clung to his sweaty clothes. The collar of his shirt rubbed like a Brillo pad.

He went straight to the bathroom and stripped out of his dirty grimy clothes. As he made to step into the tub for a shower, he noticed Dusty's bath toys Ana had bought him. Marching to the kitchen he got a plastic bag and put all the toys inside. Suddenly he could hear Dusty and he cringed. When would it stop?

He put the bag of toys in the utility closet, took a shower and went to bed, forcing himself mentally to not think. But her voice slipped through...

Dusty wasn't there on Tuesday mornings, That was us. Just us.

ANAMARIE WORKED ON the shop. Everything was going so slow. Her dad worked about two hours every afternoon and the wall wasn't even halfway done yet. Her dad could not keep up the pace of working a job and coming to help her. She had to tell him she would hire someone else. It might hurt his feelings, but she didn't think he would be too hurt.

She had decided to put in laminated wood flooring all over so that meant she had to pull up the linoleum in the bathroom. While on her hands and knees yanking linoleum, her cell buzzed. She glanced at it on the top of the commode. Bubba. If he was going to offer to help her, she would gladly take him up on it.

"Hey, sis, can you come over to the courthouse for a few minutes?"

"Courthouse? What's going on?"

"Margie's pregnant and we're getting married. We need a witness."

"Does Mom know?"

"No, we're going over there tonight to tell them."

This was not good. Her mother was going to be livid.

"I'll be right there."

Bubba and Margie said their vows in front of Judge Henley. Wyatt was there, too. Afterward, Wyatt pulled her to the side.

"Ms. Henshaw called this morning to let me know that Dusty is adjusting very well. And CPS will continue to check in every week for a while to make sure everything's okay. Just thought you might like to know. I tried calling Rico, but he won't answer his phone."

"He's taking this very hard."

"I'm sorry, and I wish there was a way I could help him."

"Me, too," she murmured almost to herself, knowing there was no one who could reach Rico. He had to heal on his own.

She went back to pulling linoleum. Her dad came in around four and put in a few studs. She had to talk to him and she was dreading it.

As he packed up his things, she said, "Dad, I appreciate your help, but I think this is getting too much for you. I'm going to look for someone else to finish this."

Her dad caught his back. "That might be a good idea. My back and my knees are about to get me. I'll be here to make sure everything is done right."

"Thank you, Dad." That went very well. Now she had to worry about her finances. She was spending everything she had in her shop and she needed to go to work to earn money.

Later that night she pushed her worries aside and thought about Rico; his gentle touch, his gentle love. No one had ever loved him but his great-grandma, and the struggle to keep her safe had caused him immeasurable pain. That's what he associated love with—pain. He had to know it was so much more than that.

She clutched the teddy bear a little tighter and Mickey edged closer as if she might need comfort. All she needed was Rico here to hold her like he always had. When would she stop wanting him?

THE NEXT MORNING Rico got up and had a ham-and-cheese roll-up for breakfast with a glass of milk. His phone binged and he glanced at it on the counter. Elias. He touched it and a photo of two little boys wrapped in blue blankets came up. He read the text below it:

The twins have arrived early. They weighed 3 lbs. 2 oz. apiece exactly. We couldn't come up with names that we could agree on so Maribel let Grandpa name them. She was heavily sedated at the time. So here they are: John Abraham Rebel the Second and John Abraham Rebel the Third. We're going to call them J.R. and Tre.

A smile tugged at Rico's face for the first time in days. He was happy for his friend and he didn't feel that pang of jealousy that he thought he might. And if the boys were anything like their father, they would probably be known as the terrors of Horseshoe, Texas.

He typed in: Congratulations. And then went to work.

For the next couple of weeks he worked from sunup to sundown. The calendar flipped over to September and hay season was winding down. On Saturday he walked into the office for another day's work.

"I'll get the round bales off the field this morning," he said.

"Paxton and Phoenix will do that," Falcon told him. "You have the day off."

"I don't need a day off."

Falcon stared right at him. "Yes, you do. You can't continue this pace. You need a break and you're taking it."

Rico could see there was no need to argue. They weren't going to let him work. He turned and walked out the door. Egan followed him.

"Rico, he's right and you know it."

"I need to work, Egan. That's all I know."

Egan sighed. "Go see Anamarie."

"I don't need to see Anamarie. I wish everyone would just leave me alone."

He was acting like a petulant child, but he couldn't change the way he felt. No one understood what was going on in his head. No one.

"Talk to her," Egan kept on. "Talk, yell, scream. Do whatever you have to do to get this out of your system."

Rico got in his truck and drove to the bunkhouse. He wasn't talking to anyone, not even for Egan. He did laundry and changed the sheets on his bed. For the first time he noticed that Dusty's drawing was missing. Ana had taken it. She had no right. The drawing belonged here in the bunkhouse. Then, the drawing was fictional just like everything else had been.

He stayed busy doing things he hadn't done in a while like washing dishes and wiping down the counters. Dusty's door was firmly closed and it always would be. Around eleven he realized he was hungry, but there wasn't much to eat. He'd have to make a trip to the grocery store. He'd do that later.

Sinking into his recliner, he turned on a football game and watched the players run helter-skelter all over the field just like his thoughts were running through his head.

Talk to her.

Our relationship wasn't about Dusty.
I saw Dusty as a way to get closer to you.
He fell asleep with those words in his head.

ANAMARIE WAS HAVING a bad week. The first carpenter she hired brought a six-pack of beer with him and he didn't last the day. The next carpenter brought his two little grandbabies with him. That didn't work, either.

She was still looking for someone else. In the meantime she searched the Internet for ways to do it herself. It couldn't be that hard. But then it was. It took someone strong to hold the two-by-fours and nail them in place.

She was trying to figure out where to start when her mother blew through the front door like a low-grade hurricane. "What are you doing to your father?"

Anamarie laid her laptop on the concrete floor. "What's wrong?"

"He's in his recliner with a heating pad on his knee. I just picked up another pad for his back."

"I'm sorry. He hasn't worked here in days."

"It's finally caught up with him and now he's sitting in his recliner expecting me to hand him stuff." She glanced around at the empty space and the partial wall. "This is nonsense. Just nonsense. You have a place of business down the street. Why do you need this?"

Anamarie took a patient breath. Her mother's ire tested her patience and her nerves like it always had. But she wouldn't give in to those guilty feelings. Her independence meant a lot to her. "I've made cakes at the bakery for many years now and you complained about it daily. You also complained about the cookies I made and every upgrade I made to the bakery. I want my own place where no one is telling me what to do. I've earned that right."

Her mother sank onto the bench that her dad used to step up on. "Why are all my kids against me?"

Ana sat by her mother. "Do you want me to be brutally honest?"

Her mother frowned. "Of course. I don't want you to lie to me."

Ana swallowed the constriction in her throat. This is the talk she and her mother should've had years ago and she had to go with her heart even if her words were going to hurt. "You're judgmental, critical and sometimes even rude."

Her mother drew back. "I am not. How dare you say that."

"How many times have you told me that I needed to fix myself up and I needed to lose weight? That's critical and it kept my low self-esteem going for years. How many times have you criticized Angie for marrying Hardy? How many times have you criticized Peggy or Patsy for the way they wear their hair or their clothes? How many—"

"Okay, okay. You don't have to be mean."

"I'm being honest."

"I'm just trying to help my kids. Hardy got Angie pregnant when she was seventeen. I'll never forgive him for that. And Patsy and Peggy, well, who knows about them. I never understood them even when they were little girls. And you, I was only trying to protect you after what that boy did to you."

"Then support me, love me, but please don't criticize me and make me feel lower than I already do."

"I… I…" Her mother brushed away a tear and Ana took her hands in hers.

"Just love us the way we are. That's all we need. And try to be more accepting of others."

"You're talking about that man, aren't you?"

"Yes, I'm talking about Rico, and Hardy

and Teresa's husband and Frank's wife and
Margie."

Her mother pulled her hands away. "Don't
get me started on Margie. I guess you know
they got married at the courthouse."

"Yes. I was a witness and I'm happy for
them. You're going to have another grandchild in a few months. A grandchild who will
live here in Horseshoe and you'll get to see
it every day. Aren't you excited about that?"

"It's just that—"

"They didn't get married in the church,"
Ana finished for her. "She's getting her first
marriage annulled through the church and
then she'll be joining. That should make you
happy."

"It's embarrassing."

"Like you got pregnant with Frank," Ana
came back at her without any guilty qualms.
"Since you've experienced the same thing, I
thought you would be more understanding."

"Anamarie, please come back to the bakery
and let's forget all this nonsense." Her mother
switched gears quickly.

"I'm not coming back to the bakery. Margie will eventually take it over."

"Not if I have anything to say about it." Her
mother lifted her chin.

"That's the way it works, Mom. A Wiznowski wife runs the bakery. That's the way it's been for over a hundred years and it's not going to change anytime soon."

Her mother got to her feet. "It's no use talking to you."

"Give Margie a chance. For Bubba. For all of us."

"I've got to go. Your dad needs a heating pad." Her mother walked out the door without another word.

She sat on the bench wondering if her mother had heard anything she'd said. She seemed to have walls just like Rico and nothing ever penetrated them. At the thought of Rico, he strolled through the front door. She froze.

What was he doing here?

CHAPTER FOURTEEN

"WHAT ARE YOU doing here, Rico?" Anamarie asked.

"Umm…"

Mickey, who was sleeping in the bed she'd bought for him, woke up and trotted over to Rico. He circled him, sniffing at his boots and then barked several times.

Rico squatted and stroked Mickey. "I stopped by to check on Mickey," he said.

She had a feeling that was a white lie. He seemed lost. The haggard lines of his face and the sadness lurking in his eyes tore at her heart. She had said that she wasn't going to talk to him, but some things were just impossible not to do.

"Mickey's fine."

Rico scratched the dog's head. "He's put on some weight."

"He loves biscuits and gravy and any kind of meat I put in it." As she watched him with the dog, it hit her that he might be here to take Mickey. "If you're here to…"

He got to his feet. "I'm not here to take Mickey. I work all day and he'd be alone and not fed. It's best if you keep him." He looked around at the empty space with the partial wall. "Who's helping you?"

"My dad."

He walked to the wall to inspect it. "It's crooked." He always took his hat off when he entered a room and it was now in his left hand. With his right hand he touched the studs. "It's not tight. It's loose and unsteady. This has to be torn out and redone."

"No, I'm not going to do that. It would hurt my dad's feelings."

"The bottom studs have to be nailed to the concrete and you'll need special tools for that."

"That's what my dad said, but he doesn't have the tools."

"We have them at the ranch. I'll be back later." He put his hat on and headed for the door.

"Rico, what are you doing?" He couldn't just waltz in here and take over. She had some pride. But then, she really needed help and she couldn't afford to be choosy.

He turned back. "I told you I would fix this for you and that's what I'm going to do." On that note, he went through the door.

She stared after him not knowing what to make of this visit. Mickey barked and she glanced down at him. "What do you think? Is this his way of saying he's sorry?"

Mickey barked again.

"Yeah," she murmured to herself. Rico had a hard time verbalizing deep emotions so she wouldn't press him for the words...just yet. He was here and that was the first step in his healing. And as the saying goes, she wasn't going to look this gift horse in the mouth. She would accept it and somewhere along the way maybe they could talk about their feelings.

And Dusty.

RICO DIDN'T KNOW what he was doing. He'd gone into town to buy groceries and he saw her SUV parked in front of her shop and he'd pulled in beside it for some reason still unknown to him. Maybe it was Egan urging him to talk, but talk was the last thing he wanted to do.

He called Falcon and told him he was taking tools from the tool shed and, as always, he said it was fine. He also told him he was taking tomorrow off. Again he said it was okay. To take all the time he needed. Sometimes the Rebels were just too nice. But he'd worked many hours for each of them and he supposed that's what families did for each other.

He gathered up everything he needed and headed back to town. He stopped at the hardware store to buy masonry screws. When he reached the shop, he gathered power tools and drills and his toolbox. His arms were full and he couldn't open the door. Then he saw her sitting cross-legged against the wall with Mickey and a laptop in her lap. He paused for a moment to stare at her.

In the empty space she looked so alone sitting there with her thoughts turned inward and for the first time the wall he built around himself pressed into his chest. He'd hurt her and he hadn't meant to do that. So much pain had sidetracked him and he was still caught in its web unable to let go. But staring at her a tremor hit his strong resolve, creating a crack in his solid steel armor.

He missed her, her smile, her positive attitude and energy she always put into everything she did. Were fiction and reality the same thing? Confusion clouded his head and he shook it away.

He would live in the moment and that was all he could do for now.

ANAMARIE WATCHED IN amazement as Rico brought in all kinds of power tools, two sawhorses, a tall ladder and some things she didn't even know what they were. He tore the partial wall out in minutes and then he used chalk and measuring tape to mark where the new studs would go.

He anchored the studs along the bottom with a power tool and masonry screws. It was solid and tight to the concrete. He then put in the horizontal ceiling studs and marked where the parallel studs would go. It was like watching a master craftsman. He knew what he was doing. She handed him things when he asked for them and they worked on into the night. She turned on the florescent lights as the darkness moved in. At nine o'clock she decided to go to the diner to get them something to eat. Rico worked on.

They sat cross-legged on the concrete eating chicken-fried steak. She'd bought Mickey biscuits and gravy and she gave him part of her steak.

"You're spoiling him," Rico remarked.

"Yeah. I need to give him dog food every now and then." They talked like casual strangers and not like two people who had been deeply in love.

"Did Wyatt get you?" She pushed the boundaries a little just to get his attention.

"No." He continued to eat without looking up.

"He said he called you and you wouldn't answer your phone."

"I have nothing to say to Wyatt."

So that's how it was. Rico blamed Wyatt for not stepping in and doing something when they had taken Dusty. She pushed the boundaries a little more.

"He said Dusty is adjusting well."

Rico stop eating, but he didn't say anything.

"He's five now. His birthday was in August. School has started and I wonder how he's adjusting to a new school with so many children. It's not Horseshoe."

Rico got to his feet. "I'm not talking about Dusty." His stern expression said *case closed*.

She let him get away with it this time, but they were going to talk and he was going to listen. Their future depended on it whether he would admit that or not.

SEPTEMBER ROLLED INTO October and Rico worked steadily on the shop. They worked together and it was like getting to know each other all over again. They only talked business and she didn't bring up Dusty again.

Her dad stopped by and it was a tense moment. He glared at Rico. "I don't like what you did to my daughter."

"I'm sorry about that," Rico said.

"Enough said." He walked over to the wall. With one hand he pushed against a stud. "It's sturdy now."

"Yes, sir," Rico replied. "I screwed it to the concrete."

"Good deal. I'll leave y'all to it."

As her dad left, she smiled at Rico and a slight grin touched his lips. Her heart jumped at the transformation. It was like watching a seedling buried in the ground pop up reaching for the sky, reaching for air and sunshine to breathe, to live. It was a beautiful sight.

EVERY CHANCE RICO had he worked in the shop. The studs were all in and then Elias helped him with the wiring. It was old and needed to be replaced. Phoenix helped him with the plumbing. Jude helped him with the Sheetrock and Quincy came when he put in the insulation. The Rebels turned out in full force to help someone they loved. Ana hoped Rico saw that.

They made a trip to Home Depot to pick out cabinets. Anamaria had a vision inside her head of what she wanted and she was sticking to it.

"Pre-stained cabinets would work," Rico said.

She looked at all the stained cabinets from off-white to black, but she kept coming back to the white ones. "I'd rather have white."

"White? Why?"

"I wanted it to look weddingly."

"Weddingly?" He was clearly confused. "Is that even a word?"

"Can't you see it in your mind?"

"No." He shook his head.

"It's all white, sparkly and fairy-tale like." He groaned.

She poked him in the ribs. "I'm not kidding."

He caught her hand and stared into her eyes and memories, beautiful loving memories, blindsided them. She couldn't look away from the joy she saw blazing there, and it seemed neither could he.

"Do you need some help?" a young man asked and the moment floated away... temporarily.

Rico looked at the young man. "Yes, we're going to take the weddingly cabinets."

"Excuse me?" The man was puzzled.

They were laughing as they left the store and little by little Ana could see the sadness leaving Rico. She saw it earlier in his eyes, too.

There was hope and at this point it was all she needed.

IT WAS FALL roundup on the ranch and Rico was busy, but every afternoon after work he headed to the shop. He spent his days off there and they had supper every night together, sitting on the concrete floor talking. They fell back into an easy routine and it was what he needed to feel normal again.

The brothers continued to help him in the shop; even Falcon showed up to help him tape and float the walls. Egan and Bubba helped put in the cabinets. Those weddingly cabinets. He smiled every time he thought of them. Paxton did the backsplash in the kitchen and

Phoenix helped him build the big island in the center and the counter out front. Ana, her sisters, Peyton, Wyatt's wife, and most of the Rebel wives had a painting party that included wine.

Rachel brought her art students in and they painted a mural in the party room. Then Remi, Paxton's wife, brought her kindergarten class and they put their handprints on the wall with their name and the date.

As he watched the kids he realized that Dusty would've been in Remi's kindergarten class and he would have been putting his handprint on the wall. For a moment he was frozen in place as the pain threatened to take him down again. Then he looked across the room and saw the sadness on Ana's face. She was thinking the same thing. But unlike him she stepped forward with a pen and drew a handprint on the wall and wrote *Dusty* inside and the date. He couldn't breathe for a moment and then she came to his side and he exhaled deeply, knowing she was his guiding light, his strength.

Maybe he wasn't so strong, after all.

OCTOBER FADED INTO November and the shop was complete. Rico and Paxton had done a wonderful job with the oak floors and they looked beautiful. The whole place was beautiful, just as Anamarie had pictured in her head—all white and silver and weddingly. It had been a family affair.

It was late on a Saturday afternoon and the weather was cold and dreary. A freeze was predicted by morning. Rico was finishing up little things like putting knobs on the cabinets. She was waiting for a chance to bring up Dusty. The talk was long overdue. Before she could think of a way to segue into it, she tripped on a cord Rico had stretched from an electrical plug.

"Are you okay?" He lifted her to her feet.

"Yeah, just injured my pride a little." She straightened her blouse as her cheeks burned with embarrassment.

"You've lost more weight." For the first time he really looked at her.

She ran her hands down her hips. "I'm into a size ten jeans now."

"I liked you better when you had curves."

Before she could stop herself, she slapped his arm. "You don't say that to a woman."

"What?" He was clueless.

"You don't tell a woman she looked better back then than she does now."

"Oh." The lightbulb finally went on. "I didn't mean it that way."

"Forget it." She walked over and sat in the middle of the shop.

He unplugged the drill and wrapped the cord around it. "What are you doing?"

"Thinking and worrying if I can make a living out of making cakes."

"It's a little late to think about that."

She stuck her tongue out at him.

He walked over and sat cross-legged in front of her. "Stop worrying. People from all over are going to be drawn to this place." He glanced at the small white wicker sofa with white-and-green striped cushions, a matching chair and a coffee table with cake books on it. "Why are we sitting on the floor? There's a sofa and a chair."

"It just feels comfortable to sit on the floor with you. We've been doing that for weeks."

"Yeah." He glanced at the posters she'd put on the wall—posters of cakes she'd made. "Those are some amazing cakes."

She didn't want to talk about cakes. She had something much more important in mind. Scooting closer to him, she said, "I want to talk."

He brought his eyes back to her. "Isn't that what we're doing?"

She scooted even closer. "I want to talk about Dusty."

"I'm not talking about Dusty."

He made to get up and she grabbed his hands. "No, Rico. It's time to talk."

He remained silent, staring at her hands locked on his. She searched for words, words he needed to hear and she prayed for the right ones.

"I don't regret the time I spent with Dusty. He was a special little boy and he showed me that I could be a mother without giving birth. I could feel all those deep emotions that mothers have, and I loved him with all my heart. I'll always be grateful for that. Up until Dusty, I thought I didn't have those feelings anymore."

Rico remained silent, and once again she would have to push boundaries that he'd erected and deal with the consequences. She scooted even closer until their knees were touching.

"Remember when we took him to the carnival and the bumper cars? He would shout 'I got you, Ana' and 'I got you, Rico' and then he would giggle uncontrollably. He had so much fun and it was a joy to watch him."

Rico still remained silent.

"Remember when we took him to the park after his grandmother's funeral? He was so sad, but soon he was laughing as I went with him up the slide and then down. He wanted to do it over and over again and his childish giggles washed away all the sadness."

"And then he found the swings," Rico said in a hoarse voice.

"Yes." Rico was talking and she had to keep him talking.

"You ruined your beautiful black dress playing with him."

"No." She shook her head. "I didn't ruin it because it helped brighten a little boy's day. And yours, too." He lifted his head and their eyes met. "You showed me I could be a woman and feel all those sensuous feelings I'd only heard about. You made me whole and complete in a way I thought I never would feel again. And those feelings had nothing to do with Dusty."

"I know." He suddenly cupped her face and pulled her to him. "I was blindsided by so much pain I couldn't think straight and I did the one thing I swore I would never do. I hurt you."

"I understood, Rico," she said, breathing in the scent of him; heat, wood and a masculinity she associated with him. A scent that reminded her of their time together.

He rested his forehead against hers. "Everyone tells me I'm a strong person, but I couldn't handle losing Dusty. I just wanted to run away from that little voice hollering at me for help and there was no way I could help him. I kept hearing 'Rico, come get me' and I ran from it. I spent days walking and running on Rebel Ranch in places I've never been before. I got lost a couple of times, but I kept going, trying to outrun Dusty's voice. I'd let him down. I…"

"No!" She stroked the hands on her face. "There was nothing you could do. If you hadn't turned him over to Darlene, you would be in jail today. Rico, there was nothing you could do."

"He wanted to stay with us," he dragged out in a throaty voice.

"Dusty had been waiting a long time for his mother to get well and for her to come get him. Things got complicated with the fight in prison and Darlene signing over her maternal rights. We thought he would be our little boy and we gave him all the love we had. I don't regret that and I know you don't, either."

"No."

"We just didn't know Darlene was still trying to get her kid back."

"She played us," he remarked with a touch of anger.

"But you kept Dusty out of foster care and you should be proud of that. I am. We gave him a home. A happy home. Now we have to let go. Rico, you have to let go of Dusty. He's with his mother like he always planned. He's happy and you have to be happy for him."

"It's hard."

"I know, but we can't have a future until you do."

He reached for her then and pulled her on to his lap, burying his face in her neck.

"Let him go, Rico. Let Dusty go."

A tremor ran through his strong body and she held him tightly as he grappled with his emotions. He was letting go.

"When Egan found me and we came home, I had this tightness in my chest, as if I couldn't breathe. I shut everyone out, even Egan. I didn't want to talk. I just wanted to live in the pain. The first day I came here I saw your car and just stopped and came in. I don't know why, but the moment I did I could breathe again. That's why I came back and came back. With you I could breathe again and I found my way back from all the pain."

"Oh, Rico."

He lifted his head and brought his lips to hers in a gentle, touching kiss. Soon all the emotions they'd shared took over and the heat from their bodies welded them together. "I've missed you," he breathed into her mouth. "I missed you so much."

His lips trailed away and she rested her face against his. "I loved you back then and I love you even more now."

"Ana…"

His phone buzzed, interrupting the moment. A second later her phone buzzed.

"Let's ignore them," she said.

"Okay."

The phones buzzed again.

They looked at each other and smiled. She kissed him briefly. "You get yours and I'll get mine and then we'll turn them off."

"Deal."

She heard him say, "I'll be right there." Her heart sank.

She clicked on to talk to Margie and heard

herself saying the same thing. "I'll be right there."

"That was Miss Kate," he explained. "They're having a meeting and waiting for me."

"Do they usually have meetings?"

"About important things."

"And they include you?"

"Yeah." He had a sheepish grin.

"You're more a part of that family than you realize."

"Yeah. I'm slowly seeing that."

She walked to him and placed her hands on his chest. "I have to go to the bakery and check out the stove. That thing is probably as old as I am and you have to jiggle the knob to turn it on. Margie had a hard time getting it to work this morning and now it won't work at all. They're getting ready to close for the day and Margie wants me to see if I can get it to work. She doesn't want any problems on Monday morning."

"Okay. You help Margie and I'll go home and see what Miss Kate wants. I'm going to shower and change into my starched jeans, white shirt and good Stetson. You go home and change into something black that will keep my blood pressure at a dangerous level.

Then we're going out to eat someplace fancy and tonight we might not come home."

She smiled into his eyes. "I love that plan."

"See you back here in about an hour or so." He kissed her in a long drugging kiss. Her knees wobbled as he walked out the door.

She touched her lips with a shaky hand and wanted to embrace all these new emotions they'd shared. But a niggling doubt was there poking at her like a mischievous child. He hadn't said the words she wanted to hear. He hadn't said *I love you*. Maybe he would have if the phone hadn't interrupted. But now she had to brace herself for the fact that after all he'd been through, he might never say them again. Could she live with that?

RICO DROVE TOWARD Rebel Ranch feeling as if the world and its demons had lifted from his shoulders. At the thought of Dusty he didn't feel that ache in his chest. With Ana's help he'd tucked it away in his heart in a special place to be remembered, but never forgotten. He could breathe. He could live now.

He couldn't imagine what the meeting was about. He just wanted to get it over with quickly and get back to Ana and their evening. If he hurried, he might have time to go to Temple to buy a ring. *Yes!* This time he was doing it right.

All the brothers' trucks were parked at Miss Kate's house and he went there. The cold north wind embraced him and he didn't even bother buttoning his coat. Nothing bothered him today. He was flying high with all the emotions inside him.

"Rico," Miss Kate said when she saw him in the kitchen doorway. "How about a cup of coffee?"

He rubbed his cold hands together. "Sounds good."

"I'm making Grandpa a mug," she said, and then leaned over and whispered, "It's decaf. If I give him the real stuff, he gets all wound up."

"I'll never tell."

She eyed him for a moment. "You're in a good mood."

"Yes, ma'am, I am." And for the first time he didn't feel any shackles or walls around him.

She handed him a mug of coffee. "Good. Let's go into the den. I want to talk to everyone."

He followed her into the large den. When he'd first come here, he'd been overwhelmed by the huge house. But then, he'd been over-whelmed about everything on Rebel Ranch.

The brothers sat on a brown leather sectional sofa watching a football game on television. The fire glowed in the stone fireplace and all Rico could feel was the warmth this family had brought him.

Egan turned off the TV.

"Hey," echoed around the room, and then they saw him and shouted, "Rico."

Grandpa sat in his recliner. "Hey, Rico. Come on in."

Miss Kate took her seat beside Grandpa and Rico took the only available seat beside Falcon on the love seat.

"Rico, this meeting is about you," Miss Kate said.

"Oh." He looked around at all their eager faces and thought this might be an intervention or something. As was his nature he didn't jump in and assure them he was okay. They had to see that for themselves.

"And it's about family," Miss Kate continued. "Whenever we mention that you're part of this family, you get this stone-faced expression."

He set his warm mug on the coffee table. He didn't know how to explain that so he took a moment. "I've always thought that to be a part of a family you had to be blood and I'm not Rebel blood. But then Dusty wasn't my blood either and I loved him as if he was my own."

"Rico…" Egan tried to interrupt, but Rico kept talking.

"I've never been part of a family. There was just me and my great-grandma so I've never been sure where I fit in here."

"I'll tell you where you fit in." Miss Kate sat forward in her chair. "I think of you as one of my sons and today I want to do something to make you feel comfortable in this family."

"You don't have to do that, Miss Kate. It's just me."

She shook her head. "No. I thought about this and spoke with the boys and Grandpa and we all agree. On December first you will no longer receive a weekly check."

She was stopping his wages. That didn't make sense.

"You will receive a monthly check just like my boys because I consider you one of them."

He took a moment for him to process that. "Thank you, Miss Kate. May I ask how much that will be?"

Falcon told him.

"Oh." He never imagined they made that much money. It was a shock.

"You see, Rico," Elias spoke up. "You've been getting the short end of the stick. You and I do most of the work and these—" he thumbed to his brothers "—yahoos receive the same money."

"We work just as hard as you do, Elias," Paxton told him. "Everyone pulls their weight on this ranch or it wouldn't be running at a profit."

"Let's keep the bickering down," Quincy suggested. "This is about Rico."

Miss Kate turned her attention to Rico. "We're doing this because we hope it will make you feel more like family. And you certainly have earned it."

She waved a hand toward his house. "That bunkhouse is yours. You can do whatever you want with it."

"Thank you, Miss Kate." Words failed him. He was overwhelmed by their generosity.

"And there's something else we thought of that might make you feel more comfortable," Miss Kate went on. "You said you never knew your father and you didn't have any attachment to the Johnson name. He was a man your mother went out with, but he said repeatedly he wasn't your father and didn't want anything to do with you."

"Yeah. My grandmother talked to him and he said he broke up with my mother a long time before she became pregnant and she wasn't shoving that baby off on him. He didn't sound like a very nice man."

"Seeing the way you turned out, whoever your father was, he must have had some good qualities. I've never met a more loyal, caring, dedicated or honest person."

Thank you was on his tongue, but he didn't say it. The word was getting redundant.

"We…" Miss Kate looked around at her boys and Grandpa. "We thought you might like to change your last name to Rebel."

Tears threatened and his throat closed up. He tried, but he couldn't push words through.

"You don't have to make a decision right now," Miss Kate added. "You can think about it. I spoke with Gabe and he said it wasn't difficult to do. He can draw up the paper and we take it to the courthouse and change your name. It's that simple. But no pressure. It's your decision and we won't think any less of you for it."

Rico swallowed the wad of tears in his throat. "Back…back in the summer when

Anamarie was planning the wedding she said she wanted a church wedding. I told her I didn't do big church weddings. She said it wouldn't be big, it would just be her family and my family. I told her I didn't have any family and then she asked me who are the Rebels? I can answer that honestly today. The Rebels are my...family."

"Yes, we are," Miss Kate said. "So does this mean..."

"Yes, ma'am. I'd be happy to take the Rebel name, but I have a question first."

"Sure, what is it?"

He looked directly at Miss Kate. "How would John Rebel feel about it?"

A smile touched Miss Kate's face. "My husband would give you this ranch for what you did for Egan. If not for you, those gang members would have killed him. There are just some things you can't place a price tag on and that's one of them. You gave us Egan back and my husband would be proud to call you his son."

"You bet he would," Grandpa said.

Rico embraced the warmth and love in the room because Ana had opened his heart and he could breathe and accept love again. He was a Rebel and every day he would strive to live up to the name.

CHAPTER FIFTEEN

FALCON GOT TO his feet and held out his hand to Rico. "Welcome to the family."

Rico stood and as he reached for Falcon's hand, Falcon grabbed him in a big hug, and then all the brothers were hugging him and he hugged them back. No walls. No stone-faced expression. His heart was wide open and accepting what this wonderful family had given him—a home.

"Get out of the way." Grandpa pushed through his grandsons to get to Rico. He wrapped his frail arms around Rico and then he looked up at him. "I know you'll do that name proud. You already have."

"Thanks, Grandpa." His throat was thick again.

Miss Kate was the last and he looked at this woman who had given him so much. She touched his face like he'd seen her do a thousand times with her sons. "I want you to be happy. I want you to feel like this is your home and we are your family."

"I do, Miss Kate. I do," he said, and then he hugged her freely for the first time.

She patted his chest. "I know you and Anamarie want a place of your own and when you find it, I will help you pay for it. I'm sorry about the McGregor property, but you'll find something."

"The McGregor property was a pipe dream. I'd never in a million years be able to afford that."

"Rebel Ranch can't even afford it," Falcon said. "I'd look for a subdivision to go in there."

"Speaking of McGregor..." Miss Kate headed for the kitchen. "Rico, you haven't picked up your mail lately and something came for you."

"I usually just get junk mail."

"This isn't junk mail!" she shouted from the kitchen, and came back with a large FedEx envelope. "It's from Robert McGregor."

"What? What would he be sending me?"

"I don't know," she replied. "It came yesterday and Grandpa signed for it and forgot to tell me."

Miss Kate handed Rico the envelope and

he stared at it for a few seconds, trying to figure out what it could be. He noticed the Weiss, Kline and McGregor law firm return address. "I can't imagine what this is. Robert McGregor thanked me after the funeral for visiting with his dad. Could this be another thank-you?"

"It's kind of big for a thank-you," Falcon remarked.

"Open it and find out," Egan encouraged.

Rico sat down, as did all the brothers, and removed a large manila envelope from the FedEx one. He undid the clasp and pulled out a legal-looking document.

"What is it?" Egan asked eagerly.

"I don't know, but there's a letter attached."

"Read it." Quincy moved to the edge of his seat, as did the other brothers, anxious to see what was inside.

Rico looked down at the page and the words seem to leap out at him. He took a deep breath and began to read:

Dear Jericho,
I'm sorry it's taken me so long to get this to you, but my wife fell two days after the funeral and fractured her hip in three places. She had to have a total hip

replacement and it didn't go well. After three surgeries and months in the hospital and rehab, she is finally home and walking with a walker. Now I have time to deal with my father's estate.

Once again I want to thank you for what you did for our family. My father and I were able to talk for the first time in forty years. We really talked without the resentment and bitterness of the past. He found peace and so have I. Now I can live my life without guilt because of you.

The last week of his life we talked about what to do with the McGregor property. A developer from Dallas had offered him a large sum of money for the land. He wanted to cut it up into one- to five-acre tracts and build a country-style subdivision. My father turned down the offer. He did not want his land divided. But first he asked me if I wanted the money. I honestly couldn't take the money with a clear conscience. Neither could my son. We don't have an interest in ranching and we never have. My son only moved to Horseshoe to spend some time with his grandfather.

The last weekend of his life we were

sitting at the kitchen table and I asked my dad what he really wanted to do with his ranch. He asked me for a pen and paper and I got it for him. Below is what he wrote on the paper. The original is at the back. I thought you might want it.

"For his random act of kindness to an old man who no one wanted anything to do with anymore, I bequeath to Jericho Johnson the McGregor Ranch in its entirety for the sum of five hundred thousand dollars. I would give the land outright, but a man has to work for something for it to mean anything to him. Jericho will love this land and care for it like I did. This is my last wish for the McGregor property. Francis McGregor."

Rico's heart raced as he flipped the pages to see Mr. McGregor's note in his own writing. He touched the scrawled letters with a shaky hand. Could this be real?

"I can't believe this," he muttered more to himself than anyone.

"Wow, Rico." Falcon looked over his shoulder. "That land is worth over two million and I'm sure that developer offered him more than that."

"I don't get this," Rico said. "I only talked to Mr. McGregor. That's all I did."

"You must have said some powerful stuff," Paxton remarked. "No one gives away that much land."

"He's not giving it away," Phoenix pointed out. "He has to come up with five hundred thousand."

"Is there anything else in the letter?" Quincy asked.

Rico flipped the pages back. "One hundred thousand is due March first of next year and then there's a balloon payment every March first until the land is paid for. Oh, man, no interest."

"Are you kidding me?" Egan looked at the document.

"That's what it says." Rico pointed to the page. "It says the money will be paid to Robert Francis McGregor, the grandson. And I'm to take this document to him next week to make it legal. Oh man, somebody tell me this is real."

"Looks real to me," Egan said and slapped Rico on the back. "It couldn't happen to a nicer person."

"What are you gonna do with all that land?" Falcon asked.

"I don't know. I'm just trying to soak this in and figure out why someone would do this. Why wouldn't Robert McGregor take the money? I don't get it."

"He told you," Quincy said. "He has no interest in the land and he wants to honor his father's wishes. I understand that and I'm sure everyone else does, too."

"What did you talk about with Mr. McGregor?" Jude asked.

"We talked mostly about his son and how hurt he was that he didn't love the ranch like he did. He had so much bitterness inside him and I told him bitterness doesn't do anyone any good. It just eats away at your soul. I told him about my past and he never judged me and he accepted me for the man I am today. And I encouraged him to accept his son for who he was. I guess I got through. He was just so lonely and I identified with that. I was happy that he and his son had made peace. I never expected anything like this."

He swallowed the lump in his throat. "I can't tell you the number of times I've driven by that place and admired it and wondered what it had looked like in olden days. Mr. McGregor showed me some old photos and it was more than I'd imagined. So many times

I wanted to ask him about the land, but I couldn't do it. I couldn't disrespect him like that and deep down I knew I would never be able to afford it. It was just a dream."

"Not anymore," Falcon said. "You have to decide what to do with it."

Falcon's voice made them think of the conversation they'd had long ago about the McGregor property and Rico knew what he was going to do. He looked at Falcon. "You said you'd like to extend Rebel Ranch across the road. I think that would be a good idea."

Falcon shook his head. "That's your property, Rico. You need to do something for you."

"I can't work that ranch by myself and I can't afford to pay anyone to help. And we're family, right?"

"Yeah."

"Then Rebel Ranch will expand across the road," Rico announced.

"That's very generous, Rico."

Rico looked down at the papers. "That's what you do for family."

"Then Rebel Ranch will pay the five hundred thousand," Miss Kate stated.

"No, I have to do that, just the way Mr. McGregor wanted me to. And he's right. It's going to mean so much more to me if I put my sweat and tears into it."

"I don't want you to have that kind of financial burden."

"Oh, Miss Kate, this burden is going to be a joy."

"That land is a little less than each of my boys will inherit from their father. I can't give you any Rebel land because it's already been gifted, but I can gift you the McGregor property. If it's going to be a part of Rebel Ranch, please let me do this."

He was blown away by her generosity and her sincerity. If they were family, he had to accept her offer. If... There was no doubt in his mind now.

"Okay. But I'll pay the hundred thousand in March. I have most of it saved up and was planning to put it on a house for me and Anamarie."

"Deal," she said with a slight smile.

Rico got to his feet, clutching the document in his hand. "I have to go. A beautiful woman is waiting for me." There were hugs all around again and he hugged Miss Kate tightly. "If I don't come home tonight, don't worry about me."

She touched his face again and he felt the

warmth of being one of her boys. "Okay. I won't. I'm so happy for you."

Rico hurried to his truck and drove to the bunkhouse. He sat in his chair staring at the document, hardly believing that it was real. Things like this didn't happen to people like Jericho, but then again, maybe they did. He found a card tucked under the letter with Robert McGregor's cell number. He called it and they talked for about twenty minutes. He reinforced everything that had been said in the letter.

"If you change your mind…"

"I'm not changing my mind," Mr. McGregor assured him.

"I don't understand why you're turning down the money."

"Jericho, I worked very hard to become a top-notch lawyer and I make good money. My parents were very frugal and spent only what they needed. A large chunk of money was sitting in savings and I shared half of that with my son. I don't need the money from the property and I wouldn't be able to sleep at night if I took it. I'm at peace with everything and I hope one day the McGregor property will be a working ranch again the way my father wanted."

"It will be," Jericho said with confidence.

"Please read the document closely. There are stipulations. The land can never be sold or divided, but there's a fifty-year limit on that."

"You don't have to worry about that. I will never sell or divide the land. My plan is to make it a part of Rebel Ranch and it will still be a ranch long after I'm gone."

"My father would be pleased. He always admired the Rebels."

"So do I."

"There are other stipulations; I will send a truck for the antique bedroom suite in my dad's room and the photos and some other things that my wife and son want. My son will take care of all of that before you take ownership."

"Sure. I'll help him load everything or whatever he wants me to do. I'd be more than happy to help."

"Thanks for your offer, but my son will take care of it. He will only be in Horseshoe for the next week. He's moving back to Dallas to join my law firm as I'm retiring to spend more time with my wife."

"I'll be in his office first thing Monday morning and if you ever need anything, you just call me." Rico gave him his cell number.

"If my wife and I are ever in that area, we'll stop by to see what you've done with the place."

"Anytime. I hope your wife continues to do well."

"Thank you, Jericho."

Rico felt he should say more and words failed him, but he forced himself to open up. He glanced at the document on his coffee table. A piece of paper that gave him more than he'd ever hoped for. "I don't have the words to thank you for what you've done for me. I haven't had a lot of good luck in life. In fact, I've had a lot of bad luck and this is just…an incredible gift. Thank you."

"Enjoy it, Jericho."

He clicked off and thought about all the good people that had come into his life lately. Things were turning around for him and…he glanced toward the ceiling and said a quiet, "Thank you." Gratitude at the kindness of the Rebels and Mr. McGregor filled his heart. Every day he would strive to be the man they had made him and every day he would give thanks for the opportunity of becoming a part of their lives. He swallowed the tears in his throat. He couldn't wait to share this with Ana.

At the thought of her he jumped up. He

was running late. He shaved and took a quick shower and put on his starched jeans, white shirt and good Stetson. They were really going to celebrate tonight.

On the way to the front door, he stopped at Dusty's room. He pushed the door open and walked in. His chest didn't cave in and his breathing wasn't labored. He'd finally let go. Wherever Dusty was, he hoped the little boy was happy. That's what he really wanted for him.

Now all he had to do was walk into a future that shined as bright as any stars he'd ever seen.

ANAMARIE HURRIED TO the bakery. This was a good day and the smile on her face showed just how important it was. Rico had finally let go of Dusty. That meant they had a future together. He still hadn't said the magic words, but tonight he would. She knew Rico and all those feelings he had inside and how hard it was to say the words out loud.

Customers were still in the bakery, buying kolaches for the weekend. She meandered around them speaking to several as she made her way to the kitchen. Margie was looking at the dinosaur stove with a frown.

"The right burner just won't turn on," Margie said in frustration.

Anamarie fiddled with it and gave up. "There are some old knobs in the storage room. I'll see if one of them will work." One of the knobs worked and they both were excited. "I've got to run," Ana said. "I've got a date tonight and I want to look my best."

"Wear something tight!" Margie shouted after her.

"Oh, please. I've already hooked him. I just need to reel him in." Ana laughed as she went out the door. She hadn't felt this good in a long time.

She showered and did her hair and then found a black dress in her closet that she'd bought for funerals and church and didn't fit her any more. After losing weight, she thought it might fit. It did, but it was sleeveless. And she wanted to wear black because Rico wanted her to. She rummaged in her closet and found the three-quarter-length black coat she rarely wore because it was never that cold in Texas. She grabbed it and went to the kitchen to make Mickey's dinner.

Hurrying back to the shop she realized she was early. Rachel's SUV was at Angie's. Anamarie went there to talk until it was time to meet Rico. Ana pulled off her coat and modeled her black dress. They said how great she looked and she never realized how wonderful that could feel. She wasn't a vain person, but if they kept complimenting her, she might turn into one. When she told them that, they laughed.

The laugh was punctuated by a loud scream from the bakery. They ran in and stopped short. Her mother lay on the floor clutching her chest. Margie knelt over her.

"She just collapsed," Margie cried.

"My chest hurts and I can't breathe." Her mother gasped for air between each word.

Angie and Ana fell down beside her. "I believe she's having a heart attack," Ana said. "Call 911."

"I'm calling." Rachel had her phone in her hand.

"Stay calm," Anamarie said to her mother. "The ambulance will be here shortly."

But inside Ana was a quivering mass of anxiety and fear. She couldn't lose her mother like this.

RICO SWERVED INTO the parking space next to Ana's SUV and jumped out, eager to see her. The place was unlocked and the lights were on, but Ana wasn't there. Maybe she stopped by the bakery? As he strolled to the building, two doors down, the cold north wind cut through his jeans and shirt. His jacket was in the truck and he wasn't going back to get it. Right now he had to see Ana. That meant seeing Miss Doris, too, but in his present mood he could face the devil.

He opened the glass door, stepped in and came to a complete stop at the sight in front of him. Miss Doris lay on the floor. Ana, Angie, Margie and Rachel knelt beside her. All of them were crying.

"What's happening?"

"I think Mom's having a heart attack," Ana replied, tears streaming down her face. He noted she wore a black dress and heels. "We called an ambulance."

Without a second thought Rico knelt by the woman who hated him more than anyone. "How do you feel, Miss Doris?"

"My chest hurts...and my arm and neck... I feel like I'm going to throw up..."

"She is having a heart attack," Rico announced. Seeing her distress he treated her as he would anyone else. "Does anyone have an aspirin?"

"I do." Angie jumped up and went into her office.

"I'm going to help you sit up, Miss Doris, to take the weight off your heart." He helped her into a sitting position and supported her back and neck. "Can you raise your legs?"

Ana helped her with her legs and Angie was back with the aspirin and a glass of water.

"Miss Doris, I want you to chew this aspirin before you swallow it. Chew it up good so it can get into your system quickly."

She did as Rico instructed.

Rico looked at Ana. "Can you get her bra off? We need to get all restrictions off her heart. We need to cut the waistband of her pants too."

Rico supported Miss Doris while Ana and Angie loosened her clothes. By then they could hear the wail of the ambulance.

"I'm dying. I'm dying," Miss Doris gasped. "Help...me."

"Stay calm," Rico instructed.

"The ambulance is on the way and you're conscious and that's good. You're going to be fine. Just stay calm."

"Rico..."

The ambulance backed up to the door and Wyatt and Bubba arrived. Two paramedics ran in and Rico told them what happened.

"You probably saved her life," one paramedic said as he checked Miss Doris's vitals. "Let's go. We have to get her to the ER now."

"Rico." Ana flew into his arms. He stroked her hair and held her close.

She wrapped her trembling arms around his waist.

"Are you okay?" he asked.

"Yeah. Just a little shaky."

They watched as Miss Doris was loaded onto a gurney by the paramedics. She didn't stir. She just lay there like a ghost of herself.

"Go with your mother," he told her. "I'll meet you at the hospital. And try not to worry."

She kissed his cheek. "Thank you." She climbed into the ambulance with Angie.

As soon as the ambulance blared into the distance quietness settled over the bakery as onlookers tried to get a peek inside. Rico could hear his heart beating in his ears. He walked back into the kitchen area and took a long breath. All the good luck he'd had today could be washed away in a heartbeat if Miss Doris died. Ana would be devastated and so would he. He didn't hate the woman. She was Ana's mother and he respected that.

But it cut deep to help a woman who thought he was vile and evil and not good enough for her daughter. His great-grandmother had taught him to never be afraid to turn the other cheek, to never be afraid to say you're sorry, and to never be afraid to admit when you're wrong. Was he wrong about Miss Doris? Could he forgive her for the things she'd said and for the way she'd treated him? The old Jericho would stand firm against her bigotry. But the new Jericho, the new soon-to-be Jericho Rebel, would be more forgiving. After all he'd been given by the Rebels and the McGregors he could do no less. For Ana and their future.

CHAPTER SIXTEEN

"LET'S GO OVER to my office and have a cup of coffee."

Wyatt's voice startled him and he realized Wyatt was still in the bakery. "I have to go to the hospital to be with Anamarie."

"Take a deep breath," Wyatt told him. "You need a minute, and I'd like to talk to you."

His insides felt like jelly and he realized he did need a moment.

"Stuart will lock up the bakery." Other than that nothing was said on their walk across the courthouse lawn to Wyatt's office. Rico sank into a chair as Wyatt went to get coffee. This wasn't how he'd planned this evening. He and Ana should be sitting in a nice restaurant staring into each other's eyes. Instead they were both dealing with a lot of unexpected pain. He had this fear deep inside that his life was always going to be like this. But he had to hold on to the joy and not let the bad take him down as it had in the past.

Wyatt handed him a cup of coffee just as Stuart came in. He and Wyatt talked for a minute.

Rico rested his forearms on his thighs, staring into the dark coffee.

"How did you know what to do?" Wyatt asked as he came back in.

"From prison. An inmate on my block had a heart attack and I helped the nurse and then I later read up on it in the library."

"You probably saved Miss Doris's life."

"It's all kind of surreal right now."

Wyatt sat at his desk with a cup of coffee in his hand. "You have a lot of people in Horseshoe who care about you. I hope you know that."

Rico nodded. "Yeah."

Wyatt scooted forward in his chair. "There was nothing I could do about Dusty."

Rico looked at his friend. "I know that now and I guess it all turned out okay. It just took me a while to realize that Dusty wasn't mine to keep." Rico sat his cup on Wyatt's desk. "I have to go to the hospital. Anamarie needs me."

Before he could get to his feet, Wyatt's cell buzzed. He clicked on and talked for a minute and then laid his cell on the desk. "Miss

Doris is going to be okay. She has to have heart surgery to put a stent in and she should be able to come home in a couple days."

"That's a relief. I have to be there for Anamarie."

Rico let the stress of the day wash over him and he slowly relaxed for the first time in an hour.

ANAMARIE PACED OUTSIDE her mother's room, waiting for Rico. He should be there any minute, but fifteen minutes later he still wasn't. Something was wrong. She could feel it. They'd come so far. Why wasn't he here? Was he going to hold a grudge against her mother for the things she'd said. He had every right to but... She needed her phone so she could call him, but it was in Angie's office.

Taking a deep breath, she ran her hands through her hair. She was a mess and she needed Rico to ease all the stress inside her. Peggy poked her head around the door of their mother's room. "Mom wants to see you."

"Where's Rico?" her mother asked as she entered. "I want to see him before I go into surgery." Her mother was still very pale and she looked so fragile with her gray hair against the white pillows. But what stood out in her mind was she'd called Rico by his name for the first time.

"He's still in Horseshoe." She really didn't know where Rico was, but she didn't want to worry her mother.

Her mother started to cry and her dad who was sitting in a chair by the bed patted her hand. "I've been so wrong about him. He saved my life."

Patsy handed her mother a tissue.

Their mother dabbed at her eyes and choked back sobs. "I'm a foolish old woman, but I would like to see him."

"I'll tell him," Anamarie said, but she had this sinking feeling that Rico wasn't coming.

To ease her frustrations she took Peggy's phone and went out to the hall to call him. He answered immediately. "Peggy?" Confusion was evident in his voice.

"No, it's me. I'm using Peggy's phone because mine is in Angie's office in my coat pocket. Where are you?"

"I'm in Wyatt's office and I'll be there soon as I can. Are you okay?"

"I am now." She's worried for nothing, but fear was a tangible thing she couldn't ignore considering the past.

"How's your mom?"

"Better. She wants to see you."

"Why?" She could almost see the frown on his face.

"To thank you for what you did today."

"Now that I'm looking forward to hearing."

"Just get here as soon as you can."

"I will."

Everything was going to be okay. She had just overreacted and soon they would put this horrible day behind them.

RICO WALKED TO his truck, which was parked at Ana's shop, and got in. He took a moment to catch his breath and then he called Miss Kate to let her know what had happened. Rumors spread like poison ivy in a small town.

Putting his phone in his pocket, he thought about Ana's phone and decided to get it for her and take it with him. Angie's door was unlocked and he went inside and found a black coat across a chair.

Stuart appeared in the doorway between Angie's office and the bakery. "Oh. I heard the door open and wondered who was coming in."

Rico held up the coat. "I'm just picking up Anamarie's coat and phone and taking them to her."

"No problem. Thanks, Rico."

As he backed out of the parking spot, Wyatt came running across the courthouse lawn waving his arms. What now? He had to go. Frustrated, he pushed a button to roll down his window.

"Come back to the office!" Wyatt shouted. "I have some disturbing news."

Rico drove to the sheriff's office not even daring to wonder what had happened. Miss Doris had to be okay. That was his only thought.

"What is it?" Rico asked, feeling edgy as he walked back into Wyatt's office.

Wyatt was on the phone talking. He stopped for a moment, putting his hand over the receiver, and said, "Dusty is missing."

The bottom fell out of his stomach. "Wh-what?"

Wyatt wrote a number on a piece of paper and hung up. "You better sit for this."

Rico sat in the chair he had just vacated, hardly able to breathe.

"Darlene Miller's neighbor said that Dusty knocked on her door about six o'clock this afternoon and asked if she would call Rico and tell him to come get him."

"Wh-what?"

"She told him to come in and that she would call you, but she called the police because she didn't know who Rico was. Dusty must've heard her. He bolted before she could catch him. He left a penny on the table and an apple was missing. She said she often gave him food and he always wanted to pay her. She also said he only had on a dark long-sleeved T-shirt and jeans, no coat, and he looked as if he'd been in the clothes for a few days."

"Damn, where's Darlene Miller?" Anger clawed at his insides.

"They don't know just yet. They're looking for her, too. Her apartment door was open and the police went in and looked around. That was Sergeant Cole Chisholm on the phone. He said the place was a mess—trash, dishes, clothes and beer cans everywhere. The electricity had been turned off and there was no food anywhere."

"So she left him alone in the apartment with no electricity or food. How long has he been in there?"

"The neighbor said Darlene left about four and the little boy wasn't with her. The police are talking to all the neighbors and gathering information. One lady said that Darlene did really well the first few months after she moved in. She waited with Dusty for his school bus and then she caught the Metro bus to work. She often took him to the park and everything seemed fine until some friends of hers started coming around. They saw her leave several times without Dusty. They just assumed she'd left him with a sitter."

"Why didn't they check? He's just a little boy."

"They didn't want to get involved."

"Where was CPS? They were supposed to be checking on her and Dusty."

"They contacted CPS and talked to the worker who handles the case. She said she'd been trying to contact Darlene for a month and every time she's had an excuse like she had to work or take Dusty to the doctor. She was going to make a surprise visit this week."

"This week? That's a little too late."

"Yeah. CPS dropped the ball on this one."

"Dusty's out there all alone looking for food just like he was when I first met him at the bakery all those months ago." Unable to sit any longer Rico got to his feet. "Why did they contact you?"

"The sergeant asked the caseworker if she knew who Rico was because Dusty was asking for you and she told him you were the guy who was keeping him while Darlene was in prison. She remembered you were from Horseshoe and the sergeant on the case is from Horseshoe, so he called me."

"Oh, man." Rico ran his hands up his face in despair. "Wyatt, I can't go through this again."

"I know, and I don't blame you. They'll find Dusty and he'll go into foster care. Darlene Miller's not going to get a third chance. I can almost guarantee you that. It's your choice and I'll support you any way you choose."

Rico frowned. "What are you talking about?"

Wyatt cleared his throat. "The sergeant asked if I could locate you and get you to come to Austin to help in the search for Dusty. He wanted someone Dusty cared about to be there when they find him."

Rico stared down at the worn linoleum squares in Wyatt's office. Invisible tracks of time and the people who had been through this office were visible on the old floor. He glanced out to the waiting area where Ana had sat with Dusty as he was drinking milk like it was his last meal. From that moment on Dusty had owned a part of his heart.

"I know how you feel about foster care," Wyatt said. "But Dusty will do fine until they find a relative or someone to adopt him."

Would he? Dusty needed someone who cared about him and Rico and Ana cared deeply for the boy. He should talk to Ana, but she had a lot of her plate with her mom facing heart surgery. He had to make this decision on his own.

Wyatt's phone rang. "It's the sergeant. Maybe he has some news." Wyatt talked for a minute and then held his hand over the receiver. "They canvassed the neighborhood and haven't found him and they haven't found Darlene Miller, either. Are you willing to help? It's your choice."

He really didn't have a choice. His conscience didn't give him one. "Tell the sergeant I'm on my way."

Wyatt hung up and pushed a piece of paper across the desk. "That's the sergeant's number. As soon as you reach Austin call him and a patrol car will escort you to the apartment complex."

"Thanks, Wyatt."

Wyatt stared at him for a moment. "You're doing the right thing."

Rico stuffed the paper in his pocket. "After what happened today, I can't heap this on Anamarie, too. She loves Dusty and I need to know that he's okay before I tell her."

"Then wait until you get back."

Rico nodded and walked out.

In his truck he pulled out his phone and called Peggy's number. "Can I speak to Anamarie, please."

"Rico, where are you?" Ana's anxious voice came on. "You said you were coming."

"I'm sorry, but I'm going to be late." They were the only words Rico had for the situation facing him.

"No, Rico, please don't do this. She's an old woman and she just wants to say she's sorry for the way she's treated you."

Her voice weakened and so did he, but he knew what he had to do. "I just need a little time. That's all I'm asking."

"Just come to the hospital and we'll talk through it. Just you and me like we always do. Please, Rico, don't shut me out again. Don't shut my family out."

"You just have to give me some time. I'll call you in a couple of hours. I promise. Trust me."

"Rico..."

He ended the call and headed for the highway, his heart breaking at what he'd just done.

RICO HAD HAULED a lot of cattle for Rebel Ranch and he knew shortcuts to I-35 that went into Austin. He'd gone about a mile down the interstate when his phone buzzed. It was Wyatt. Maybe they'd found Dusty.

"What's up?" he said into the phone.

"I gave a state trooper the description and license plate of your truck and he's going to come up on you in a few minutes. He'll pass and then get in front and lead you into Austin. Once you're in Austin a police car will take over. Sergeant Chisholm will be waiting."

"Thanks, Wyatt. I owe you."

"Paid in full, Rico. Paid in full."

He didn't have time to think as he noticed a highway patrol car in his rearview mirror. It passed him just as Wyatt had said and then switched lanes to get in front of him. The man motioned with his hand as if to say "Let's go." And go they went. Fast, the siren blaring all the way into Austin. The traffic was heavy, but when people heard the siren they slowed down and pulled over to let the patrol car through. Rico kept his focus on the car and tried not to think about Ana or what he was going to find at the end of the trip.

When they reached the city limits, the patrolman waved and switched lanes to let Rico through. A white Austin police car was waiting. He turned his siren on just as the patrolmen had and they had no problem navigating the heavy traffic. They crossed the Congress Avenue Bridge and then they turned left. Rico lost track of the streets as he followed the car through a maze of apartment complexes.

The police car stopped at an apartment complex on the right. Police cars were everywhere. Some officers had spotlights as they searched the grounds for Dusty. As Rico got out of his truck the cold north wind whipped around him. He reached for his jacket and slipped into it. Dusty was out in this weather without a jacket and at that moment he wanted to strangle Darlene Miller.

An officer in a dark blue uniform and heavy jacket walked up to him and held out his hand. "Sergeant Cole Chisholm."

"Jericho Johnson." He shook the officer's gloved hand. "Thanks for the escort service. We made it in record time. Any news?"

Sergeant Chisholm shook his head. "We've canvassed the neighborhood and gone door-to-door talking to people. Several people saw him playing on the stairs, but after that no one has seen him. No one is lingering outside today. We called his name over and over and got no response."

"Have you located Darlene Miller?"

"No, but we will. She has a lot to answer for. The electricity was turned off yesterday at 4:00 p.m. They had no heat last night, but lots of blankets were on the beds. There were no sheets, though, and no food in the house. We put a police lock on the door and will come back tomorrow to take pictures. We weren't able to do that tonight because of the darkness."

"I don't understand how she could leave him all alone without food or heat. She was supposedly off drugs and wanted to raise her son." But then he did understand. His mother had left him the same way. Addiction was a powerful thing and it overrode every emotion a person had. That didn't excuse Darlene or help the situation. It was just tragic. Because of the weather, finding Dusty now was a life-or-death situation.

"I think she's been in a downward spiral for the last month according to the information we discovered. She hasn't been at work this week and Dusty hasn't been in school for three days."

"Did the school contact CPS?"

"Since it's Saturday, we couldn't reach anyone at the school. We have a call in to the principal, but he's away for the weekend. He should hear something soon, though. But a neighbor whose little boy catches the bus with Dusty said he hadn't been at the bus stop for three days."

Rico couldn't think about what Dusty had been through. It was too painful. He just wanted to find him. "What do you want me to do?" Rico asked. "He needs to be found and fast."

"We haven't had much luck calling his name and I thought if you did he might respond if he's hiding somewhere."

"Let's go," Rico said as he stepped up on the curb.

"Hold on," the sergeant said as his phone lit up. Rico could only hear the sergeant's side. "We'll be right there."

"What happened?" Rico asked.

"He's been spotted at a convenience store two blocks from here. Follow me."

Rico jumped back into his truck and followed the police car around the corner and pulled into a small convenience store. He was out of his truck before it came to a complete stop and ran into the store followed by the sergeant. An Indian man met them.

The sergeant showed the man a photo of Dusty. "Is this the kid who was in here?"

"Yes, yes. That's him. He put a penny on my counter for a bag of potato chips. He looked hungry so I let him keep them. But I asked him 'Where's your mother?' He said he didn't know. Then he says to me 'Would you call Rico and tell him to come get me?' Then I saw Amber alert on TV." He pointed to the TV behind the counter. "It was him and I told him I would call Rico. I called police and when I turned around he was gone. I looked all over store, and he's not here."

"Didn't you hear the Amber alert earlier?" the sergeant asked.

"I heard it on TV, but I didn't pay much attention because I was busy. It's Saturday and kids from neighborhood come in for candy and sodas. I have to watch them 'cause they steal."

"How long ago was he here?" The sergeant kept firing questions.

"I called right away. Maybe ten minutes. You came fast."

"A little boy's out in this weather, lost," the sergeant reminded him.

"Yes, yes, yes."

The sergeant spoke to the officer behind him. "I want every inch of the store searched." And then he spoke into a mic on his shoulder. "The boy is ten minutes out from the convenience store. Spread out and start searching using the store as a radius."

The sergeant then turned to the clerk. "Do the security cameras work?" He looked up at the cameras in each corner.

"Yes, they do."

"View the footage," he said to another officer. "And see if anyone is around the kid as he leaves the store."

"Yes, sir."

Rico and the sergeant walked outside into the dark night. Streetlights were on each corner, but otherwise it was very dark and very cold. Dusty was out there all alone and scared.

"It's very strange that he leaves a penny for the food he takes," the sergeant remarked.

"His grandmother had custody of him while Darlene was in prison and she told him that you have to pay for what you get. He's very serious about paying for what he gets."

He told the sergeant how he'd met Dusty. "After his grandmother's death, my fiancée tried to explain to him that you don't pay for a gift and we were making progress until the judge ordered him back to his mother." His gut still tightened at the thought.

"You care a lot for that little boy."

"My fiancée and I got really attached to him. He's such a good kid and he doesn't deserve this."

"We'll find him."

But would it be in time?

CHAPTER SEVENTEEN

ANAMARIE'S MOTHER'S SURGERY went well and she was resting in recovery. But she had obsessed for almost an hour about Rico before the nurses came to take her to surgery. Then her older sister Teresa and her husband arrived as did her brother Frank and his wife.

The whole family waited outside the recovery room. All Ana could think was where was Rico? It wasn't like him to be so stubborn and unforgiving. But her mother had been very cruel to him. But—there was always that *but*. If Rico couldn't accept her mother into their lives, what kind of future did that leave them? Yet he never hesitated in helping her mother. So why wasn't he here? Questions went round and round in her head, but the answers eluded her.

THE OFFICERS DID a thorough job of checking the convenience store and the surrounding area. Rico ran down the street calling Dusty's name with no results. The boy seemed to have disappeared once again.

When Rico was about to lose hope, the sergeant got a call. Dusty was spotted at a Metro bus stop. Rico followed the sergeant's patrol car back toward the apartment complex. The big bus was stopped on the street and cars were going around it. Officers were directing traffic as the sergeant had ordered the bus not to leave. The driver and a woman stood outside.

"What happened?" the sergeant asked as they walked up to them.

"That kid that's on the Amber alert—I saw him," the driver said, his shoulders hunched in a big coat.

"Where?"

"I stopped to pick up two people here." He pointed to the bus bench. "And then this lady—" he pointed to the woman behind him "—came up to get on and a man grabbed her arm and started pulling her away and she started screaming. I got off the bus to see what was going on and if she needed help. The man told me to get out of his face. That's when the kid walked up and asked if the bus went to Horseshoe. I was startled because he came out of nowhere. I asked him where his

mother was and the man started shouting pro-
fanities at me. I realized I needed to call the
cops. When I pulled out my phone, I saw the
Amber alert. I turned around and the kid was
gone."

"What about the man?"

"He ran away when I pulled out my phone."

"Did the kid get on the bus?" Rico asked.

The man shook his head. "No."

"Did you look?"

"No. He was out here, not on the bus."

Rico got on the bus. He didn't wait for per-
mission. There were five people in seats on
their phones and he showed them Dusty's picture and they all said they hadn't seen the boy.
He searched every seat and every space on
the bus and Dusty wasn't there. He gritted his
teeth. Damn! This would've been a place for
him to get warm. Where was he?

The sergeant was dealing with the driver
who was complaining about his bus schedule. He was behind and he needed to go. Once
again the officers were searching another area
for Dusty and Rico's hope of finding him was
as cold as his hands in his pockets.

"What do you think?" the sergeant asked.

"Don't let this bus leave," Rico replied.

"Why? The kid's not on it."

"I know. I just have this feeling. Dusty and his mother used the Metro buses to go places and Dusty knows it will take him somewhere and he's hoping it's Horseshoe and home. He's here. I know it. I can feel him."

"Mr. Johnson..."

"He's here, just give me a minute."

"Okay. What do you suggest?"

"Get the people off the bus."

"Mr. Johnson, it's cold outside and it seems like a big order when you didn't find him the first time."

"Get the people off the bus. He's afraid and he's not going to come out with everyone around."

The sergeant ordered everyone off the bus. There was a lot of grumbling, especially from the driver. Everyone huddled in their coats as they waited. Rico stepped back onto the bus and went down the aisle. The sergeant stood by the driver's seat.

"Dusty, Dusty, it's Rico. I'm here. Dusty, can you hear me? Dusty, come out. Dusty!" Over and over he called his name going up and down the aisle with no results. Despair settled in his chest, but he wasn't giving up. He looked toward the sergeant.

"He's not here, Mr. Johnson. I'm sorry."

"No. He's here."

"Mr. Johnson, these people need to get back on the bus. They're cold. And I can't hold this bus much longer without good reason."

"Dusty!" He screamed the word and it bounced off the walls of the bus. "It's Rico."

Nothing but silence answered him. He balled his hands into fists, not wanting to admit defeat. That would mean Dusty was still out there cold and afraid.

"Mr. Johnson…"

"Okay." He turned toward the sergeant and as he did he heard something like a whimper. "Did you hear that?"

The sergeant walked farther into the bus. "Yes. It sounded like a kitten or something."

"Dusty, where are you? It's Rico." Rico hurried toward the sound at the back of the bus and that's when he saw him. He was crunched into a ball on the floor at the back of the last seat. He was like a part of the seat and no one had noticed him. "Come out, buddy." Rico squatted and reached in to touch him. Dusty uncurled and flew into his arms.

"Rico, Rico, Rico, Rico, Rico…" He sobbed on to Rico's shoulder and he couldn't stop saying Rico's name. He was cold and his body trembled and Rico wanted to hurt Darlene Miller for what she'd done to her son.

"Shh, shh." He tried to calm him as he slipped out of his coat and wrapped it around him. The stuffed dog Rico had won for him at the carnival was held tightly in one arm. It was filthy, but Dusty wouldn't let it go.

"Rico, Rico, Rico…"

"It's okay, buddy. I'm here." He stroked Dusty's face as he continued to calm him. "It's okay. I'm here."

The sergeant stood nearby shaking his head. "Unbelievable. Is he okay?"

Dusty heard the sergeant's voice and clung even tighter to Rico. "Don't let him take me, Rico."

"Shh. No one's going to take you. I'm here." He couldn't really make that promise, but for now he had to say something.

"An ambulance is on the way," the sergeant said.

Dusty continued to sob on his shoulder. "It's okay, buddy. Everything's going to be okay."

"I peed my pants," he choked out.

"It's okay. Don't worry about it."

"I'm…wet."

"Okay." Rico looked at the sergeant. "There's

a blanket in the back of my truck. Could you get it please?"

"Sure."

"Okay, buddy. I'm going to take off your clothes and we have to do it fast because you're cold."

"'Kay."

His pants, socks and shoes were soaked and dirty. Rico didn't know how long he'd had them on. The sergeant came back with the blanket, some wipes and a plastic bag. Rico quickly cleaned Dusty and wrapped the blanket around him completely, so just his face was showing. He then wadded the clothes into a ball and stuffed them into the bag and handed them to the sergeant.

"Throw them away. He won't need them again."

"The ambulance is here," the sergeant said, and Rico carried Dusty off the bus into the ambulance.

"His temperature is 95. He has hypothermia," the paramedics said, reaching for blankets. "We have to warm him up."

They reached the hospital ER and rushed them in. A doctor checked Dusty. "His temperature is now 96. He has a slight case of hypothermia, but his toes and fingers have nice blood circulation. We'll continue to work with him and he should be fine. He's dehydrated and we need to get fluids into him. I could start an IV." The doctor looked at Rico. "Do you think you could get him to drink something?"

"Yes." He stroked Dusty's hair. "Hey, buddy, do you think you could drink some water for me?"

Dusty nodded.

The nurse brought some apple juice and a glass of water. Dusty drank thirstily and Rico continued to encourage him to drink.

"I'm hungry," Dusty announced.

"I can fix that," the nurse said and left the room. Soon she was back with chicken nuggets, ketchup, mashed potatoes and milk courtesy of the cafeteria.

As Rico watched Dusty eat he had to wonder when was the last time he had any food? Why hadn't someone noticed this little boy was in danger? It made him so angry. But he had to concentrate on Dusty and not the anger inside him.

Sergeant Chisholm stood in the doorway and a woman rushed past him into the room. Her hair had been tousled by the wind and her tortoiseshell glasses were askew. A purse was over her shoulder and a briefcase in her hand. CPS worker, no doubt.

"I'm Barbara Elliott, caseworker for Darlene Miller and Dusty. I'm here for Dusty Miller."

All Rico's anger simmered to the surface. "You should have been there a month ago."

She glanced at him and straightened her glasses. "And who are you?"

Rico looked at Dusty who was looking at him with big eyes. "The nurse will stay with you and I'm going to step outside and talk to this lady. I'll be right there. You can see me."

Dusty started to climb out of the bed. "Don't leave me, Rico. Don't let them take me."

Rico kissed his forehead. "No one's taking you. Stay right here and I'll be back."

"'Kay."

Now Rico had to make good on his promise. In the hallway, he said to the woman, "You're not taking him."

She bristled instantly. "Who are you?"

"Jericho Johnson. Dusty lived with me while Darlene was in prison."

"Well, Mr. Johnson, I'm with CPS and you can't give me orders."

"Do you know what he's been through tonight?"

She backpedaled quickly. "I haven't been given all the details, but I was notified that Darlene Miller had left him alone. I have to put Dusty into foster care until we can get this sorted out. I found a nice place. The couple has six children, but they have room for one more."

"He'll be sandwiched in like another piece of ham. After what his mother has done to him, he needs special attention and he will get that from me."

"I have to follow the rules."

He took a step toward her and she took a step backward. "If you're following the rules, why haven't you been checking on him? If you had, he wouldn't have gone through hell tonight."

"I did, but then I got the flu and got behind. Darlene was a good mother and always kept her appointments. Until recently…"

"She played you. Just like she played me. Darlene Miller is an expert at playing people. And if we hadn't found him, he probably would've died of hypothermia. And that's on you. So as of right now, tonight, Dusty Miller is going home with me where he will be safe and where he will be cared for and loved."

"You don't have the authority to do that."

Rico was about to unload big time when the sergeant stepped into the conversation. "Ms. Elliott, I called Mr. Johnson to see if he could help with the search."

"Why would you do that?"

The sergeant told her everything that had happened that night. "Dusty has been looking for Rico, asking people to call him. He wants to go home to Horseshoe. That's why he was on that bus. That little boy needs to get his wish. I've been with Mr. Johnson searching for Dusty and it's very evident to me how much he cares for him. If it hadn't been for him, we wouldn't have found Dusty so quickly. Mr. Johnson had custody of him before and in my opinion that's where Dusty should go tonight. Not into a strange home. And I'm here to see that he goes there. I might lose my job over this. But sometimes you have to make a gut call when you know it's right."

"I had no idea he'd been through so much."

"Electricity was turned off yesterday," Rico told her. "And there was no food in the house."

"Oh, I'm so sorry." The woman turned three shades of white.

"CPS dropped the ball on this one and Dusty shouldn't have to suffer anymore."

"I'll call my supervisor." She stepped away to make the call. Rico wanted to tell her it didn't make any difference what the supervisor said. He was still taking Dusty. They would need an army to stop him. Or maybe just Sergeant Chisholm. The sarge was one of the good guys.

Ms. Elliott was back in a minute. "My supervisor has agreed that you can take him, but you have to sign some papers and I need your address and cell number." She juggled her briefcase to remove papers.

Rico signed and gave her all the information she needed.

"Mr. Johnson, this isn't permanent. A judge will rule on this very soon."

"Just don't contact me tomorrow. I need time to calm him down and to reassure him that this won't happen to him again. Do you understand?"

"Yes, sir."

The sergeant was on his phone and he slipped it back into his pocket. "They found Darlene Miller. A neighbor called the police about loud music in an apartment complex across town. The police had to knock the door in and they found four people. Two DOAs and the other two are at another ER fighting for their lives. Ms. Miller is one of them."

"Oh, no." Ms. Elliott was truly shocked. "She was doing so well."

"That's what CPS visits are about, Ms. Elliott. To make sure that she is doing well," Rico reminded her.

"I know. I'm so sorry. You would not believe our caseload. We are just overloaded with kids whose parents abandon or abuse them. It's a nightmare, and I deeply apologize that Dusty suffered because of me. I wish there was something I could do."

Rico turned toward Dusty. He didn't want to hear anymore. The night couldn't be undone. As he took a step, he thought of something. "Do you have any children's clothes in your car? I know some CPS workers carry them for emergencies."

"Yes, yes, I do. I'll be right back." She was eager to help and that eased a little bit of the anger in Rico.

Dusty was sitting up drinking milk and talking to the nurse about the stuffed dog clutched in his hand. When Ms. Elliott came in, Dusty immediately started to scramble away to Rico.

"It's okay, buddy. She's not taking you anywhere."

"I have a pair of sweatpants, a T-shirt, two pairs of underwear, three pairs of socks and a hoodie."

"Perfect. Thank you."

"Mr. Johnson, I really am sorry this happened."

He looked at her and the anger was gone. She really was sorry. "I know."

"Sorry to interrupt, but I need to get insurance information." A woman with papers on a clipboard stood in the doorway.

"He's on Medicaid," Ms. Elliott told her, and glanced at Rico. "I got this."

Rico dressed Dusty and wrapped the blanket around him with the hood of the hoodie over his head. The nurse brought in the discharge papers and he walked out into the cold night with Dusty in his arms.

He stopped short when he stepped through the sliding glass doors. His truck was waiting there. He'd forgotten about his truck. He glanced back and saw the sergeant standing behind him.

"Thank you."

"No problem. Just take care of that little boy. I'll send you pictures of the apartment and details of what happened tonight in case you need it in court."

Rico strapped Dusty in, making sure he was warm. He'd put all three pairs of socks on him so his feet would be too. "I'm going to close the door," he said to Dusty, "but I'm going around to the driver's side and we're going home."

"'Kay."

Rico held out his hand to the sarge. "Thank you for calling me."

"When it comes to a kid, I don't leave any stone unturned."

They shook hands vigorously and then Rico did something he wouldn't normally do. He hugged the sergeant and walked around to the driver side and got in. That's when he noticed the white police car in front of him. Another escort. The sarge really didn't leave any stone unturned.

Traffic was heavy this time of night. People were going to bars and clubs and out for a night of partying and others were just going out for the evening. With the escort, they made it through Austin quickly. At the turn for the interstate the police car pulled over and the officer waved out the window. Rico waved back as he made the turn.

There were a lot of good people in Austin, but his focus now was on Horseshoe and Ana. He had to call her. When he did, it rang on the passenger side of his truck. He'd forgotten he had her coat and phone. Man, it had been almost four hours since he'd left. He hoped she trusted him enough to be waiting.

ANAMARIE'S MOTHER WAS resting comfortably in recovery and the doctor suggested they all go home. She would be moved to a room tomorrow and would need them. But the family would feel better if someone would stay. Patsy volunteered and Peggy drove Anamarie to the shop to pick up her car.

"Stuart and I are going to get a bite to eat. Do you want to come with us?"

"Are you kidding me? The last thing I want to be is a third at dinner. I'll see you tomorrow. Thanks for the ride."

Anamarie headed for Angie's office where she'd left her coat with her phone and keys in the pocket. Angie had given her the key, but the door was unlocked. She flipped on the lights and glanced at the chair where she'd left her coat. It wasn't there.

Stuart walked in from the bakery. "I heard the door and wondered who it was."

"Have you seen a black coat? I left it in this chair."

"Jericho picked it up and said he was taking it to you."

"Oh. He never arrived."

"That's odd. Rico and Wyatt talked for a bit in his office and then I assumed Rico went to Temple."

She couldn't figure this out. He picked up her coat to bring to Temple. Why hadn't he arrived? And why was he talking to Wyatt? Something had happened. Fear wrapped around her heart in a tight squeeze, but she shook it off.

"My car keys were in my pocket."

"I'll take you home," he offered. "I locked up earlier, but got called away. I came back to put the table and chairs back in place for Monday."

"I'm sure Margie will appreciate that."

In minutes they were in his patrol car and drove to her house. He waited while she ran in and grabbed the spare key and a jacket. The cold air bit through her clothes and her arms were like popsicles.

When she finally made it into her house

the second time, Mickey barked his head off, wanting food. She gave him dog food soaked in milk and collapsed onto her sofa. She should just take a shower and go to bed, but she didn't have the energy. She grabbed the blanket she had on the sofa and curled up to get warm. The heat was on, but she was chilled to the bone.

Since Wyatt was the last one to talk to Rico, she wanted to call him and ask about Rico. But she didn't have a phone and Wyatt was at home with his family and she couldn't disturb him. So she would do what she'd been doing since she'd met Rico. She would wait. He had asked her to trust him and she had to do that and try not to blow his reaction out of proportion.

The warmth of the house and the blanket lulled her into a peaceful sleep. Her last thought was: Where was Rico?

ANA WOKE UP and wondered where she was and then it all came rushing back. Her mother. The heart attack. And Rico. Pushing the blanket aside, she noticed Mickey curled up at her feet. No wonder her feet were so warm. She scratched Mickey's head and got up. She had to call Rico and realized again that she didn't have her phone.

She hurried to her bedroom and pulled on a pair of knee-high boots and grabbed a big jacket and slipped into it. In the kitchen she grabbed her spare car keys and walked to bakery to get her car so she could head for Rebel Ranch.

Rico had promised two hours and now it was over four. The only place he could be was the ranch. He had a lot of explaining to do and she wasn't going to stop until she found him. It was past ten o'clock and lights were on at Quincy's, Falcon's and Miss Kate's. Elias and his family now lived in the big house with Miss Kate and grandpa. She drove over the entrance cattle guard and to the bunkhouse.

There were no lights. Just total darkness. Rico wasn't there, nor was his truck. She glanced out at Rebel Ranch and the vast landscape. Several spotlights were on, but there was no movement of any kind. It was cold and dark and everyone was inside, even the animals.

Where was he? Why hadn't he come to the hospital as planned? She had no answers. She had to trust him, as he'd asked. She drove back to her house to wait. That's the only choice she had. Living without Rico wasn't an option. She loved him too much.

As she drove into her garage, Rico's truck pulled up behind her. For some reason that made her angry. Why had he put her through this horrible night? This wasn't how a relationship was supposed to work. Of course, she hadn't had too many so she wasn't sure. But she knew she was mad at being treated like this. She had a lot to say.

He exited his truck with her coat in his hand. That made her even madder. She yanked it out of his hands. "Where have you been?" Her words were full of anger and it jarred her senses. Normally she wasn't an angry person. She wasn't going to let him get off so easily.

"I've been waiting and waiting for you. You said two hours and now it's after ten. My mother has been asking to see you and I had to calm her before the surgery. She's worried you're never going to forgive her for the way she's treated you. It's important to me that she approves of our relationship. But for some reason, known only to you, you did a disappearing act. What kind of relationship do we have when you can't talk to me? I know my mother hurt you, but…" She shook her head.

"I'm not talking about this anymore tonight. I'm exhausted and might say something I regret." She swung toward her back door.

"How's your mother?"

She turned to face him and the cold wind stung her cheeks, but she didn't feel it. There was such warmth in his voice and that's what she felt all the way to her heart.

"The surgery went well and she's in recovery. She should be able to come home in a couple of days."

"I'm glad for you and your family."

"Rico, I needed you tonight."

"I know, and I'm sorry I wasn't there. When I explain where I was, I think you'll understand."

Her outside lights were on and they could see each other clearly. The worry lines around his eyes were prominent and the scar seemed to stand out. He was worried.

She took a step toward him. "It better be a good explanation. I mean so good that I won't ever think about it again. So good that…"

He reached for her hand. "I'll show you."

He led her toward his truck. The back passenger window was halfway down and there was someone in Dusty's car seat.

She peered closer and her heart dribbled painfully. "Is that...is that Dusty?"

He nodded.

"Did you kidnap him?"

"No." And he told her a story that chilled her more than the weather. "Oh, Rico, no."

"I was so afraid I wasn't going to find him in time. He just wanted to come home. I talked to Gabe and he said we have a good chance of getting custody this time."

"What? Wait. When did you talk to Gabe?"

"On the way from Austin."

"You called Gabe, but you didn't call me." A bad feeling simmered in her gut. She wanted to push it away, but she couldn't.

"I did. I had your phone, though, and it buzzed on the passenger side of my truck."

"You could have called anyone in my family and they would have gotten in touch with me. You didn't try very hard, Rico, and this is an important decision we should have made together."

"Ana, I didn't have time."

"You knew about Dusty the last time I talked to you and yet, you said nothing."

"I didn't want to worry you with every-thing that was going on with your mother, and I didn't know what I would find in Austin. I was just trying to protect you."

"I don't need you to protect or mollycoddle me. I'm a strong woman and what I need is a man who trusts that I can handle life, a man who allows me a voice in our relationship, a man who doesn't shut me out and a man who considers my feeling, my wishes."

"Ana, please…"

"Is Darlene still alive?" She ignored the plea in his voice.

"Yes, but Gabe and Wyatt feel we have a strong case."

"You talked to Wyatt, too?"

"Y-yes."

"You talked to everyone but me."

"Ana…"

"Did it even cross you mind that Darlene will recover and she's going to want her son back?"

"Wyatt said…"

"I don't care what Wyatt said. Darlene is good at working the system. She will hire the same lawyer who got her out of prison and a judge will listen because she's a mother and she has rights. They will jerk Dusty out of our arms once again." As the words left her mouth, she wanted to reach into the truck and grab Dusty, kiss him and feel his little body in her arms and listen to his childish giggles, but she couldn't let that weakness sway her. "Do you remember the pain, Rico? You were gone for days and I didn't know where you were or if you were okay. You shut me completely out of your life."

"It's different now. Together we can do this."

That niggling fear inside her wouldn't let go and then it hit her. Her freezing hands curled into fists and she jammed them into the pockets of her jacket. She drew cold air into her lungs to cool her heated thoughts. "You once told me our relationship was all about Dusty. I guess you were right...about you, but not for me. I really love you, but I can't put myself through that pain again. I barely survived the first time."

"Ana, no!"

She ran to her back door, tears streaming down her face. As she yanked open the door, Mickey shot out and darted to Rico, barking. She hit the button for the garage door and it buzzed down, shutting out the night, shutting out her entire world and everyone who mattered to her.

CHAPTER EIGHTEEN

RICO DROVE HOME SPENT. The talk with Ana had robbed him of his last bit of energy and he blocked out everything, especially her words.

He carried Dusty into the bunkhouse and put him to bed, making sure he was covered and warm. Mickey's barking had woken him briefly, but he was exhausted and out for the night.

Rico collapsed into his recliner and his thoughts played hopscotch, jumping from one wrong to another, but one thing was very clear. He'd screwed up so bad Ana wasn't ever going to forgive him or love him again. He'd hurt her. He winced at the knowledge. How could he have gotten this so wrong? And what did he do now?

He saw the McGregor papers lying on the coffee table. They meant nothing without her. He reached back and flipped off the light, submerging himself in darkness, and drifted off to a place where only pain lived. A place he was very familiar with.

He awoke at five to searing pain in his heart. If Miss Doris hadn't had the heart attack, he and Ana would've been together and they would've made the decision about Dusty together. The way it should have been. But now he had to fight for Dusty alone and be prepared to handle the outcome. Without Ana. That created a pain so deep in his chest that he had trouble breathing.

Dusty awoke at six and wanted his boots. Rico put them on him and he ran around the bunkhouse with Mickey chasing after him. The trauma of the night before seemed a lifetime away. While Dusty played, Rico called Miss Kate and told her what had happened. He couldn't talk about Ana and the walls he'd happily destroyed were taking root once again. He could feel them.

Rico gave Dusty a good bath and cleaned his fingernails and toenails. He had no clothes to put on him so he dressed him in the same clothes. Later, he drove to Temple to buy the boy some clothes and to get his hair cut. First, he had something he needed to do.

Miss Doris was sitting up in bed with a breakfast tray in front of her. "Oh, Rico, I'm so glad you're here." She glanced at Dusty on his shoulder. "You have the boy."

"Yes, ma'am." And he told her a little bit about last night.

Miss Doris looked around him. "Where's Anamarie?"

"I'd rather not talk about it."

"Okay."

Rico was surprised she was so amenable. He felt sure she had a dozen or more questions, but he wasn't discussing Ana.

"Thank you, Rico, for what you did yesterday."

"I'm glad you're feeling better," was all he could say.

"I've been an old fool, judgmental and stupid. I'm so sorry for the way I've treated you. You're everything Anamarie said you were—a wonderful man."

Rico left soon after. He couldn't stay and listen to all the praise. He wasn't a wonderful man. After shopping at Walmart, which was the only place open, they went home. Dusty was clingy and Rico knew he had to talk to the boy.

Dusty sat in his lap, his head on Rico's chest. "Tell me what happened."

Dusty lifted his head and twisted his fingers like he always did when he was nervous or excited. "My mommy's still sick."

"I know, buddy."

Dusty knew his mother was on drugs. That was so awful for a little boy. His and Dusty's stories were much alike and maybe that's why they'd connected so strongly.

"I not go back." Dusty shook his hand. "I stay here with you and Ana."

He'd told Dusty that Ana's mother was in the hospital and she needed to be there with her. He couldn't tell him Ana wasn't coming back. He could barely think it in his head. But soon he would have to face that possibility.

RICO SPENT THE afternoon on the phone with Gabe and Wyatt going over details so he would have a strong case and a good chance of getting custody. Then he called the principal to see if he could get Dusty back into school while he was here. There was no problem. The principal put Dusty in Remi's kindergarten class so he would feel comfortable.

Dusty was excited to go back to school. He left him safely in Remi's hands and headed back to Temple.

He had a lot to do today and seeing Robert Francis McGregor was at the top of the list. He was early, but the office was open. The lawyer was packing, putting books and things in boxes.

They shook hands and Rico took a seat.

"I've said thank you so much that it seems rather lame for this kind of gift."

"It's enough, Mr. Johnson." The lawyer pulled some papers forward. "I'm doing a transfer of title for tax reasons."

"Sounds good to me, but I wanted you to know that in about two hours I'm meeting Miss Kate Rebel at the courthouse and I'm changing my name to Rebel."

"I'll update the papers, but it won't be finalized until March first when I receive the hundred thousand."

"You'll have it before then."

"I have no doubt."

The lawyer handed Rico some keys and then held out his hand. "I'll notify you when the truck comes to pick up the items my parents want."

"Sure. I'll be there to make sure everything is loaded."

"I'm glad you came in early because I wanted to let you know that I'm closing the office for good on Wednesday because of the Thanksgiving holiday. From now on our

transactions will be through my Dallas office." He handed him a business card. "All
the information is there if you need to ask
a question. Thank you for being so kind to
my grandfather. He looked forward to those
mornings you spent with him and there
wasn't much in this world he looked forward
to anymore."

They talked a few minutes more and Rico
left. Outside in the truck he took a moment.
It was Thanksgiving week. With everything
that was going on he'd forgotten. He'd been
looking forward to the holidays with Ana.
Their first holiday and now he would spend
it alone.

HE MADE IT back to Horseshoe in time to
meet Miss Kate at the courthouse. When
Miss Kate's truck drove in, Rico got out and
paused as seven more trucks followed. All
the brothers had come for the name change.
His connection to the Rebels was rock solid
and they were all he had in this time of angst.

Gabe met them inside the courthouse
and handed a clerk some papers for a name
change. It was simple and in a matter of minutes Rico became Jericho Johnson Rebel.

There were handshakes and hugs all around

as they made their way out of the courthouse. Quincy and Rico stood beside Grandpa as he made his way down the steps.

Everyone left to go back to work, but Gabe stayed behind and soon Wyatt walked up. Once Wyatt was there, Gabe said, "I have some bad news. Connie Grimes has filed for custody of Dusty. Wyatt pulled some strings and Judge Carvel worked it into his schedule on Wednesday before the holiday break. It's at one o'clock."

"What?" Rico was numb, but not surprised. Ana was right. They were going to jerk Dusty around some more and Rico would be left to deal with the pain.

"She has a good job and so does her husband. They live in a good neighborhood in Austin. This is a problem as the judge always wants to place a child with family."

"I got this." Wyatt spoke up. "Don't worry about it."

What could Wyatt do now that he couldn't do before?

ANA WENT THROUGH the motions of everyday life, not allowing herself to think of what she was losing. She wasn't his maid or his housekeeper. She wanted to be his lover, his wife, his life partner. She needed to know that she counted.

On Sunday she cried most of the day with Dusty's drawing clutched to her chest, getting caught up in all the emotions that plagued her. That afternoon she got herself together enough to go see her mother. Her eyes were red and blotchy and she knew her mother was going to ask questions. But it didn't keep her from going.

As soon as Anamarie walked into the room, her mother asked, "What's wrong?"

Luckily her mother was alone. Frank and Teresa had spent the morning with her and she was exhausted from all the company. Her father had gone home to take a nap.

"Anamarie?"

"What?" Ana brought her thoughts back to her mother, and to keep her from asking more questions she added, "Patsy said the doctor gave you a good report and you might go home tomorrow."

"Yeah." Her mother was sitting in a comfy chair with pillows propped behind her back. "I don't know, Anamarie." Her mother picked at the blanket over her lap. "I'm getting older and I'm thinking of turning over the bakery to Bubba and Margie. You were right, she's good at making kolaches. And I can spend more time with your dad."

Anamarie's mouth fell open and she quickly closed it. "Mom, did you hit your head when you fell?"

"Why?" Her mother glanced up. "You think I'm talking out of my head?"

"Well, it's not like you to be so docile."

"When you have a close call with death, it changes everything and now I can see how relentless and unyielding I've been. I want to cherish my children and to be a part of their lives. Teresa and Frank want us to come visit and I think Willard and I will do that. I want to see more of my grandchildren."

Anamarie sat on the bed, completely flabbergasted by her mother's change of attitude.

"Now, tell me why you've been crying."

Anamarie bit her lips and decided to be completely honest and tell her mother what had happened.

"I knew something was wrong when Rico came with the little boy."

"He came and had Dusty with him?"

"Yes, but he was half asleep on Rico's shoulder. From what Rico said, he'd been through a rough night."

Don't think about it. Don't think about it,

she kept repeating in her head. She had to be strong.

"I know how you're feeling," her mother said, and that was an odd thing for her to say because her mother never knew what Anamarie was feeling. "When I married your father, he was a momma's boy. He thought his mother was God and I always came second. It took me a lot of years to realize he loved us in different ways."

"This is not the same, Mom."

"I don't think that's true. You don't feel loved and I didn't, either. Rico's the type of man who has this need to help people. That's why he helped Egan and that's why he went into that school to help those kids. He's the type of man who never thinks of himself. You told me over and over what a wonderful man he is and now you have to ask yourself is that true or not."

Ana slid from the bed. "I have to go."

"Think about what I said. You love Rico. Are you willing to lose him over this?"

She couldn't shake her mother's words. They kept running through her head. She went to sleep that night with the question pounding in her head. Was she willing to lose Rico?

Rico tried to get through each day as best he could for Dusty's sake, but he kept thinking about Dusty's aunt. Could she be a good mother? He wasn't going to set himself up again to get knocked down. If the court was leaning toward Connie, he had to know if she would treat Dusty as her own. On Tuesday, he went to see Wyatt, but he was out. Rico had to pick up Dusty so it had to wait until tomorrow and Wednesday was the hearing. Time was running out. Rico had to make a decision.

Early Wednesday morning Rico caught Wyatt in his office. Taking a seat in the wood chair he'd used a lot lately, he said, "I'd like to talk about Connie Grimes."

Wyatt frowned. "Connie Grimes? Rico, there's no way she's going to get Dusty."

"You can't say that for sure and I need to know something about her."

"Rico…"

"Tell me all you know."

Wyatt sighed. "She's a shopaholic and likes expensive things. She owes money everywhere and Wendy spent most of her life paying Connie's bills. The husband owns a bar and works nights. Does that sound like they'd make good parents?"

"No, but…"

Wyatt frowned. "What's this about? You're giving up too easy and that's not you."

Rico had no choice but to tell him what happened. "I screwed up, Wyatt. I screwed up real bad."

"So, every man screws up. Didn't you know that?" Wyatt pointed toward Anamarie's shop. "Go over there and talk to her. Talk this out. This is the most important thing you'll ever do in your life. I know you, Rico. You cannot give up on that little boy."

"I don't want to, Wyatt, but I don't want to get my heart crushed again, either. And I have to think about Anamarie."

"Go," was all Wyatt had to say.

Rico walked across the courthouse lawn to Ana's shop. He could see her inside moving around in the kitchen. What they said now would determine their future. And Dusty's. Their decision had to be a mutual agreement between two people who loved each other. And this time he wasn't going to get it wrong. He just hoped she listened.

ANAMARIE GOT A call for a wedding cake and she decided to make it weddingly. She smiled for the first time in days. Then she looked up and saw Rico standing in her doorway. He was here!

She took a deep breath and walked to the front area. "What is it, Rico?" She tried to keep her voice calm while inside butterflies swarmed her stomach.

With his hat in his hand, he asked, "Could we talk?"

"Sure." She braced herself for what was to come, but didn't know how much longer she could resist him. His strong, honed features were sharp and pronounced and pain was vivid in his dark eyes. Her heart ached for the pain he was going through. Pain she'd inflicted on him because of her insecurities.

"Connie Grimes has filed for custody of Dusty."

"What?"

"She and her husband want to raise him. She's Dusty's aunt and a judge will look at that. I was thinking about withdrawing from the custody hearing and allow Dusty's aunt to raise him."

"Why would you do that?" She couldn't believe her ears.

He twisted his hat in his hands and then he looked up, those gorgeous dark eyes gazing right into hers as if he could see right into her soul. "I can survive losing Dusty, but I can't survive losing you."

"Oh..." Her trembling hand touched her mouth and she wanted to say so many things, but emotions congealed in her throat.

"I'm sorry I didn't try harder to get in touch with you, but I couldn't leave Dusty in the hell he was in. He asked for me and I couldn't ignore that."

"And you shouldn't have. Dusty needed you and he still does. My problem is not with Dusty. I love him as much as you do. My problem was that you made me feel like a surrogate mother. I just wanted to know I counted in your life as more than a mother for Dusty."

He looked down at his hat and then back at her. "I've loved you since the first moment I met you. Do you remember where that was?"

She swallowed hard. "At...at the bakery."

"I came in to buy kolaches for Egan's dog, and your mother and that other lady wouldn't wait on me. They ignored me. Then you came over and asked, with a smile as big as Texas, 'May I help you?' Do you know what words ran through my mind when you asked that?"

"No." She held her breath.

"For the rest of my life."

"O-h."

"I love you. I will always love you."

"Oh, Rico." She flew into his arms. He grabbed her and held her tight against his chest. "I love you. I love you," she breathed against his lips. His hat fell to the floor and he took her lips in a passionate kiss. Her doubts drifted away, as did everything else. They had each other and that's what Ana wanted. She had his love.

He rested his forehead against hers. "Now we have to decide what to do about Dusty."

She leaned back and looked into his eyes. "Is there any question?"

"I was raised by my great-grandmother, as you know, and Dusty might benefit from being raised by a relative."

She touched the scar on his face, feeling the rough edges and cringing at how it had been put there. "I don't want you to give up on Dusty. You love him, and can you honestly believe Connie Grimes will be a good parent?"

He caught her hand and kissed her fingertips. "I want to keep Dusty for you, for us. I want him to be the child you can never have. That's always been my wish."

Through a smile she blinked back a tear.

"Then let's fight for him and together we can handle the outcome."

He held her tight, his chin resting on her head. She snuggled closer, just needing to be near him to feel his warmth, his love. "When's the hearing?"

"Today at one."

She pushed back. "Rico, we don't have much time."

"I know."

She made a decision in an instant. "Let's get married. Wyatt can marry us."

"No, I want you to have the big wedding."

"I don't need the big wedding and all the trappings. I just need you in my life for good. And we need to start that adventure today."

He gave in easily and she took his hand and they walked across the courthouse lawn to Wyatt's office.

Wyatt was alone, talking on the phone. "Come in," he said, his hand over the mouthpiece. After he hung up he asked, "What can I do for you guys?"

"Can you marry us?" Rico asked.

"Huh…yeah…huh…" Clearly, they'd shocked the sheriff.

Wyatt fumbled around and pulled out a big

book and a small book. They held hands and stood in front of Wyatt's desk.

"I haven't done this in a while so you'll have to bear with me," Wyatt said. "First I need some information." They answered all of Wyatt's questions and Wyatt filled out the form. "I almost forgot to put Rebel on here."

"Rebel?" Ana asked.

Wyatt looked at Rico. "You haven't told her?"

"I haven't had time." Rico turned to her. "That's what the meeting with the Rebels was about. Miss Kate asked me to change my name. She said she sees me as one of her sons. I was going to tell you on Saturday night."

"Oh, that's wonderful. You are a Rebel." She hugged him until Wyatt interrupted.

"Let's get back to the wedding." Wyatt picked up the little book and started the ceremony. In minutes they said *I do* and were married. They didn't have rings, but that didn't matter. They shared a long kiss and Wyatt took pictures with his phone.

"Something to remember this day," Wyatt said with a smile.

They hugged Wyatt and then got into Rico's truck and drove to the ranch. They held hands the whole way and several times she reached over to kiss his cheek. She couldn't seem to stop touching him. She was so happy. When they reached the bunkhouse, Ana stepped into the house where she'd shared so much love. In that moment she knew she was home. This was where she belonged.

AFTER RICO CALLED Gabe to update the filing with Ana's name, he swung her up into his arms and carried her into the bedroom. A long time later they lay entwined just savoring the moment. Then he told her about the McGregor gift.

Her eyes grew big. "Rico, that's unbelievable. You made Mr. McGregor's last days happy." She stroked his face. "You're such a wonderful man."

"I'm going to work very hard to make the McGregor property a showplace once again and I'm going to work even harder on Rebel Ranch so it will always make a profit. I don't have to prove myself to Miss Kate, but I want her to know how grateful I am for the life she's given me."

They talked until it was time to go to the courthouse and they were now both strong enough to face whatever happened.

THE COURTHOUSE WAS ablaze with Christmas. The town was getting a jump on the holiday. Two big wreaths adorned the large double doors. A bare twenty-foot Christmas tree stood on the lawn waiting to be decorated after Thanksgiving. In the foyer there was a smaller tree and more wreaths were on all the office doors. Fresh Douglas fir garlands and red bows hung everywhere and poinsettias were in every available space. A pine scent hung heavy in the air.

The courtrooms were upstairs and it was much the same. Two bigger courtrooms were to the right and the small family courtroom was to the left. Everything was quiet and no one was around.

The door suddenly opened, shaking the wreath on it. "Court in ten minutes," the woman said.

"Thanks, Brenda," Ana replied.

"You know her?" Rico asked as they walked in to the room.

"Oh, yeah. Brenda's been around forever. She comes into the bakery."

One day he hoped he would know everyone in this small town, but since he was a loner he only knew the people he came into contact with. Now that he had officially plunged into the Rebel clan he had a feeling that would change.

The judge's bench was straight ahead with the US and the Texas flag behind it. Two small tables were in front of the judge's bench with two chairs at each. Other chairs were scattered about. The room would only hold about twenty people.

"Where is everyone?" Ana asked as they took seats at one of the small tables.

As the words left her mouth, Connie Grimes and a tall man who Rico assumed was her husband walked in, followed by a young woman who had to be the lawyer. They sat at the other table.

Rico looked back at the door wondering where Gabe was. He should've been here by now. And Wyatt? He felt sure Wyatt would be here.

Ana touched his thigh. "It's going to be okay," she whispered, and he settled back and waited for the gut-wrenching decision.

Just as Brenda came out of the side door, Gabe rushed in with files under his arm and a briefcase in his hand. "Sorry, I'm late but I was on the phone with Sergeant Chisholm. Darlene Miller is showing signs of waking up and he's over at the hospital to see if he can get any information that would help us." Gabe looked around. "Where's Wyatt?"

"He's not here," Rico replied. "Is Darlene going to recover?" That was upmost in his mind.

"Don't know yet. It's touch and go at the moment, but the sergeant will keep us informed."

"The Honorable Judge Harvey Carvel," Brenda announced, and the judge walked in and took a seat at the bench. The man was probably in his sixties with thinning gray hair, and wore a black robe. Rico had lived in Horseshoe for a lot of years and he'd never met the man.

Before the judge could speak, Wyatt walked in with a big folder in his hand. He took a seat behind them.

The judge stared at him. "Wyatt, what are you doing in my courtroom?"

"I have a personal interest in this case, Judge."

"Okay." The judge looked down at the file in front of him. "We are here today to decide custody of minor child Dustin Miller. Connie Miller Grimes, an aunt, has filed for custody, as has Mr. Rebel…" The judge blinked and glanced at Rico. "Is that correct?"

"Yes, Your Honor," Rico replied. "I've become a member of the Rebel family."

"I see." The judge pushed his horn-rimmed glasses up the bridge of his nose. "As I was saying, Mr. Rebel and his wife have also filed for custody." He folded his hands over the file. "I would like to say that I'm extremely sorry for everything this little boy has gone through and take the responsibility of finding him a forever home personally. As of today I am terminating Darlene Miller's maternal rights."

Connie's lawyer got to her feet. "Your Honor…"

"And you are?" the judge asked.

"Sharon Hildebrand, attorney for Connie Miller Grimes."

"Go ahead."

"Mrs. Grimes is the biological aunt of Dustin Miller. She sincerely wants to raise her nephew. At best a child should be given the opportunity to be raised by family."

"I agree, Ms. Hildebrand. I always try to place children with relatives. In later years they are grateful for that and to have a connection to the family they were born into."

No, no! They couldn't do this again. Rico

was screaming inside, but he remained silent. He had to trust in justice this time. Ana reached for his hand and he held it just to know he wasn't in this alone.

Wyatt got up and slapped a big folder in front of the judge. "There's everything you ever wanted to know about Connie Miller Grimes."

"Wyatt, this is highly unusual and I take offense at you interrupting my court."

"Read it." Wyatt jabbed a finger at the folder.

Footsteps sounded outside and Rico looked back to see Miss Kate, Grandpa and the brothers walk in, followed by Miss Doris, Willard and the Wiznowski clan.

"Miss Kate, this is a closed courtroom," the judge told her.

"It's okay, Harvey. We won't make a sound."

Before the judge could reply, shouts echoed outside the courtroom. "What's going on, Wyatt?"

Wyatt looked out of the only window in the room. "This doesn't look good, Harvey."

Ana's phone binged and she showed it to Rico. It was a video of what was going on outside. People were carrying signs that read: Justice for Dusty. Justice for Dusty and

Rico. Justice Today. He saw the principal, the owner of the hardware store who wouldn't sell anything to him unless Falcon approved, the auto parts store owner who did the same thing, the president of the bank who called Miss Kate the moment he had walked in— he was afraid Rico would rob the place—the owner of the feed store who also refused to sell him anything until Miss Kate had a stern talk with him. People who had shunned him for years were everywhere carrying signs.

"Most of the town is out there," Ana whispered. "They're supporting you."

"No, they're supporting us."

Ana shook her head. "No, this is about you and your involvement in this community. You're a big part of it."

For the first time he had to admit that maybe he was.

"Wyatt, get those people off the courthouse lawn."

"I can't, Harvey. They're protesting peacefully and it's legal. Just make a ruling and let's get this over with."

Gabe's phone binged. He took it and then stood up. "Your Honor, Darlene Miller just passed away."

"Oh, my poor sister," Connie wailed and her husband put his arm around her shoulders.

"I'm sorry for your loss, Mrs. Grimes," the judge said.

"Your Honor, there's more," Gabe interrupted. "I've been in contact with Sergeant Chisholm of the Austin Police Department. He was at the hospital and said that Darlene was conscious for a few minutes. She became agitated and the nurse asked if she wanted to write something. She had a breathing tube and couldn't speak. This is what she wrote." Gabe took his phone to the judge and laid it in front of him. "It's barely legible, but I think you can read it."

The judge read the message and Ana clutched Rico's hand. "What do you think she wrote?"

"I don't have any idea. We just have to wait." But he held on to her hand as if his life depended on it.

The judge looked at Connie. "Mrs. Grimes, I'd like for you to hear what your sister wrote. As Gabe has said, it's barely legible, but her message is clear." He took a breath and read from Gabe's phone. "Dusty. Home. Take Mr. Johnson. Not sister."

"She doesn't mean that," Connie spat.

"Your Honor." Ms. Hildebrand got to her feet. "Mrs. Grimes is his blood aunt and…"

"Ms. Hildebrand, you're not going to pull that one on me. You see, I did some checking on Connie Miller Grimes. I didn't want to make the mistake I made with Darlene Miller. I wanted to be sure that little boy gets the home he deserves after all he's been through. So I talked to the neighbors of Wendy Miller. She's had custody of Dusty on and off since he was born. This last time she had him a little over a year. She received government assistance for Dustin because she had no income except for her disability check. You know what I found, Mrs. Grimes?"

"Those old busybodies hate me and would say anything to hurt me."

"I've known these ladies all my life and they're as honest as the day is long. Every first of the month you showed up on your mother's doorstep for Dusty's government check and she signed it over to you."

"I was going through a rough time and needed the money. Mom understood that."

"I seriously doubt that, but you were her daughter and she always wanted to help you. But in doing that you took food from your nephew's mouth. Toward the end of the month they had very little money. Dustin would bring a half a peanut butter and jelly sandwich to school with part of an apple. That's how much you thought of your nephew and you have the nerve to come in here today to file for custody. I'm throwing out your claim."

"Your Honor…" Ms. Hildebrand wasn't giving up.

The judge picked up the file Wyatt had laid on his desk and handed it to Brenda who stood to the side. "Give this to Ms. Hildebrand. I'm sure it's everything she doesn't know about Connie Miller Grimes."

"I object." The lawyer was hanging tough.

The judge ignored her. "I'm awarding full custody of the minor child Dustin Miller to Jericho Johnson Rebel and Anamarie Wiznowski Rebel."

Ana threw her arms around his neck and he held her so tight his arms hurt. They'd won. Dusty was now their little boy.

Before the judge could bang his gavel, Gabe grabbed papers out of his briefcase and walked to the bench. "Your Honor, these are adoption papers I filed back in June. If you would sign them today, it would give Dustin Miller his forever family."

"My pleasure." The judge signed the papers and then banged his gavel. "This court is adjourned."

Rico held onto Ana, hardly believing that it was over. Ana sobbed onto his chest, "We have a son, Rico, the most wonderful little boy in the whole world. He's ours and no one can ever take him again."

She couldn't seem to stop crying. He cupped her face in his hands and wiped away tears with his thumbs. "Hey, don't fall apart on me now."

"I'm not. I'm just so happy." She kissed his hand. "I love you. I thought no one would ever love me or that I would ever have a child of my own. You have given me everything."

"Hey." He touched her lips gently. "I love you right back. You gave me love and I will be grateful for that every day that I'm with you." He wrapped his arms around her and they stood as one for now and always.

He was a husband, a father and a part of a big family. And the community that once had shunned him had accepted him and supported him today in a way he'd never expected. If he ever doubted there was a God, he didn't anymore. Someone had a hand in everything that had happened to him. Someone supreme and more powerful than any man on earth.

Shouts echoed from outside; they'd heard the good news. Jericho Johnson Rebel had finally found a place where he belonged.

He'd found home.

EPILOGUE

TUESDAY MORNINGS HELD a special place in Rico and Ana's hearts. They decided to get married the second time on Tuesday morning before Christmas in the small Catholic church with family and close friends.

Rico had something he wanted to do before the ceremony. He called Peggy and met her at the Talk of the Town Beauty Shop. He had his hair cut to shoulder length and Peggy asked if he minded if she sent it to a company that made wigs for cancer patients. Of course, he agreed. He didn't tell Ana about the haircut. He wanted it to be a surprise and he hoped it didn't backfire on him.

Ana was at her house getting ready. She didn't want Rico to see the dress. Miss Doris had taken it up for her and he couldn't wait to see her in it. Dusty was with her and he would pick him up later to take to the church. Everything was going according to plan.

They had told Dusty about the adoption

the day they had been awarded custody. He knew about adoption because Paxton and Remi's daughter Annie had been adopted and he asked if Rico and Ana were his momma and daddy now. They said yes and he seemed to relax and know he was their little boy forever.

They worried about telling Dusty about his mother, but Dusty took it out of their hands. One night as Rico sat in his recliner and Ana cooked supper, Dusty played on the floor with Mickey. He got up and crawled into Rico's lap, twisting his little fingers and Rico knew he was worried about something.

"Daddy, did my mommy go be with Grandma in heaven?"

"Yes, buddy," he answered without hesitation.

Dusty laid his head on Rico's chest and cried.

Rico gathered him close. "It's okay, buddy."

Ana came and took him and he cried on her shoulder. She kissed his cheek and smoothed his hair, making it all better.

"My mommy's not sick anymore," Dusty muttered through his tears.

Ana kissed him again. "No, baby boy, she's

not. She's smiling at you and happy you're with us. It was her last wish."

Dusty raised his head. "Really?" It was clear Dusty was feeling a little sad for his mother and Rico knew Darlene loved the boy. Her last act proved that, but she couldn't shake the addiction.

"Yes, now come help Momma make supper." And just like that the sadness was gone.

Rico and Ana had paid to have Darlene's body brought to Horseshoe and to be buried in the Horseshoe Cemetery next to her mother. It had put a strain on their finances, but Ana had sold her house to Peggy and Stuart who were getting married in June, and that had helped. They would have done it for Dusty anyway. They hadn't taken him to the cemetery yet, but they would when they thought he was ready.

All these thoughts ran through his mind as he stood at the front of the church with Egan and Dusty. Ana couldn't choose among her sisters, so they decided to have Egan and Rachel stand up for them. Ana had coordinated their clothes. He wore starched jeans, white shirt, a black Western bolo tie and a black tuxedo jacket, the same as Egan and

Dusty. Today he wanted everything to be just as Ana wanted.

They didn't have to decorate the church. It was already decorated for Christmas in white and gold and as festive as the courthouse. His thoughts stopped as he noticed all the people in church. They were packed in the pews, stood at the back, along the sides and in the foyer. They hadn't invited all these people. Rico and Ana had been in the spotlight lately and maybe the town just wanted to share this day.

The "Wedding March" music started and Rico focused on the back of the church. Rachel came first and then his breath stalled as he saw Ana all in white on her father's arm. She was the most beautiful sight he'd ever seen. "Here Comes the Bride" played and she walked down the aisle like an angel. She missed a step when she noticed him, but quickly recovered. Miss Doris met them halfway and they continued to the foot of the altar. Rico was so busy watching Ana that Dusty got away from him and ran to Ana.

"Look, Momma." He pointed to Rico. "Daddy cut his hair."

Laughter filled the church and Dusty scooted a little closer to him.

The priest continued the ceremony. "Who giveth this woman in marriage?"

"My wife and I do," Willard answered.

Rico walked to Ana and lifted her veil and saw her smiling blue eyes that he would remember for the rest of his life. He took her arm and led her to the altar and the waiting priest. Dusty danced around in front of them until Rachel snagged him.

They said their vows, slipped on the gold bands they would wear for a lifetime, and sealed it with a kiss they would continue later.

A flurry of rose petals greeted them as they walked from the church.

After shaking hands and hearing congratulations for thirty minutes, they got in the truck and drove to Rebel Ranch for the reception.

Ana reached out and ran her hand around his neck. "I married a stranger. A handsome stranger."

"I'll introduce myself later." He winked at her.

"You didn't have to cut your hair for me."

"I didn't," he told her. "I said I would cut it when I was free and I'm free. Finally free to live my life the way I want."

Her face split into a smile. "I can't stop smiling. This is the happiest day of my life."

"Mine, too."

Ana had spent most of the week making the wedding cake. She insisted on doing it and it had turned out incredible. It had five layers with a bride and groom on top. A trellis of roses cascaded down one side and spilled out onto several small cakes around the bottom. On the other side was a waterfall that spilled from the top, down the cake to the bottom layer which was all water. Behind the waterfall was a photo of them. The whole cake was edible and everyone "oohed" and "ahhed" over it.

Later they left to spend two nights and days in Austin at a posh hotel. It was all they could afford and it was all they needed. They especially needed this time together alone. Dusty stayed with Egan's family and they worried he might miss them, but Dusty seemed fine, eager to play with Justin and Jordy. They had come a long way since May.

They returned in time to celebrate Christmas with the family. Their house was as festive as the courthouse. Decorations were everywhere. Ana had insisted on a big tree and they had to move the toy box to get it in.

Dusty was enthralled with all the bright decorations and he lay on the floor with Mickey staring at the shining tree.

It made Rico realize that with very little money Dusty probably never had a very big Christmas and he had to wonder if they even had put up a tree. Dusty was mesmerized by everything, especially the presents under the tree. Rico and Ana planned to make it a Christmas Dusty would never forget.

They would have Christmas dinner at the Wiznowskis', but Christmas Eve was at Miss Kate's and it was a loud, joyful occasion. Dusty giggled, laughed and smiled and it was good to see him so happy. When the kids opened gifts, he didn't offer to pay for them. He tore into his gifts with glee. He was getting it, finally.

Dusty fell asleep in a chair with Justin and Annie. Rico gathered him in his arms, and Egan and Paxton each picked up their child, and the family stood around the Christmas tree and sang "Silent Night." Eden, Falcon's daughter, led the singing.

Afterward, they walked home. It was a clear cool night and they needed the exercise after sitting and eating most of the day. Dusty was asleep on Rico's shoulder. His shirt was

out of his jeans and he'd lost a sneaker somewhere. They'd find it tomorrow. Ana linked
her arm through his as they made their way
to the bunkhouse.

A star shot across the bright sky.

"Did you make a wish?" Ana asked.

"I don't need to. I have everything I ever
wanted."

She leaned her head against his shoulder.
"Me, too."

"I was thinking about something, though…"

"What?"

"Ms. Henshaw has called me about four
times apologizing for what happened to
Dusty and she always says if we need anything to just call her. I was thinking I might
call her and tell her if a baby comes available
that we might be interested in taking it."

"Oh, Rico." Ana stopped in her tracks and
stared at him. "Are you serious?"

"We'll be moving into a five-bedroom
house and we'll have plenty of room. There
are a lot of kids in foster care who just need
someone to care about them."

She stood on her tiptoes to kiss his cheek.
"You know I've said this before, but you're
the most wonderful man alive."

He didn't know about wonderful, but he

sure was the luckiest. Even after his horrific past, he'd managed to survive and embrace life once again with a woman he loved. Tomorrow they would spend their first Christmas with their child and they hoped that Dusty would never forget the awe and wonder of Christmas and the love of his parents.

Yep, he'd gotten lucky. He glanced toward the sky and said a silent, "Thank You."

* * * * *

Watch for the next story in Linda Warren's TEXAS REBELS miniseries,
To Save a Child,
coming in March 2020,
only from Harlequin Heartwarming!

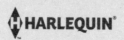

Get 4 FREE REWARDS!

We'll send you 2 FREE Books plus 2 FREE Mystery Gifts.

Love Inspired® books feature contemporary inspirational romances with Christian characters facing the challenges of life and love.

FREE
Value Over
$20

Get 4 FREE REWARDS!

We'll send you 2 FREE Books plus 2 FREE Mystery Gifts.

Love Inspired® Suspense books feature Christian characters facing challenges to their faith... and lives.

FREE Value Over **$20**

YES! Please send me 2 FREE Love Inspired® Suspense novels and my 2 FREE mystery gifts (gifts are worth about $10 retail). After receiving them, if I don't wish to receive any more books, I can return the shipping statement marked "cancel." If I don't cancel, I will receive 6 brand-new novels every month and be billed just $5.24 each for the regular-print edition or $5.99 each for the larger-print edition in the U.S., or $5.74 each for the regular-print edition or $6.24 each for the larger-print edition in Canada. That's a savings of at least 13% off the cover price. It's quite a bargain! Shipping and handling is just 50¢ per book in the U.S. and $1.25 per book in Canada.* I understand that accepting the 2 free books and gifts places me under no obligation to buy anything. I can always return a shipment and cancel at any time. The free books and gifts are mine to keep no matter what I decide.

Choose one: ☐ **Love Inspired® Suspense Regular-Print** (153/353 IDN GNWN)   ☐ **Love Inspired® Suspense Larger-Print** (107/307 IDN GNWN)

Name (please print)

Address _____ Apt. #

City _____ State/Province _____ Zip/Postal Code

Mail to the Reader Service:
IN U.S.A.: P.O. Box 1341, Buffalo, NY 14240-8531
IN CANADA: P.O. Box 603, Fort Erie, Ontario L2A 5X3

Want to try 2 free books from another series! Call 1-800-873-8635 or visit www.ReaderService.com.

---

*Terms and prices subject to change without notice. Prices do not include sales taxes, which will be charged (if applicable) based on your state or country of residence. Canadian residents will be charged applicable taxes. Offer not valid in Quebec. This offer is limited to one order per household. Books received may not be as shown. Not valid for current subscribers to Love Inspired Suspense books. All orders subject to approval. Credit or debit balances in a customer's account(s) may be offset by any other outstanding balance owed by or to the customer. Please allow 4 to 6 weeks for delivery. Offer available while quantities last.

Your Privacy—The Reader Service is committed to protecting your privacy. Our Privacy Policy is available online at www.ReaderService.com or upon request from the Reader Service. We make a portion of our mailing list available to reputable third parties that offer products we believe may interest you. If you prefer that we not exchange your name with third parties, or if you wish to clarify or modify your communication preferences, please visit us at www.ReaderService.com/consumerschoice or write to us at Reader Service Preference Service, P.O. Box 9062, Buffalo, NY 14240-9062. Include your complete name and address.

THE FORTUNES OF TEXAS COLLECTION!

18 FREE BOOKS in all!

Treat yourself to the rich legacy of the Fortune and Mendoza clans in this remarkable 50-book collection. This collection is packed with cowboys, tycoons and Texas-sized romances!

YES! Please send me **The Fortunes of Texas Collection** in Larger Print. This collection begins with 3 FREE books and 2 FREE gifts in the first shipment. Along with my 3 free books, I'll also get the next 4 books from The Fortunes of Texas Collection, in LARGER PRINT, which I may either return and owe nothing, or keep for the low price of $5.24 U.S./$5.89 CDN each plus $2.99 for shipping and handling per shipment*. If I decide to continue, about once a month for 8 months I will get 6 or 7 more books but will only need to pay for 4. That means 2 or 3 books in every shipment will be FREE! If I decide to keep the entire collection, I'll have paid for only 32 books because 18 books are FREE! I understand that accepting the 3 free books and gifts places me under no obligation to buy anything. I can always return a shipment and cancel at any time. My free books and gifts are mine to keep no matter what I decide.

☐ 269 HCN 4622   ☐ 469 HCN 4622

Name (please print)

Address   Apt. #

City   State/Province   Zip/Postal Code

Mail to the **Reader Service:**
IN U.S.A.: P.O. Box 1341, Buffalo, N.Y. 14240-8531
IN CANADA: P.O. Box 603, Fort Erie, Ontario L2A 5X3

*Terms and prices subject to change without notice. Prices do not include sales taxes, which will be charged (if applicable) based on your state or country of residence. Canadian residents will be charged applicable taxes. Offer not valid in Quebec. All orders subject to approval. Credit or debit balances in a customer's account(s) may be offset by any other outstanding balance owed by or to the customer. Please allow three to four weeks for delivery. Offer available while quantities last. © 2018 Harlequin Enterprises Limited. ® and ™ are trademarks owned and used by the trademark owner and/or its licensee.

Your Privacy—The Reader Service is committed to protecting your privacy. Our Privacy Policy is available online at www.ReaderService.com or upon request from the Reader Service. We make a portion of our mailing list available to reputable third parties that offer products we believe may interest you. If you prefer that we not exchange your name with third parties, or if you wish to clarify or modify your communication preferences, please visit us at www.ReaderService.com/consumerschoice or write to us at Reader Service Preference Service, P.O. Box 9049, Buffalo, NY 14269-9049. Include your name and address.

50BFT19R

Get 4 FREE REWARDS!

We'll send you 2 FREE Books <u>plus</u> 2 FREE Mystery Gifts.

FREE
Value Over
$20

Both the **Romance** and **Suspense** collections feature compelling novels
written by many of today's bestselling authors.

YES! Please send me 2 FREE novels from the Essential Romance or
Essential Suspense Collection and my 2 FREE gifts (gifts are worth about
$10 retail). After receiving them, if I don't wish to receive any more books,
I can return the shipping statement marked "cancel." If I don't cancel, I will
receive 4 brand-new novels every month and be billed just $6.99 each in the
U.S. or $7.24 each in Canada. That's a savings of at least 13% off the cover
price. It's quite a bargain! Shipping and handling is just 50¢ per book in the
U.S. and $1.25 per book in Canada.* I understand that accepting the 2 free
books and gifts places me under no obligation to buy anything. I can always
return a shipment and cancel at any time. The free books and gifts are mine
to keep no matter what I decide.

Choose one: ☐ **Essential Romance**   ☐ **Essential Suspense**
  (194/394 MDN GNNP)   (191/391 MDN GNNP)

Name (please print)

Address _____ Apt. #

City _____ State/Province _____ Zip/Postal Code

Mail to the **Reader Service**:
IN U.S.A.: P.O. Box 1341, Buffalo, NY 14240-8531
IN CANADA: P.O. Box 603, Fort Erie, Ontario L2A 5X3

Want to try 2 free books from another series! Call 1-800-873-8635 or visit www.ReaderService.com.

He

On ReaderService.com, you ca

- Try 2 free books from any series

- Access risk-free special offers

- View your account history & manage payments

- Browse the latest Bonus Bucks catalog

Don't miss out!

If you want to stay up-to-date on the latest at the Reader Service and enjoy more Harlequin content, make sure you've signed up for our monthly News & Notes email newsletter. Sign up online at ReaderService.com.